THE GODS WILL HAVE BLOOD

Anatole France (Jacques-Anatole-François Thibault) was born in Paris in 1844, the only son of a book-dealer. His childhood and education, mostly self-acquired through voracious reading, are described with tenderness, humour and some licence in *Le Livre de mon ami* (1855), *Pierre Nozière* (1899), *Le Petit Pierre* (1918) and *La Vie en fleur* (1922).

Soon after leaving schoool he obtained employment with a publishing company. During the next twenty years, besides bibliographical and cataloguing work, his work as publisher's reader and the writing of prefaces for editions of the classics, he contributed to various reviews and published a study of Alfred de Vigny (1868). *Les Poèmes dorés* (1873) and *Les Noces corinthiennes*, a poetic drama (1876), mark the beginning of his creative work proper, and both show the strong influence of the Parnassiens. From 1876 to 1890 he was an assistant librarian at the Senate, which gave him ample free time for his writing. He also became a regular contributor to *Le Globe* and *L'Univers illustré*, and published *Jocaste et le Chat maigre* (1879) and a highly successful novel, *Le Crime de Sylvestre Bonnard* (1881). In 1888 he became literary editor of *Le Temps*, a leading daily, and about this time became associated with Mme Arman de Caillavet, whose *salon* was a centre of French literary life. He entered actively into the world of contemporary letters and by 1897, a year after his election to the *Académie française*, had come to dominate that world. The decisive shift in his career as a writer came with his participation in the Dreyfus case on behalf of the convicted Jewish officer. It marked the first stage of his emergence as one of the 'representative men' of his epoch, and brought about his conversion to socialism. Subsequent works reflected this sharpened humane concern and a powerful distrust of clerical obscurantism, seen particularly in his pungent satirical portraits of French social and political life in the four volumes of the *Histoire contemporaine*.

Anatole France was awarded the Nobel Prize for Literature in 1921. His last years were spent in retirement in his Touraine property, La Béchellerie. He died in 1924.

Frederick Davies was widely known as the translator of the plays of Carlo Goldoni, of which *Four Comedies* has been published in the Penguin Classics. He was a Fellow Commoner of Churchill College, Cambridge, where he translated Goldoni's *Memoirs*. Frederick Davies also translated *Three French Farces* and Daudet's *Letters from My Windmill* for the Penguin Classics, as well as a number of plays by Molière and Labiche. He was the editor of the *Diaries of John Cowper Powys* and he also wrote two novels for children. Frederick Davies died in February 1990.

ANATOLE FRANCE

THE GODS WILL HAVE BLOOD

(Les Dieux ont soif)

TRANSLATED WITH
AN INTRODUCTION BY
FREDERICK DAVIES

PENGUIN BOOKS

PENGUIN BOOKS

Published by the Penguin Group
Penguin Books Ltd, 27 Wrights Lane, London W8 5TZ, England
Penguin Putnam Inc., 375 Hudson Street, New York, New York 10014, USA
Penguin Books Australia Ltd, Ringwood, Victoria, Australia
Penguin Books Canada Ltd, 10 Alcorn Avenue, Toronto, Ontario, Canada M4V 3B2
Penguin Books (NZ) Ltd, Private Bag 102902, NSMC, Auckland, New Zealand

Penguin Books Ltd, Registered Offices: Harmondsworth, Middlesex, England

First published (in French as *Les Dieux ont soif* in 1912)
This translation first published in Penguin Classics 1979
Reprinted in Penguin Books 1990
10

This translation and Introduction copyright © Frederick Davies, 1979
All rights reserved

Printed in England by Clays Ltd, St Ives plc
Set in Monotype Garamond

The translator wishes to acknowledge gratefully the help of Jean
and Roderick McKie in the transcribing and typing of several
drafts of the manuscript during the translating of this novel

For EDWARD THOMPSON, *in appreciation
of our long association with the works
of Carlo Goldoni*

INTRODUCTION

In 1896, Anatole France was elected a member of *l'Académie française*, a highly coveted honour in those days as well as good business for an author. In 1921, he was awarded the Nobel Prize in Literature.

Anatole France's election to *l'Académie française* was not without much opposition. His attacks on Church and State had earned him many enemies on the Right. One of the aristocratic establishment said to him on the eve of the election: 'Everything in your writings, monsieur, shocks my beliefs. But genius is a gift of God. I should oppose the will of heaven if I did not vote for you.' Another promised to vote for France, but trusted he would not be successful, 'since I have never heard of a case where a superior man was elected the first time'. On hearing of this, France remarked dryly: 'He must have made several applications himself.'

His award of the Nobel Prize in 1921 was in spite of his vehement denunciations of the Versailles Treaty and his continuous attacks on the Catholic Church. Some of his books had been banned in libraries before the award. After it, all his books without exception were 'placed on the Index' by the Roman Curia because of 'excess of utterances that were communistic and anti-clerical in tone'. When he went to Stockholm to receive the Prize he is reported to have said regarding the Treaty of Versailles: 'The most horrible of wars was followed by a treaty which was not a treaty of peace but a prolongation of the war.'

In 1896, as was customary for a newly elected member of *l'Académie française*, France had to deliver a eulogistic address about his predecessor. He had succeeded to de Lesseps' chair and in his address there was nothing that could offend any of the traditionalists. For that reason it has been much cited by those critics who wish to prove France's essential conservatism. The address was delivered by France, attired in the customary broidered costume of green and black, wearing the cocked hat, and with the useless sword at his side, in a crowded amphitheatre before the élite of Paris. Such a numerous and brilliant assembly had not been seen for years. Among the Ambassadors, Ministers of State, Princes and Dukes who witnessed the scene was a boy, Pierre Champion, who later wrote:

I recall the packed amphitheatre . . . Finally Anatole France arrived in his uniform. I had glimpsed him sometimes in our bookshop, with his well-groomed and lively air, his charming courtesy . . . In religious silence, he stood and read his speech, in praise of Ferdinand de Lesseps . . . I had to re-read the *éloge* later, to appreciate its courage and its simple beauty.

Twenty-one years later, in 1927, when Anatole France had been dead over two years, the man who was elected to take his place and sit in his chair at *l'Académie française*, delivered a very different address about his predecessor – an incident worth recalling, since it indicates in essence most of the reasons for the decline of the popularity and fame of Anatole France.

The twenty-five years before the First World War, the period of Anatole France's enormous popularity and fame, had been largely characterized by a predominance of Naturalist and socialist literature – the great reputations in England and France had been those of Shaw, Wells, Bennett, Zola, Rolland and Anatole France – largely in reaction against the Romanticism of the earlier part of the century. But, during those twenty-five years before the First World War, a growing disillusion and weariness had been gaining expression in the writings of a small coterie who became known as the Symbolists. Their writings were later to achieve a short but widespread influence after the war. For, when the war ended in the impoverishment and exhaustion of all the European nations involved, a general disillusion with politics and with all attempts to organize mankind in the service of some common ideal caused Western literature to become receptive to a less idealistic attitude, indifferent to action and unconcerned with social groups. Yeats, Eliot, Joyce, Proust became the heirs of the Symbolists. These writers wrote in isolation, uninvolved with, and disengaged from, the issues of the time. None of them would have rushed, risking their literary reputations and the loss of their friends, as Zola and France did, to the defence of a Dreyfus.

In 1927, one of this new generation of writers, Paul Valéry, was elected to *l'Académie française* to fill the chair left vacant by the death of Anatole France, and had the customary honour of delivering the address on his predecessor. On this important occasion, Paul Valéry behaved in a most unconventional way. The uniforms of *l'Académie française* were always passed on from generation to generation, and a new member had to fit himself as best he could from such old uniforms as were available. Paul Valéry, however, astounded the Academicians by appearing in a smart, new uniform made for him by a fashionable tailor. The address on Anatole France which he then read was received with even greater astonishment.

Instead of the usual eulogy, Valéry delivered what can hardly be described as anything but a vicious attack. In all his own writing, France had always maintained the lucidity and simplicity of the French tradition, against which Valéry and the Symbolists had rebelled. France, moreover, had occasionally poked fun at the Symbolists, and had even said that he could 'never believe in the success of a literary school which expressed difficult thoughts in obscure language'. Valery took his revenge. In what should have been his complimentary obituary upon Anatole France, Valéry became the first to enumerate most of the charges which have been made against France since his death. Valéry referred to the gossip that, if it had not been for Madame Arman de Caillavet, France would never have accomplished anything; to the repetitiveness, the mechanical neatness of form, in the novels of a man who had lived long enough to produce inferior as well as good ones; to the digressive nature of much of France's work which tends to turn some of his novels into abstract discussions about God, democracy, justice; to France's prudence, with the implication that he was timid and insincere, conveniently forgetting that the man who had failed to defend Symbolism, had invited popular hatred and the loss of his friends, by coming to the defence of the Jewish Dreyfus; and finally he referred, his last patronizing disparagement, to Anatole France's humble origins, concluding that in view of his lack of formal education, France had really done very well.

Anatole France was born Jacques-Anatole Thibault, in Paris in 1844, the only child of François Thibault, an old soldier and a devout Catholic, who kept a small bookshop on the Quai Malaquais, specializing in rare books and manuscripts, and who, when writing bibliophile articles, signed himself France Libraire, France being short for François in his native Anjou. The son of a shoemaker in Anjou, Anatole's father had taught himself to read and write during his military service. As a shopkeeper he lacked business instincts and, as Anatole mentions later, would prefer to read his books than to sell them. His shop, however, became a meeting-place for scholars and authors, and this daily contact as a boy with thinkers and writers, with wits and critics must have played a vital part in the development of Anatole France as a psychologist and stylist.

France himself was later to declare: 'Ah, home is a fine school.' He hated the school his parents sent him to: the Jesuit College Stanislaus. He resented the gibes of teachers and students and would play truant along the quais of the Seine. When the Professor's report was: 'Progress nil: conduct bad', and his father had brought himself to accept the Professor's verdict that the boy would never accomplish anything in the arts or the sciences, his mother whispered something to him that he never forgot: 'Be a writer, my son. You have brains and you will make the envious hold their tongues.' His mother was Flemish, unfailingly optimistic and practical, important qualities in the household with an absent-minded father. She was, moreover, an accomplished story-teller and her only child proved an avid listener. Among his last words on his deathbed, France, that only child, who had become not only the famous writer she had foreseen, but also 'a genial mocker at life', an epicurean who believed in the importance of but two things, beauty and goodness, called upon the name of his mother. Some critics, incidentally, have seen in France 'a mother's boy'. Be that as it may, the extreme licentiousness of his late 'teens and early twenties soon exhausted the patience of both his mother and father, and for a time, until his marriage and the publication of his second book in 1872, he lived in a garret, often on the verge of starvation.

France's first literary efforts were in verse and he had many poems published in the smaller reviews. It was in one of these that he first signed himself 'Anatole France', in allusion to his father's pseudonym. The best of his poems were published in a collected edition in 1872: *Les Poèmes dorés*. They show the influence of the ancient classics, an influence which was to remain with him all his life. His first published work was in 1868: *Étude sur Alfred Vigny*. At the age of twenty-one he found employment in the Senate library under Leconte de Lisle – a position which, like Daudet's first employment in Paris, was more or less a sinecure and allowed him plenty of time for writing. His first attempts in prose narrative, two short novels, *Jocaste* and *Le Chat maigre*, were published in one volume in 1879. They show the influence of Daudet and of Dickens and lack his later distinctive style, that complex blend of irony, pity, sensuality, love of beauty and worldly wisdom. This style, or manner, was first revealed with the publication in 1881 of *Le Crime de Sylvestre Bonnard,* his first full-length novel. The book is about a philologist, a passionate hunter after rare manuscripts, whose gentle nature and generous heart make him an endearing figure, and Anatole France has justly been credited with the creation of a new genre: the 'bookish' novel, in which the scholar's temperament, preoccupations and 'angst', whimsically bound up with the trifles of everyday life, become the very subject-matter of the novel. This idea of *le bon maître*, the gentle, eccentric, life-loving philosopher-teacher, he developed in his next novel in 1882, *Les Désirs de Jean Servien*, a story of the Commune in which the Marquis Tudesco di Venezia, lover of poetry and good wine, undertakes the education of a poor book-binder's son.

In 1885 he published *Le Livre de mon ami*, a delightful selection of his childhood memories. In 1886 he joined the staff of *Le Temps* and in 1888 became its literary editor. In this position he was able to use to the full his individual qualities: the many facets of his great intelligence, his ability to allow his imagination and prodigious memory to play around a wide variety of themes – qualities which in themselves imply his limitations as a writer – his inability, or rather, marked reluctance, to undertake sustained work. As a critic, he became the leading impressionist of his time, maintaining the subjectivity of all critical judgements.

In 1889 appeared a volume of stories, entitled *Balthasar* after the first of them. This was followed in 1890 by *Thaïs*, a story about a courtesan of Alexandria converted by the monk Paphautius. In 1891 France left the Senate library after a dispute with Leconte de Lisle. A volume a year ensued during the next five years. In 1892 came *L'Étui de nacre* containing fifteen stories, the best being *Le Procurateur de Judée*. Then, in 1893, came *La Rôtisserie de la Reine Pédauque*, one of his masterpieces, in which he develops *le bon maître* into the type of character which was to recur in many of his succeeding novels – the lay saint – reaching its apotheosis in the character Brotteaux des Ilettes in *Les Dieux ont soif* (*The Gods Will Have Blood*).

The real hero of *La Rôtisserie de la Reine Pédauque* is not Jacques Ménétrier, the rotisseur's son who becomes a book-dealer: it is the Abbé Jérôme Coignard, humanist and theologian. France, indeed, was so delighted with his own creation, that in spite of Coignard's violent death, he brought him to life again the following year in *Les Opinions de Jérôme Coignard*.

A change of style is apparent in his next novel, *Le Lys Rouge*, in 1894. The change was largely owing to the liaison he had begun with a married woman, Madame Arman de

Caillavet, who held every week in her house in Paris what were among the last of the famous Parisian salons. France's own marriage, in 1877, to Valerie Guérin, by whom he had one child, a daughter Suzanne, though undoubtedly a *'mariage de convenance.'* had been a happy one for a while but incompatibilities led to a divorce in 1892, and for almost twenty years France was to be captivated and largely dominated by Madame Arman de Caillavet. He finally rebelled against her assumption, and that of others, that his literary eminence would never have been achieved without her.

In 1909 he sailed to South America, having deliberately accepted an invitation to lecture there and, as deliberately, refused to allow Madame Arman to accompany him. On the ship he immediately began an affair with an actress, Jeanne Brindeau, continuing it openly on his arrival in South America knowing full well that word of it would reach Madame Arman. When his secretary, Brousson, remonstrated with him, France gave him his return ticket. On his own return, five months later, there was an attempted reconciliation with Madame Arman. It was unsuccessful and her death a few months later was hastened by his break with her.

There is no doubt that for several years France suffered poignant remorse at his treatment of the woman who had been the great love of his life, yet his release from her domination appears to have brought about a rejuvenation. Now well into his sixties he began a number of love-affairs with women much younger than himself. What was eventually, however, to prove more significant was his installation as his housekeeper of Emma Laprevotte, Madame Arman's maid. She was thirty-nine, a woman who knew her place and kept to it. That place, in France's house and heart grew swiftly, but it was not until 1920, four years before his death, that he married her.

Meanwhile, Emma's presence, even though it comforted France did not restrain him. That perhaps was partly why he had chosen her to live with him; there would be no need to behave himself in front of Emma who knew all about him. In the year following her advent into his home, there began what was probably the only other serious love-affair of his life. He had met an American, aged thirty-five, twice married, and now the wife of a Monsieur Gagey. She was his audience for much of *The Gods Will Have Blood*, on which he was working at the time. When it was finished, she wrote to him that it was in part hers since so much of it had been created under her very eyes. France appears to have seen the warning light. Sensing this, she wrote him a letter telling him she had never had much happiness, that her hold on life was very light and it would not take much to make her release it. France answered the letter but not the implied appeal. Madame Gagey killed herself with an overdose of sleeping pills. France attended the funeral where he had to face the accusations of Madame Gagey's husband. A few days later he left for Cap d'Antibes with Emma.

If Madame Gagey, with some justification, could claim to have played a part in the creation of *The Gods Will Have Blood*, so too might have Madame Arman, for it had been begun in her company. But ultimately, *The Gods Will Have Blood* belongs to France himself, more so than any of his novels. For it is the most personal of them all.

The novel which first showed the influence of Madame Arman was *Le Lys Rouge* in 1894. This was written during their first journey together in Italy and is a tale of passion and jealousy, with characters identifiable in real life, and with fine descriptive scenes of Florence. France's next two novels *Le Jardin d'Épicure* and *Le Puits de Sainte-Claire* in 1895 show a return to his more meditative manner. On 23 January 1896, France was elected to *l'Académie française* and had reached a height of fame that was to continue for the next twenty years. Soon after his election the Dreyfus affair became a national political issue and, with Émile Zola, Anatole France came to the defence of Dreyfus.

The 'affair' is the main theme of four of his next six novels. He gave them the collective title *L'Histoire contemporaine*. they are *L'Orme du mail* (1897), *Le Mannequin d'osier* (1897), *L'Anneau d'amethyste* (1899), and *Monsieur Bergeret à Paris* (1901). These four loosely constructed novels contain some of France's most imaginative writing: in them he attacks intolerance, injustice and dictatorship, and eloquently advocates free universal education, the separation of Church and State, social reform, the organization of labour, and the rights of minorities. It was as a result of the Dreyfus affair that he eventually became a supporter of the Russian Revolution and a member of the Communist Party, and that his novels increasingly assumed the character of social satire culminating in 1908 with his *L'Île des pingouins* which stands with Swift's *Gulliver's Travels,* Voltaire's *Candide* and Orwell's *Animal Farm* as one of the most searingly satirical indictments of human folly.

In 1903 his *Histoire Comique* had told of the neutralization of a guilty passion by the suicide of the wronged lover – by no means a comic story. And in 1905, his *Sur la pierre blanche* contains a picture of a future world with no towns – by no means unworthy of H. G. Wells.

A few months before the publication of *L'Île des pingouins* in 1908, there had at last been published, in two volumes, his monumental *Vie de Jeanne d'Arc*, over which he had procrastinated for years. It was his chief bid for consideration as an historian, but it proved unpopular largely because he expounds the thesis that Joan of Arc was the victim of hallucinations, without military talent, of low intelligence, and only a tool in the hands of the clergy. A premonition of its adverse reception was probably the cause of the speed with which he wrote *L'Île des pingouins*, which was published a few months later to overwhelming acclaim, and so remedied the blow to his reputation.

In 1912, at the age of sixty-eight, Anatole France published the book which is regarded as his masterpiece. Like many of his novels, *The Gods Will Have Blood* had first appeared serially, under the title *Évariste Gamelin*. In it, France breaks free from the bonds of classical restraint and reveals his own deeply felt personal emotions more openly than in any of his novels. The book is, nevertheless, written in the same style which he had developed over the years: a style impregnated with echoes of, and allusions to, the classical writers of the ancient world, and it is probably the marriage of such a style to a content so charged with emotion that caused Professor G. M. Trevelyan to observe, in passing, in his Clark Lectures of 1953: 'I know I should be sorry to read *Les Dieux ont soif*, one of the world's best historical novels, in anything except the French of Anatole France, which is not its robe but its skin.'

And France's synthesis in this novel of classical style with romantic content also illustrates Paul Morand's generalization to the effect that French writers are never younger, never more free from restraint, than when they have passed their sixtieth birthday. In this respect, André Maurois has pointed out that, 'Voltaire wrote his best book, *Candide,* at sixty-five, and Anatole France his *Les Dieux ont soif,* at sixty-eight.'

The Gods Will Have Blood is not only the greatest novel Anatole France wrote, it is one of the greatest of French novels. All great literature universalizes some fundamental human problem. *The Gods Will Have Blood* is the only one of France's novels to achieve this. It is artistically a perfectly balanced portrayal of human aspirations and failings. One of its two main themes recurs in many of France's novels but in no other is it so well integrated into the narrative. It is the pathetic discrepancy between human ideals and thoughts on the one hand, and between human actions and passions on the other. In this novel, France has recast Lord Acton's aphorism: 'All ideals corrupt, fanatic ideals corrupt fanatically.' The artist Gamelin could be any young terrorist of today led by his ideals to the fanatic and indiscriminate killing of innocent people in the name of 'justice' or 'freedom'. France universalizes this theme by drawing a parallel between the fanatic Gamelin and the mad Orestes. This is brought out vividly when the poor, young artist is explaining his painting of Orestes and Electra to the Citizeness Rochemaure. He cites the passage in Euripides' *Orestes* which inspired his painting and explains the tragic situation he has tried to represent. The parallel is emphasized later when Gamelin has been appointed to the Revolutionary Tribunal through the influence of the Citizeness Rochemaure and sends hundreds of people to the guillotine, including his own brother-in-law and the Citizeness Rochemaure herself. France constantly reminds the reader that Gamelin's political fanaticism is identical with the crazed Orestes' persecution by the Furies. Suffering under the illusion that his merciless 'justice' is the best way to serve humanity, he becomes a monster. Throughout the novel Gamelin grows more and more like the Orestes in his painting.

This objectively impersonal historical theme is closely interwoven with another theme, deeply personal to France himself: the conflict between love of life and the gift of thought; the gift of foreseeing the tragic possibilities and inevitabilities of life: poverty, loneliness, and death for oneself and those one loves.

In various forms, this theme also recurs in many of his books, but, again, in none other is it so well integrated, nor so free from bitterness. With it, France came close to the theme that Sartre was later to exploit: the tragic solitude of the thinker in a hostile community. In general, France's conclusions are bitter, especially in his creation of the character Monsieur Bergeret in the four volumes of L'Histoire contemporaine, where he seems, like Flaubert, to have found most of his inspiration in the deep bitterness of all thought, a bitterness that with Flaubert reached a point of exasperation in Bouvard et Péchuchet. 'By the mere fact that he thought, he was a strange being, disturbing and suspect to all.' . . . 'Monsieur Bergeret is to be pitied, for he thinks.' These are examples of two of France's comments on Monsieur Bergeret. And when the reader is first introduced to Brotteaux des Ilettes in The Gods Will Have Blood, France makes Brotteaux say of his puppets, 'These are my creatures. From me they have received a perishable body, free from joy and sorrow. I've not given them the power of thought, since I'm a benevolent God.'

The protagonist of the impersonal historical theme set in the fifteen months immediately preceding the fall of Robespierre is Évariste Gamelin, a poor artist, an idealist, courageously caring for his artistic integrity and for his widowed mother. The protagonist of the theme deeply personal to France himself is Maurice Brotteaux des Ilettes, a cultured aristocrat, who under the old régime had possessed wealth, rank, estates, beautiful women and beautiful works of art, but who now possesses only a worn, puce-coloured coat, a copy of Lucretius, and his epicurean philosophy of life.

The accusation made by some critics that France's characters are static is completely refuted by the character of Gamelin. France is at pains to show that Gamelin as a boy and as a young man was far from heartless. His mother relates incidents from his boyhood revealing his extreme sensitivity. He is shown early in the book giving away half his small ration of bread to a woman with a child whom he passes in the street, strangers but obviously ill and in greater need than himself, and then telling his mother he had eaten his share of the bread so that she might take hers without misgivings. Before the end of the book this same man has so changed, and France makes the change appear completely convincing, that he is prepared without a qualm to send his only sister to the guillotine.

This development of character, this change in Gamelin, is most apparent in his relationship with his mistress, Élodie Blaise, the daughter of a picture-dealer. Hers is a hard-won victory, seducing the pale, ascetic young idealist. And she gets far more than she bargained for. As the fanatic flame of Gamelin's idealism burns fiercer and fiercer and his hands become red with the blood of countless innocent people, France, with a psychological insight in advance of his time, causes her to experience the horrible delights of sexual masochism.

The relationship between Gamelin and Élodie Blaise is also the occasion for one of the supreme examples of France's use of irony. The circumstances in which he uses it is also a refutation of another accusation that critics have brought against France: that he interposes himself between the reader and his characters and tells the reader what he should feel. In no way does France tell the reader how he should feel about the relationship between Gamelin and Élodie. There is no indictment, no denunciation; all is in the style of classical restraint. France merely uses the expedient of making Élodie say exactly the same words when she parts at the end of the book from her new lover, Desmahis, as she said when she parted from Gamelin on the night they first made love.

France's mastery of irony permeates the book. He wishes to convey that, though he has to focus the reader's attention on the grim activities of the men of the Revolutionary Tribunal, everyday life went on much as usual: people went to work, women gossipped, children played with their dogs in the street. Even the names of the Revolutionary leaders, now synonymous with the French Revolution, often meant nothing to the ordinary people. France brings this home with the same devastating ironic effect as when at the end of his famous short story *The Procurator of Judaea* Pontius Pilate is asked if he remembers a man named Jesus from Nazareth who was crucified for some crime, and Pilate after thinking deeply for a few moments murmurs: 'Jesus? Jesus – of Nazareth? I cannot call him to mind.' For when Gamelin, having heard with horror of the assassination of Marat, is hastening to pay his last respects to the murdered leader, he is stopped in the street by an old woman who asks him: 'if this Monsieur Marat who had been assassinated was not Monsieur le Curé Mara, from Saint-Pierre-de-Queyroix'.

The personal theme represented by Maurice Brotteaux des Ilettes is made doubly significant by Emma Laprevotte. Some years after her installation in his house, when she was considerably more to France than his housekeeper, though not yet his wife, she told a friend Marcel le Goff: 'In *Les Dieux ont soif* Monsieur France has imagined what would happen to himself in a time of trouble, deprived of his possessions, of his books, of all his belongings – he was Brotteaux.'

The characters of Brotteaux and Gamelin are an aspect of France's achievement in *The Gods Will Have Blood* which no critical appreciation of his work appears to have noted. With these two characters he succeeds in one of the most formidable tasks an author can undertake: the presentation of a very good man and of a very bad man. Apart from Dostoyevsky, few authors have attempted the creation of either, and Dostoyevsky's saints and criminals too often appear to inhabit the world of William Blake, Milton or Dante, rather than the world of ordinary men and women. Among the few novelists who have made the attempt with any success to create a good man in a credible world are Anthony Trollope with the Rev. Septimus Harding in *The Warden*, Elizabeth Bowen with Major Brutt in *The Death of the Heart,* and Georges Simenon with Louis Cuchas in *The Little Saint*.

Anatole France is one of the very few authors who have successfully portrayed both a very good man and a very wicked man in the same novel. And there is irony and paradox in his creation of both. For Gamelin, who worships Rousseau and believes in the essential goodness of men, aims at doing good and yet his every action, under the influence of this aim, is evil. Brotteaux des Ilettes, who believes in the essential evil of men, aims merely at enjoying 'the pleasure there is in life itself', and yet his every action, under the influence of this aim, is good.

In real life, contact with a genuinely good man does not leave us with the impression that he is like ourselves only better; that somehow he makes a more successful struggle to do right than we do. On the contrary, he appears to live on some other level than ourselves. A very good man gives us the impression he has gone beyond ethics. He does not seem to know that he is good. So when, at the end, Brotteaux is seated beside the young prostitute, whom he has befriended with no ulterior motive, as the tumbril takes them both to the guillotine, the old aristocrat contemplates the young girl's white breasts and 'is filled with regret for the light of day' (one of the many deliberate classical allusions by France) – and we know that in Brotteaux we have experienced what a genuinely good man must be like. What is more, we feel that he does not know that he is good. France has made sure that we shall feel this by the scene a few pages earlier when the monk, Father Longuemare, asks the atheist, Brotteaux, to pray for him: 'Monsieur, I ask you one favour: this God in Whom you do not yet believe, pray to Him for me. It is possible that you may be nearer to Him than I am myself: a moment and we shall know. Only one second, and you may have become one of the Lord's most dearly beloved children. Monsieur, pray for me.' France has made us come to recognize, like the monk has done, true goodness when we see it.

In his creation of Gamelin, France with classical symmetry brings the Orestes theme full circle. At the beginning of the novel Gamelin explains his painting of Orestes and Electra to the Citizeness Rochemaure in the following words:

'Hennequin painted the madness of Orestes in a masterly manner. But surely it is the grief of Orestes that appeals to us even more poignantly than his madness . . . In order that he might revenge outraged justice, he had repudiated Nature, made himself into a monster . . .'

Towards the end of the novel, when Gamelin learns from his mother that his sister Julie, who has married an emigré, has returned to Paris, he threatens that he will have her sent to the guillotine if he finds her:

The poor mother, white as her coif, let her knitting fall from her trembling hands and murmured in a sighing voice, fainter than the faintest whisper: 'I did not want to believe it, but I see it is true: he is a monster . . .'

The identification is complete: the mother has recognized the wickedness of her son.

Anatole France's subtle prose style has been the delight and despair of critics. It is possible here only to indicate briefly its two main features. France's two chief stylistic devices were his use of startlingly unusual contrasts and antitheses and his use of the right word, the ideal *mot juste*. Without his use of contrast and antithesis none of the tragic or ironic implications which France aimed at could have been achieved. The series of sharp contrasts in the opening paragraphs of *The Gods Will Have Blood* fill the solemnity of the church of the Barnabites with the fear of the Terror and achieve the effect of creating the tense, tragic atmosphere of the time. A very different, more ironic, effect is achieved a little later in the book when we come to the series of contrasts between Brotteaux's pleasant past life and the almost comical jobs he has to undertake in order to keep alive after the Revolution.

France's aim is that of oxymoron, to startle, surprise or

amuse the reader. This device is most apparent in his choice of seemingly incongruous adjectives and in the juxtaposition of apparently contradictory nouns and adjectives. At the close of the first chapter of *The Gods Will Have Blood* France describes the men of the Revolutionary Committee as working with 'fanatic patience' and 'serene fanaticism'. Later we find Gamelin admiring the 'reasoned dogmatism' of the leaders of the Revolution, and the girl Athénaïs being described as the 'innocent prostitute'.

The second main element in France's style is his preoccupation with the smallest unit of language. To France, the 'word' was sacred, chosen for all time. His life-long search for the right word in the right place derived from his conscience as a verbal artist. He sought perfection, knowing full well it was unattainable. What made the search for the ideal *mot juste* more difficult for France was that, like many foreign students of the French language, he could never master the agreement of past participles! He once told a young friend, 'My greatest pleasure is to purify my style, to weigh the true, the etymological meaning of each word, for each word is an individual which has its own origins, its ancestors, its birth, its ups and downs, in short its history.'[1]

And he admitted to Frank Harris that even in his old age writing remained for him 'horribly difficult'. How difficult, is amusingly illustrated by an incident related by the sculptor, Bourdelle. Whilst working on his bronze bust of France, Bourdelle had one of those spells of discouragement which every artist knows. France then showed him one of his own manuscripts, its pages covered with erasions, alterations, corrections, and whispered to Bourdelle: 'Only idiots think themselves perfect.'

Though France took special care to avoid repetition of a word or words, he knew well what he was doing – and what he was making Élodie Blaise do in the eyes of the reader – when he made her use the same words to her new lover as she had used to Gamelin.

1. Madame Demont-Breton: *Les Maisons que j'ai connues*, p. 160, 'Lettres d'Anatole France à Jules Breton', Plon, 1927.

This search for perfection had its dangers: it was, to some, too successful. Critics have found his novels too well-written, almost monotonous in their perfection. Yet the testimony of others far outweighs them. Maurice Barrés[1] wrote: 'Say what you like, first and foremost Anatole France has preserved the French language.' And in France's own lifetime, Gregh[2] wrote: 'He is already a classic, and with reason. No one has ever written better in the French language.'

The paradox of France, the man, is thus reflected in his books. For though their content and thought became increasingly of the Left in their social and political implications, his style in its constant defence and maintenance of all that was best and traditional in the French language increasingly belonged to the Right. This paradox is aptly epitomized in an anecdote concerning Emma Laprevotte. After twenty years as the dominant voice in his country's literature, France had become the 'Grand Old Man' of literature. Literary pilgrimages were made to the house, La Béchellerie, near Tours, where he had made his last home and where he was always addressed as 'Master' by his admirers. Emma Laprevotte, who had once been Anatole France's mistress's maid and now was Madame France, would mutter on hearing this: 'Master! Master! Why do you call him Master? He's only master of his soup, when he eats it, and even then only when it's in his mouth.'

The reaction against him was more against the inflated reputation bestowed upon him in his lifetime than against his books. In these troubled, confused, permissive times, no books would be more appreciated than his if their intelligence and humour were more widely known.

Note

This novel begins in April 1793, just before the final crisis in the struggle for power between the Girondists and the Jacobins.

1. Maurice Barrès: *Mes Cahiers*, Plon, 1929.
2. F. Gregh: *La Fenêtre ouverte*, Paris, Fasquelle, 1901.

The Girondists, so named because many of their members in the Convention came from the Department of the Gironde, had been the guiding power in the course of the Revolution during the previous three years. But, with the need to repel the invading armies of Austria and Prussia and to subdue the revolt against the Revolution in La Vendée, the people of Paris, the sans-culottes, began, through their elected representatives in the Paris Commune, to accuse the Girondists of 'moderatism' in the prosecution of the war, and even of treason after General Dumouriez, who had been a Girondist minister, had deserted to the enemy. It had become known, also, that several of the leading Girondists had tried to save the King from the guillotine.

All this increased the influence of the Jacobin Club, the main stronghold of the Republicans led by Danton, Robespierre and Marat, over the people of Paris who, through their Paris Commune, constituted a force which could make or break the ministers in power at the National Convention.

When, therefore, the Girondists using their majority in the Convention had Marat impeached before the Revolutionary Tribunal, which the Convention had instituted just before the novel begins and which, with its arbitrary power to impose death-penalties, was to become the main instrument of the Terror, the sans-culottes of Paris celebrated Marat's acquittal by a popular insurrection, which Anatole France omits from the novel. This was followed by the troops of the Paris Commune besieging the Convention and refusing to allow its members to leave until they had agreed to the arrest of the Girondist ministers.

The Girondists' hold over the Convention was thus broken and replaced by that of the Jacobins. How the Jacobins, led by Danton and then by Robespierre, dealt with the critical situation which faced them and France, how they saved Europe from despotism by means of despotism and were themselves finally destroyed, is the essential background to this novel.

THE GODS WILL HAVE BLOOD

(Les Dieux ont soif)

I

VERY early one morning, Évariste Gamelin – artist, pupil of David,* member of the Section du Pont-Neuf, formerly Section Henri IV – was to be seen approaching the ancient church of the Barnabites, which had served for three years, since the 21st May, 1790, as the meeting-place for the general assembly of the Section.* The church towered high above a pinched gloomy square close to the iron-barred Palais de Justice.* On its classical façade, decorated with inverted corbels and ornamental capitals, battered by weather and mutilated by man, the symbols of religion had been smashed with hammers and above the door was inscribed in black letters the slogan of the Republic: 'Liberty, Equality, Fraternity – or Death'.

Évariste Gamelin strode purposefully up the nave: the arches, which for so long had heard the holy offices of the day chanted by the surplice-clad brothers of the community of St Paul, saw now the red-capped patriots gather to elect the municipal magistrates and to discuss the daily affairs of the Section. The saints, pulled from their niches, had been replaced by the busts of Brutus, Rousseau and Le Peltier. The tablet of the Rights of Man stood on the plundered altar.

In this nave on two evenings each week the public meetings were held, from five o'clock until eleven o'clock. The pulpit, decorated with the tricolour, served as a rostrum for the speakers' harangues. Opposite, on the Epistle side, for the women and children who came to these gatherings in quite large numbers, rose a high, rough-planked platform.

On this particular morning there was seated before a desk at the foot of the altar, wearing his red cap and carmagnole,* one of the twelve members of the Committee of Surveillance –

*Asterisked words are annotated at the back of the book, pp. 252–54.

the Citizen Dupont *aîné*, a joiner from the Place de Thionville. On the desk were some glasses and a bottle, an inkwell and a pen, and a sheaf of papers containing the text of a petition urging the Convention to expel forthwith the twenty-one unworthy members.

Évariste Gamelin picked up the pen and signed. The working-class magistrate said,

'I knew you'd come and put your name to it, Citizen Gamelin. Made of the right stuff, you are. That's the trouble with this Section; there aren't enough like you. Lukewarm most of them. No moral backbone. I've put it to the Committee of Surveillance that all those who don't sign this petition don't get their certificate of citizenship.'

'I'd sign with my blood,' said Gamelin, 'to get these Federalist* traitors banished. They were behind Marat's impeachment. Let them all be done away with.'

'Apathy – that's what's wrong with this Section,' Dupont *aîné* went on. 'We've nine hundred citizens with the right to vote, yet there aren't fifty who attend the Assembly. Yesterday, there were only twenty-eight of us.'

'Then the citizens will have to be made to come,' said Gamelin. 'Fine them, if they don't.'

The joiner frowned and said quckily, 'Ah, yes! But if they all came, the militant patriots would be outnumbered . . . Come, Citizen Gamelin, won't you join me in a glass of wine to the health of all good sans-culottes? . . .'*

Gamelin turned away. On the walls of the church, on the Gospel side, were the words: '*Comité civil, Comité de surveillance, Comité de bienfaisance*'. Beside them had been painted in black a hand whose forefinger pointed along the passage leading to the cloisters. A few yards beyond this passage, he came to the door to what had been the sacristy and on which was inscribed: '*Comité militaire*'.

Gamelin pushed it open and found the secretary of the Committee seated writing at a large table laden with books, papers, steel ingots, cartridges and samples of soils containing saltpetre.

'*Salut,* Citizen Trubert. How are you?'

'Me?... I couldn't be better.'

The secretary of the Military Committee, Fortuné Trubert, invariably made this reply to those who troubled themselves about his health, less to inform them of his welfare than to cut short all conversation on the subject. At the age of twenty-eight, he was dry-skinned, thin-haired, hectic-cheeked and bent-shouldered. An optician on the Quai des Orfèvres, in 1791 he had given up the very old house he owned to an ageing clerk so that he could devote himself to his municipal duties. He had inherited from a charming mother – who had died when he was twenty and whose memory was still cherished by a few old men of the district – her beautiful, gentle, yet smouldering eyes, her pallor and her timidity. To his father, who had been carried off by the same illness before he was thirty, he owed his industry and integrity. Without ceasing writing, he said:

'And you, citizen, how are you?'

'Quite well. Anything new?'

'Not a thing. As you see: all's quiet here.'

'And the situation?'

'The situation is still the same.'

The situation was disastrous. The first army of the Republic surrounded at Mayence; Valenciennes besieged; Fonteray taken by the Vendéens; Lyons in revolt; insurrection throughout the Cévennes with the frontier open to the Spaniards; two-thirds of France either invaded or in revolt; Paris within reach of the Austrian cannon, without money, without bread.

Fortuné Trubert went on writing calmly. The Sections had been instructed by decree of the Commune to arrange the levy of twelve thousand men for the Vendée and he was making out orders for the enrolling and arming of the contingent that the Section Pont-Neuf, *ci-devant* Section Henri IV, was required to contribute. All muskets had to be handed over to the requisitioned men. The National Guard of the Section would be armed with pikes and fowling pieces.

'I've brought you the list of the bells which must be sent to the Luxembourg for converting into cannon,' said Gamelin.

Évariste Gamelin, though without a penny to his name, was

on the list of militant members of the Section; the law allowed this privilege only to citizens rich enough to pay a contribution equivalent to the value of three days' work; and a further ten days were demanded for an elector to be eligible for office. But the Section Pont-Neuf, obsessed with equality and jealous for its autonomy, held that every citizen who had paid for his National Guard uniform out of his own pocket should be eligible to vote and to hold office. Thus it was that Gamelin was a militant citizen of his Section and a member of the Military Committee.

Fortuné Trubert put down his pen.

'Citizen Évariste,' he said, using the familiar form of address now compulsory, 'kindly go to the Convention and ask for orders to be sent us for the digging up of the cellar floors and for the washing of the soil and flagstones for saltpetre. It's not enough to have cannons. Cannons need gunpowder.'

A little hunchback, pen behind ear and papers in hand, entered the former sacristy. He was the Citizen Beauvisage, of the Committee of Surveillance.

'Citizens,' he said, 'we've had bad news: Custine has evacuated Landau'.

'Custine's a traitor!' exclaimed Gamelin.

'He will be guillotined,' Beauvisage said.

Trubert, in his usual gasping voice, reacted with his usual calm:

'The Convention has not created a Committee of Public Safety for nothing. Custine's conduct will be the subject of an inquiry. But whether an incompetent or a traitor, he will be replaced by a general resolute for victory, and *ça ira*!'*

He leafed through some papers, glancing over them with his tired eyes:

'In order that our soldiers may do their duty without any unease or worry, they must feel sure that those they have left behind them are being cared for. If you are of this opinion, Citizen Gamelin, you will demand with me, at the next assembly, that the Benevolence Committee joins with the Military Committee to help indigent families which have a relative in the army.'

He smiled and hummed:

'*Ça ira*! *ça ira*! . . .'

Working twelve and fourteen hours a day at his plain wood table in defence of his imperilled country, this humble secretary of one of the Section's committees saw no disproportion between the immensity of the task and the paucity of his means, so much did he feel himself at one with the common effort of all patriots, so much did he identify himself with the nation, so much was his own life part of the life of a great people. He was one of those who after each defeat prepared, with fantastic patience, the impossible yet certain victory. For victory had to be theirs. These little men, who had demolished the throne itself and turned upside down the old order of things, this Trubert, a little optical mechanic, this Évariste Gamelin, an unknown artist, did not expect the least mercy from their enemies. For them the alternatives were victory or death. Hence their serene fanaticism.

II

ON leaving the church of the Barnabites, Évariste Gamelin proceeded towards the Place Dauphine, renamed the Place de Thionville in honour of that impregnable city.

Situated in the most frequented quarter of Paris, this square had lost for nearly a century now the stately beauty it had once possessed: the large houses on three of its sides, built uniformly of red brick surmounted by a chain-like series of white stone arches for the luxurious splendour of officers of State in the reign of Henri IV, had had their imposing slate roofs replaced by two or three miserable plaster storeys, or had even been demolished for the ignoble construction of shabby whitewashed houses, and there could now be seen only a series of irregular, squalid, poverty-stricken façades, pierced with countless narrow, unevenly spaced windows brightened by flowerpots, birdcages and washing hung out to dry. A multitude of working people lived there: jewellers, metal workers, clock-makers, opticians, printers, laundresses, seamstresses, milliners and a few elderly lawyers who had not been swept away in the tempest which had destroyed the royal courts of justice.

It was morning and it was spring time. The early sunshine, heady as sweet wine, laughed against the walls and slid gaily through garret windows. The sash of every casement window had been raised, and below each could be seen a housewife's dishevelled head. The clerk of the Revolutionary Tribunal, stepping out of his house on his way to work, patted the cheeks of the children playing under the trees as he passed them. From the direction of the Pont-Neuf could be heard the crier's voice denouncing the treason of Dumouriez.

Évariste Gamelin lived on the side of the square next to the Quai de l'Horloge in a house dating from the time of Henry

IV which would still have had a handsome appearance but for a small, tiled attic which had been added during the reign of the last but one of the tyrants. To adapt this building, owned by some former dignitary, to the convenience of the bourgeois and artisan families which it now housed, numerous partitions and false floors had been constructed. This was why the Citizen Remacle, concierge-cum-tailor, lived in an entresol as confined in height as it was in width, where he could be seen sitting cross-legged on his work-bench, his bent head almost touching the ceiling, stitching away at a National Guard uniform, whilst his wife whose stove had no chimney apart from the well of the staircase, poisoned the other tenants with the reek of her stews and fried fish, and whilst their little daughter Joséphine, her cheeks smeared with molasses and beautiful as a little angel, sat in the open doorway playing with Mouton, the joiner's dog. The Citizeness Remacle, as big-hearted as her back was broad and her bosom ample, was thought to bestow her favours on her neighbour, the Citizen Dupont the elder, one of the dozen members of the Committee of Surveillance. Her husband, at least, strongly suspected it and the whole house used to be filled with the noise of their alternate quarrels and reconciliations. The upper floors of the house were occupied by the Citizen Chaperon, gold- and silversmith, who had his shop on the Quai de l'Horloge, by a health inspector, by a lawyer, by a gold-beater and by several employees at the Palais de Justice.

Évariste Gamelin climbed the old-fashioned staircase as far as the fourth and last floor where he had his studio and a bedroom for his mother. Here ended the wooden stairs laid with tiles which succeeded the grand stone staircase of the first floors. A ladder, fastened to the wall, led to an attic. At that moment, climbing down it, was a large man, rather elderly but with a handsome pink and florid face, who was holding with difficulty an enormous package of wares, yet singing to himself, 'I have gone and lost my servant!' He stopped his song to bid a polite good day to Gamelin who greeted him fraternally and helped him down with his package, for which the old man thanked him.

'You see here,' he said, taking up again his burden, 'some puppets I'm going to sell to a toy merchant in the Rue de la Loi. I've a whole village of people in there. They are my creatures. From me they have received a perishable body, free from joy and sorrow. I've not given them the power of thought since I'm a benevolent God.'

He was the Citizen Brotteaux, *ci-devant* aristocrat and collector of revenue and taxes.* His father, having enriched himself by the latter means, had bought himself the former: a title. In the good old days, Maurice Brotteaux had styled himself Monsieur des Ilettes and had given elegant suppers which the fair Madame de Rochemaure, wife of a Public Prosecutor, had often enlivened with her bright glances – a finished gentlewoman whose loyal fidelity was never impugned so long as the Revolution left Maurice Brotteaux in possession of his offices and emoluments, his hotel, his estates and his noble name. The Revolution swept all of them away. Now he had to earn his living by sitting under the arches of doors painting portraits, by making pancakes and fritters on the Quai de la Mégisserie, by composing speeches for members of the Assembly, by giving dancing lessons to the young citizenesses. At the moment, up in his garret which could be reached only by climbing the ladder and in which it was impossible to stand upright, Maurice Brotteaux, enriched by a pot of glue, a ball of string, a box of water-colours and numerous scraps of paper, was constructing puppets which he sold to wholesale toy merchants who resold them to the pedlars who hawked them up and down the Champs-Élysées at the end of a pole, glittering attractions for young children's eyes. In the midst of public disorder and of the great misfortune that had overwhelmed him, he still kept his serenity, finding recreation and amusement in reading his Lucretius which he carried constantly in the capacious pocket of his puce-coloured frockcoat.

Évariste gave the door of his lodging a push and it swung open. His poverty saved him the trouble of locks, and when his mother, from habit, pushed back the bolt, he would say to her: 'What's the point? People don't steal second-hand furniture – still less second-rate paintings.' In his studio, under a thick layer of dust and with their faces turned to the wall, were piled the paintings of his student days, when, according to the fashion, he had portrayed scenes of gallantry, depicting with a sleek, timorous brush, arrowless quivers and birds in flight, hazardous sports and dreams of bliss, all polished off with goose-girls and the breasts of shepherdesses flowering like roses.

But this manner had never suited his temperament. The cold treatment given to these scenes attested to their painter's uncompromising singleness of heart. His fellow students had not been wrong: Gamelin had never impressed them as a painter of erotic scenes. Today, though he was not yet thirty, these subjects seemed to him dated: relics of a time long past. He recognized in them the degrading effects of the monarchy and the shameful corruptive influences of the Courts. He accused himself of having been taken in by such a contemptible style and of having demeaned his genius by such enslavement. Now a citizen of a free people, he drew strikingly vigorous charcoal sketches of Liberty, of the Rights of Man, of the French laws, of the Republican Virtues, of proletarian Hercules overwhelming the Hydra of Tyranny, and putting into each of them all the ardour of his patriotism. But alas, they brought him not even a pittance. The times were bad for artists. It was certainly not the fault of the Convention – hurling its armies on every frontier against the kings of Europe – proud, calm and resolute in the face of the Coalitions of a Europe, which, false and ruthless to itself, was tearing itself to pieces with its own hands – no, certainly not of the Convention, which was making the Terror the order of the day, which was establishing for punishment of conspirators a pitiless Tribunal to which it would soon be giving its own members to be devoured – no, most certainly not the Convention, which, despite all of this, was calmly, thoughtfully, befriending all things beautiful, was reforming the calendar, building schools, ordering societies of painters and sculptors to be formed, giving prizes to encourage art, organizing annual exhibitions, opening the museum, and, following the example of Athens and of Rome, imparting a sublime distinction to the celebration of festivities and of public obsequies.

But French art, once so widely appreciated in England, Germany, Russia and Poland, now found closed every outlet to foreign countries. Amateurs of painting, dilettanti of the fine arts, great aristocrats and financiers, all were ruined, had emigrated or were in hiding. The men whom the Revolution had enriched, peasants who had bought up national property, speculators, army contractors, gamblers of the Palais-Royal, did not yet dare show their wealth, nor did they care, for painting meant nothing to them. It needed the reputation of Regnault or the adroitness of young Gérard to sell a picture. Greuze, Fragonard, Houin were reduced to poverty. Prud'-hon could scarcely earn bread for his wife and children by drawing subjects which Copia reproduced in stippled engravings. The patriotic painters Hennequin, Wicar, Topino-Lebrun were starving. Gamelin, unable to meet the expenses of a painting, to hire a model or to buy paints, abandoned his vast canvas of *The Tyrant Pursued to Hades by the Furies* after barely sketching in the main outline. It blocked up half the studio with its half-finished, threatening shapes, huger than life, and with its vast brood of green snakes each darting forth two sharp, forked tongues. In the foreground, to the left, could be discerned Charon in his boat, a wild-looking, haggard figure – a powerful study, well-conceived, but which smelt of the art school. There was far more of genius and originality in a canvas of smaller dimensions, also unfinished, which hung in the best lit corner of the studio. It was of Orestes, whom his sister Electra was holding in her arms on his bed of pain. The girl was putting back with a moving tenderness the matted hair that hung over her brother's eyes. The head of the hero was tragic and fine, and in it was a marked resemblance to the painter's own face.

Gamelin cast many mournful glances at this composition; sometimes his fingers itched with the craving to be at work on it, and his arms would stretch longingly towards the boldly sketched figure of Electra, only to fall back again helpless to his sides. The artist in him was burning with enthusiasm, his spirit aspired to great achievements. But he had to exhaust his energy on pot-boilers which he executed indifferently, because he was bound to please the taste of the vulgar and also because he had no skill to impress trivial things with the mark of genius. He drew little allegoricial compositions which his comrade Desmahis engraved cleverly enough in black or in colours and which were bought at a low price by the Citizen Blaise, a print-dealer in the Rue Honoré. But the trade was going from bad to worse, declared Blaise, who for some time now had declined to purchase anything.

This time, however, made inventive by necessity, Gamelin had conceived a new and happy thought, as he at any rate believed – an idea that would make the print-seller's, the engraver's and his own fortune: a patriotic pack of cards in which for the king, queen, knave of the old régime he substituted figures of Genius, Liberty, Equality. He had already sketched out all his designs, had finished several and was eager to pass on to Desmahis those which were ready for engraving. The figure which seemed to him to be the most successful represented a volunteer soldier, dressed in the three-cornered hat, blue coat with red facings, yellow breeches and black gaiters, seated on a big drum, his feet on a pile of cannon-balls and his musket between his knees. It was the 'citizen of hearts', replacing the knave of hearts. For more than six months Gamelin had been drawing volunteers with loving care. He had sold some of these in the first flush of enthusiasm. Quite a number hung around the wall of the studio. Five or six in water-colour, in gouache, in charcoal and white chalk, lay scattered on the table and chairs. Back in the month of July, 1792, when in all the squares of Paris platforms were erected for enrolling recruits, and when all the taverns were decorated with green foliage and resounded with shouts of 'Long live the Nation. Live free, or die!' Gamelin had been unable to cross the Pont-Neuf or pass the Hôtel de Ville without his heart beating at the sight of the beflagged marquee where magistrates in tricolour scarves were inscribing the names of the volunteers to the sound of the Marseillaise. But for him to have joined the army would have meant leaving his mother to starve.

Preceded by the sound of her painfully drawn breath, the

widowed Citizeness Gamelin entered the studio, sweating, palpitating, going red in the face, the National cockade hanging untidily from her bonnet and almost dropping off. She placed her basket on a chair and, remaining standing the better to regain her breath, began complaining about the high price of food.

She had been the wife of a cutler in the Rue de Grenelle – Saint-Germain, at the sign of the Ville de Châtellerault until the death of her husband, and now she lived with her son, the artist, trying to keep house for him on almost nothing. He was the elder of her two children. As for her daughter, Julie, formerly a fashionable milliner's assistant in the Rue Honoré, it was best to forget what she had become: it was not advisable for it to be known that she had emigrated with an aristocrat.

'Dear God!' sighed the citizeness, showing to her son a podgy cob of wholemeal bread. 'With the price of bread what it is, they could at least make it out of pure wheat. And no eggs, no vegetables, no cheese anywhere in the market. If we have to go on eating chestnuts, we'll end up becoming chestnuts.'

She was silent for a time, and then went on:

'Out there in the street, I've seen women who did not have a thing for their children to eat. The poor are suffering great misery. And it will go on like this until things are back as they were.'

Gamelin frowned and said;

'Mother, the scarcity we're suffering from is caused by the monopolists and speculators who starve the people and conspire with our enemies outside the country to turn the citizens against the Republic and to destroy liberty. This is what the plots and treasons of the Brissotins, the Pétions and the Rolands has led to! Perhaps it will be best if the workers in the army do march on Paris and massacre the remaining patriots that the famine's not destroying quick enough! There's no time to lose. Flour must be taxed, and any person, whoever he is, who speculates in the food of the people, who foments rebellion or who comes to terms with the enemy, must be guillotined. The Convention has just set up an extraordinary

Tribunal to put conspirators on trial. It is made up of patriots – but will they have the devotion to duty to defend our beloved country against all its enemies? We must put our trust in Robespierre; he is incorruptible. Above all, we must trust in Marat. He is the one who really loves the people, who realizes their true interests and serves them. He was always the first to unmask the traitors and frustrate plots. He's not only incorruptible; he is without fear. He alone is capable of saving the Republic in its peril.'

The Citizeness Gamelin shook her head, causing the carelessly placed cockade to fall out of her bonnet.

'No more of that, Évariste: your Marat is a man like any other, and no better than any other. You're young, you're full of illusions. What you say today about Marat, you said yesterday about Mirabeau, about La Fayette, about Pétion, about Brissot.'

'Never!' shouted Gamelin, who had genuinely forgotten.

After clearing the litter of papers, books, brushes and chalks from one end of the table, the citizeness fetched the earthenware soup bowls, two pewter bowls, two iron forks, the cob of wholemeal bread and a jug of poor wine.

Mother and son ate their meal in silence, finishing off with a small scrap of pig's fat. The mother put hers on her bread, raising each piece solemnly to her mouth on the point of her knife and chewing decorously with her toothless jaws the food that had cost so much.

She had left the best part of the food for her son, who still sat deep in thought with a faraway look in his eyes.

'Take some and eat, Évariste,' she kept saying to him with an almost rhythmic regularity. 'Take and eat.'

And on her lips these words took on the solemnity of a religious command.

She renewed her lament on the cost of food. Gamelin repeated his claim that taxation was the only remedy for these evils.

But she persisted:

'There isn't any money. The émigrés have gone off with it all. No one trusts anyone. Everybody's desperate.'

'That's enough mother! Be quiet!' shouted Gamelin. 'What's it matter if we suffer hardships for a short while? The Revolution is going to make the whole human race happy for ever and ever!'

The old woman dipped her bread in her wine: her mood mellowed and a sweet smile lit her face as she recalled the days of her youth, when she had danced on the grass on the King's birthday. There came into her mind, as it now increasingly did, the day when Joseph Gamelin, master-cutler, had asked for her hand in marriage. And all the little details poured out again. Her mother had said to her, 'Get dressed. We are going to the Place de Grève, to Monsieur Bienassis, the goldsmith's shop, to see Damiens drawn and quartered.' They'd had great difficulty pushing their way through the crowd. And there, in Monsieur Bienassis' shop, the young girl had found Joseph Gamelin, dressed in a fine rose-pink jacket, and she had known at once what the outcome would be. All the time that she was seated at the window to see the regicide torn with red hot pinchers, drenched with molten lead, pulled apart by four horses and thrown on to the fire, Joseph Gamelin, standing behind her, had showered compliments on her complexion, her hair and her figure.

The old woman drank the last drop of her wine and continued her memories of things long past.

'I brought you into the world sooner than I expected, Évariste, because of a fright I had on the Pont-Neuf. Yes, I was nearly knocked down by a crowd running to see the execution of Monsieur de Lally. You were so small when you were born the surgeon thought you wouldn't live. But I knew all right. God would be good to me and preserve you. I brought you up as well as I could – not a care or an expense did I deny you. It's only fair to say, dear Évariste, that you've always shown me you've realized that. Yes, even from a child, you've always tried to repay me in every way you've been able to. You've an affectionate and tender nature. Not like your sister. Oh, I know she's not bad at heart, but she was always selfish and uncontrollable. She never had your feeling of pity for those less fortunate than yourself. Why, when other naughty children used to rob birds' nests, you'd try to make them give the little birds back to their mother, and many a time you never gave in until you'd been cruelly kicked and beaten. When you were only seven, you'd never start quarrelling with bad boys. You used to walk quietly along the street reciting your catechism; and you'd bring home all the poor people you met to help them, until I had to give you a good beating to make you stop. The sight of anybody suffering used to make you burst into tears. And what a handsome young fellow you became when you got older. It always surprised me you never seemed to realize that – not like most good-looking boys who become conceited coxcombs and only have eyes for the girls.'

What his old mother said was true. When he was twenty Évariste had had a grave, charming face, a beauty at once austere and feminine, the features of a Minerva, goddess of wisdom. Now his gloomy eyes and pale cheeks were evidence of a sad restless spirit. But his glance, when he turned to his mother, took on for a moment the gentleness of his youth.

She went on:

'You could have made use of your advantages to run after the girls, but it gave you more pleasure to stay with me in the shop, and sometimes I had to tell you to let go of my apron-strings and go and enjoy yourself with your friends. Until the day I die, Évariste, I shall bear witness that you have been a good son. Since your father died, you've looked after me without a thought for yourself, though you were able to earn so little, you've never let me want for anything, and it's not your fault if we're both now miserable and penniless. It's the Revolution that's to blame for that.'

He made a reproachful gesture but she shrugged her shoulders and went on:

'I'm not an aristocrat. I've seen those mighty people in all their power and I'll grant you they abused the privileges their power gave them. I've seen your father beaten by the Duc de Canaleilles' servants because he didn't get out of their master's way quick enough. Least of all did I like that Austrian woman:* she was too proud and did nothing but spend money. As for the King, I thought he meant well, and it took his trial and condemnation to make me change my mind about him. All in all, I've no regrets for the old régime, though I did have some good times in those days. But don't you ever tell me the Revolution will bring equality, because men'll never be equal. It's just not possible. They can turn the country upside down and inside out, there'll always be the big people and the little people, the fat ones and the thin ones.'

While she was talking away, she was clearing the plates from the table. The artist had stopped listening. In his mind the vague design was shaping for a sans-culotte, in red cap and carmagnole, which would replace the discredited knave of spades in his pack of cards.

There was a scratching sound on the door and a girl entered, a country lass, fatter than she was tall, red-haired, bandy-legged, her left eye hidden under a wen, her right eye so pale a blue it appeared almost white, her teeth sticking out between enormous lips.

She asked, if he was Gamelin the artist, whether he could make her a portrait of her fiancé, Ferrand (Jules), a volunteer with the army in the Ardennes.

Gamelin answered that he would willingly do it when the gallant warrior returned.

The girl asked with a gentle insistence whether it might be done at once.

Smiling in spite of himself, the artist protested that he could not paint a portrait without seeing the person to be painted.

The poor girl remained silent: she had not foreseen this difficulty. With her head drooping over her left shoulder, her hands clasped across her stomach, she stayed dulled and dumb, almost as if crushed with grief. Touched and amused by such simpleness, the artist, to take the poor girl's mind off her misfortune, put into her hand one of the volunteers he had painted in water-colour and asked if that was what he was like, her fiancé in the Ardennes.

She glanced miserably at the paper and gradually her one eye came to life, then glowed, then shone; her wide face expanded into a radiant smile.

At last she exclaimed: 'It's him! It's Ferrand (Jules) to the life! It's the spitting image of Ferrand (Jules).'

Before the artist had time to think of taking the paper out of her hands, she folded it over carefully with her thick red fingers and made it into quite a little square which she slipped next to her heart between her corsets and her shift, handed the artist an assignat* for five livres, bade them good-night and went out limping and light-hearted.

III

THE afternoon of the same day, Évariste paid a visit to the shop of Citizen Jean Blaise, print-seller and also dealer in ornamental boxes, book-binding materials and games of all kinds, in the Rue Honoré, opposite the Oratoire, near the Messageries, under the sign of the *Amour Peintre*. The shop, on the ground floor of a sixty-year-old house, was entered beneath a vaulted archway whose keystone bore a grotesque horned mask. The semi-circular opening below the arch was filled with an oil painting representing *Le Sicilien ou l'Amour Peintre* after a composition by Boucher, which Jean Blaise's father had placed there in 1770 and which the sun and the rain had been wearing away ever since. On either side of the door similar openings, glazed with the largest panes obtainable and with a nymph's head on the keystone arches, offered to the public gaze the prints then in fashion together with the latest novelties in coloured engravings. On that particular day there could be seen 'gallant' scenes by Boilly, treated in his graceful if rather stiff manner, *Leçons d'amour conjugal* and *Douces résistances*, which used to scandalize the Jacobins and which the purists had denounced to the Society of Arts; the *Promenade publique* of Debucourt, with a fop in canary-coloured breeches stretched out languidly the length of three chairs, a group of horses by the young Carle Vernet, air-balloons, the *Bain de Virginie,* and figures after the Antique.

Among the citizens passing and repassing in front of the shop, only the most ragged and tattered stopped before the beautiful windows, quick to seize any chance to share, if only with their eyes, in the good things of this world. Their mouths wide open, they paid their homage, while the aristocrats merely glanced, frowned, and passed on.

As soon as he came in sight of it, Évariste fixed his eyes on

44

one of the windows above the shop, the one on the left, where there was a pot of red carnations behind a balcony of twisted ironwork. This was the window of the bedroom of Élodie, Jean Blaise's daughter. The print-dealer lived, with his only child, on the first floor of the house.

After stopping for a moment in front of the *Amour Peintr*, as if to take a deep breath, Évariste lifted the hasp on the door. He found the Citizeness Élodie, having just sold a couple of engravings by Fragonard *fils* and by Naigeon, carefully chosen from many others, anxiously holding up to the light the assignats received in payment, to examine with her beautiful eyes the delicate and intricate curves and lines of the watermark before locking them up in the cash-box, for business was being ruined by the large number of forged notes that were being circulated. As under the old régime, counterfeiters of the national currency, any who forged the King's signature, were punished by death; yet plates for printing assignats were to be found in every cellar; thousands of counterfeit notes were smuggled in by the Swiss, whole packets being put into circulation in inns; every day the English were landing bales of them on the coasts to ruin the Republic's credit and reduce patriots to destitution; and so Élodie was continually in fear of receiving bad money and in even greater fear of passing it on and so being treated as an accomplice of Pitt, though by nature she was optimistic, and certain she would be able to extricate herself should such a contingency arise.

Évariste stood gazing at her with a grave expression which conveyed deep love more strongly than any smile could. She looked at him with a little mocking pout and a coy glance from her sloe-black eyes, an expression she had adopted now that she knew he loved her, for she did not mind his knowing she knew, since such an expression provokes a lover, arouses him to feel sorry for himself and so forces him to declare his love, if he has not done so already – as Évariste had not.

Having put the assignats in the cash-box, she took a white scarf out of her work-basket and continued with some embroidery she had begun on it. Industrious and coquettish, as if

45

by instinct she knew how to fascinate with her needle and at the same time make some pretty thing for herself; her manner of sewing differed according to the onlooker: she sewed capriciously before those whom it amused her to see made a little miserable. She now began to sew carefully in front of Évariste, in whom she desired to arouse a serious affection.

Élodie was neither very young nor very pretty. She could have been considered plain at a first glance. A brunette, olive-skinned, from beneath the wide, white handerchief knotted negligently round her head, and from under which escaped ringlets of gleaming blue-black hair, her eyes of fire glowed as though scorching their sockets. Her round, laughing, slightly snub-nosed, almost peasant-like face with its prominent cheek-bones and voluptuous appeal, reminded the artist of the Borghese fawn, which, though seen only in a plaster-cast, he worshipped as the epitome of god-like mischief. A faint down accentuated the full curve of her lips. Her rounded breasts, held taut by the crossed fichu in fashion that year, seemed made for love. Her lissom waist, her lithe slender legs, her whole body moved with a primitive and delicious charm. Her glance, her breath, the quivering delight of her flesh, all of her cried out for love and gave promise of its passionate fulfil-ment. Behind the counter of that shop, she seemed like a nymph of the dance, a bacchante of the opera, shorn of her lynx skin, of her bacchanalian staff, of her garlands of ivy, checked, concealed by magic beneath the common exterior of a housewife by Chardin.

'My father isn't here,' she said. 'Wait a little for him; he won't be long.'

Her small brown hands made the needle fly over the fine linen.

'Is this pattern to your liking, Monsieur Gamelin?'

Gamelin was incapable of pretence. And love, boosting his courage, increased his frankness.

'You embroider skilfully, citizeness, but, if you wish me to speak frankly, the pattern you've made isn't simple enough or plain enough; it's inflated by the affected taste which lasted too long in France in the art of dress, furniture and wainscoting; all these clusters and garlands recall that pitiful, paltry style everybody favoured under the tyranny. Taste is undergoing a renaissance. Oh, I know we've a long way to go yet! In the days of the infamous Louis XV the art of decoration had something Chinese about it. They used to make potbellied chests of drawers, with ridiculously contorted handles, fit only for putting on the fire to warm good patriots. It's simple things that are beautiful. We must go back to antiquity. David designs beds and armchairs from scenes on Etruscan vases and from wall-paintings of Herculaneum.'

'I've seen those beds and armchairs,' said Élodie. 'They are beautiful! Everybody will soon be wanting them. I do adore the Antique like you.'

'In that case, citizeness,' Évariste replied, 'if you had trimmed the scarf with a Greek border, with ivy leaves, with serpents or crossed arrows, it would have been worthy of any Spartan girl . . . or of you. But you can still keep this design by simplifying it, reducing it to straight lines.'

She asked him what she should leave out.

He bent over the scarf: his face brushed against the blue-black ringlets of Élodie's hair. Their hands came together on the linen; their breath brushed each other's cheeks. At that moment, Évariste tasted bliss infinite and measureless; yet, as he felt his lips approaching Élodie's lips he was filled with fear lest the young woman should feel offended, and he drew back brusquely.

The Citizeness Blaise was in love with Évariste Gamelin. To her he was magnificent, with his great ardent eyes, his fine oval face, his pallor, his long, black hair parted in the middle and falling on to his shoulders, his grave demeanour, his cold reserve, his unapproachableness, his severe manner of speech, always devoid of flattery. And, because she loved him, she endowed him with all the pride of an artistic genius who would one day blaze forth masterpieces and make his name famous; and since she believed this she loved even the more. The Citizeness Blaise had no liking for masculine purity; her morals were never offended by a man yielding to his passions, to his tastes, to his desires. She was in love with Évariste, who was

47

virtuous; she was not in love with him because he was virtuous; but she appreciated the advantage it gave her in that she would never have cause for jealousy, suspicion, or fear of rivals.

All the same, at the moment she did consider him a little too reserved. If Racine's Aricie, who loved Hippolyte, admired that young hero's aggressive virtue, it was in the hope of triumphing over it, and she would have been quick to complain at a moral severity which refused to yield for her sake. And as soon as the opportunity arose, she more than half declared her love, to force him to declare his. Like the tender-hearted Aricie, the Citizeness Blaise was not disinclined to believe that in some matters of love it was up to the woman to make the advances. 'The most loving natures,' she was fond of telling herself, 'are the most timid; they have need of help and encouragement. Besides, they are so guileless, a woman can go half-way and even further without their realizing it, if she is tactful enough to make it appear that it is they who are making the bold attack and gaining the glorious victory.' What made her more confident of the outcome was that she knew very well (there was indeed no doubt about the matter) that Évariste, before the Revolution had given him the aura of a hero, had like any other mortal been in love with a woman, a quite ordinary creature, the concierge at the Academy of Arts.

Élodie, who was far from being an ingenuous girl, knew quite well there were different kinds of love. And the feeling she had for Évariste was sufficiently strong to make her consider him as a possible partner for life. She was quite ready to marry him, but did not expect her father would approve the union of his daughter with a poor and unknown artist. Gamelin had nothing; the print-dealer's business transactions entailed huge sums of money. The *Amour Peintre* brought him a great deal, the share-market even more, and he was in partnership with an army contractor who supplied the Republic's cavalry with inferior hay and damp oats. In other words, the cutler's son was a very insignificant person compared with a publisher of prints and engravings known throughout Eur-

48

ope, related to the Blaizots, to the Basans, to the Didots, and a frequent guest in the houses of the Citizens Saint-Pierre and Florian. It was not that she held her father's consent to be indispensable, as any obedient daughter would have. Her father, widowed early in life, easy-going and carefree by disposition, as great a runner after women as he was after business, had never taken much interest in her, had allowed her to grow up in complete freedom, without advice, without affection, careful not to supervise, indeed rather to ignore, the conduct of this girl in whom, as a connoisseur, he recognized that mettlesome spirit and those powers of seduction which are far more potent than a pretty face. Too warm-hearted to be over-prudent, too intelligent to be over-rash, circumspect even in her pleasures, her love affairs had never made her forget the social proprieties. Her father had continued to be infinitely grateful for this prudence, and as she had inherited from him a good business sense and a liking for making money, he remained unworried as to why so marriageable a daughter still stayed at home, where she was worth a housekeeper and four clerks to him. At twenty-seven, she felt experienced and old enough to manage her own life, and in no need of asking the advice or following the wishes of her still-young, easy-going and carefree father. But if she were to marry Gamelin, it would be necessary for Monsieur Blaise to find an opening for such an impoverished son-in-law, an interest in the business, a guarantee of regular work such as he already gave to a number of artists; in other words, provide him with a means of livelihood. And that the one would offer and the other accept, she deemed impossible, so little sympathy was there between the two men.

This difficulty was giving the fond and prudent Élodie some thought. The idea of a secret union with her lover caused her no alarm. Her philosophy saw nothing to be condemned in such a union: something which would be quite possible in view of her independent way of life, and to which Gamelin's honourable and virtuous character would give a binding and reassuring strength; but Gamelin was having difficulty in providing for himself and in supporting his old mother: it hardly seemed likely that in so straightened an existence there would be room for a love-affair, reduced even to its most primitive level. Moreover, Gamelin had still not spoken of his feelings nor of his intentions. The Citizeness Blaise had strong hopes of compelling him to do so shortly.

She brought her thoughts and her needle to a sudden halt.

'Citizen Évariste,' she said, 'this scarf doesn't please me so long as it doesn't please you. Draw me a pattern please. And whilst you're making it, like Penelope I'll undo what I've done during your absence.'

He replied with grave enthusiasm:

'It is as good as done, citizeness. I will draw for you the blade of Harmodius: a sword entwined in a garland.'

And, taking his pencil, he sketched swords and flowers in the sober, unadorned style he loved. And, at the same time, he expounded his tenets.

'The French are a reformed people,' he said, 'and they must repudiate all their legacy of servitude: bad taste, bad drawings, bad design. Watteau, Boucher, Fragonard worked for tyrants and slaves. Their paintings reveal a complete absence of clear style and clear line; a complete unawareness of nature and of truth. Masks, dolls, fripperies, childish nonsense. Posterity will despise their frivolous works. A hundred years hence all Watteau's paintings will have rotted away in attics. By 1893 art students will be covering the canvases of Boucher with their own rough sketches. David has shown the way: he is going back to the Antique; but even he has still not attained true simplicity and greatness. Our artists have still many secrets to learn from the friezes of Herculaneum, from Roman bas-reliefs, from Etruscan vases.'

He spoke long on Antique beauty, then returned to Fragonard, whom he pursued with irrepressible hatred.

'Do you know him, citizeness?'

Élodie signified with a nod that she did.

'You know also the splendid Greuze. No doubt he looks rather ridiculous with his scarlet coat and his sword. But, beside Fragonard, he could be taken for a philosopher of ancient Greece. I met that senile old dodderer Fragonard not long ago, tottering along under the arcades of the Palais-Égalité, wagging his tail, elegantly powdered, lecherous, hideous. The very sight of him made me long for some strong-armed friend of the arts to string him up on a tree and flay him alive like Apollo did to Marsyas, as an eternal eternal warning to all bad painters.'

Élodie looked up and gazed steadily at him with her bright sensual eyes.

'You know how to hate, Monsieur Gamelin. Does that mean you know also how to lo— '

'Is that you Gamelin?' interrupted the light, tenor voice of the Citizen Blaise as he entered the shop, high-boots squeaking, watch-charms tinkling, coat-tails flying, the corners of an enormous cocked hat descending to his shoulders.

Élodie put her embroidery back into her work-basket and went up to her bedroom.

'Well, Gamelin! Have you brought me something new?' demanded the Citizen Blaise.

'Possibly,' replied the artist.

And he outlined his plan.

'Our playing-cards are a disgraceful contrast to the new order. The very names of king and knave offend patriots' ears. I've planned and designed a pack of new Revolutionary playing-cards in which kings, queens and knaves are replaced by Liberties, Equalities and Fraternities. The aces are called Laws. When a player makes his call he says Liberty of clubs, Equality of spades, Fraternity of diamonds, Law of hearts. I think the designs are quite inspiring. I intend having them engraved in copperplate by Desmahis, and to patent them.'

And taking some of the finished designs in water-colour from his portfolio, the artist held them out to the print-dealer.

The Citizen Blaise turned his head, ignoring them.

'Take them along to the Convention, lad. They'll give you a vote of thanks. But don't think you'll ever make a sou out of your new invention, which isn't new. You'll have to get up earlier in the morning. Yours is the third pack of Revolutionary playing-cards I've had brought to me. Your friend Dugourc offered me one last week, a piquet set with four

Geniuses, four Liberties, four Equalities. Somebody else suggested a set with philosopher heroes, Cato, Rousseau, Hannibal, and heaven knows who else! ... And theirs had the advantage over yours, my friend, in being poorly drawn and cut in wood with a pen-knife. It shows how little you know the world if you think card players want cards designed in the style of David or with engravings in the manner of Bartolozzi! And you're under an even bigger illusion if you think it's necessary to go to all that trouble to make playing-cards conform with modern ideas. The good sans-culotte does that for himself. He simply says "The Tyrant!" or "The big pig!" and goes on using his dirty old cards and never thinks of buying a new pack. The best market for playing cards is at the Palais-Égalité: my advice is to go to the gambling houses there and offer the croupiers and punters your Liberties, Equalities, your ... how d'you call them? ... your Law of hearts – then come back and tell me what sort of reception you got!'

The Citizen Blaise seated himself on the counter, flipped some grains of snuff off his yellow nankeen breeches and looked at Gamelin with gentle pity.

'Do allow me to give you a word of advice, citizen. If you want to make something of your life, give up your packs of patriotic cards, forget about your revolutionary symbols, your Hercules, your Hydras, your Furies pursuing traitors, your geniuses of Liberty – and paint me some pretty girls. Citizens' enthusiasm for self-reformation diminishes with time; men's love for women never. Paint me some rosy-fleshed women with small feet and little hands. And get into that thick head of yours that nobody cares a damn anymore about the Revolution; everybody's sick to death with the sound of the word.'

At last, Gamelin struck back:

'Sick to death! Of the Revolution? Of events that will reverberate down the ages – the establishment of liberty, the victories of our armies, the fall of tyrants? Who could not but be inspired by such happenings? The creed of the sans-culotte Jesus lasted almost eighteen hundred years – and the religion of Liberty will have been done away with after barely four years' existence?'

Jean Blaise went on with an air of superior complacency:

'You live in a dream; I see life as it is. Believe me, my friend, the Revolution's become a bore: it's lasted too long. Five years of rapture, five years of brotherly love, of massacres, of endless speeches, of the Marseillaise, of bells ringing to man the barricades, of aristocrats hanging from lamp-posts, of heads stuck on pikes, of women with cannons between their legs, of little girls and old men in white robes on flower-bedecked chariots, the prisoners, the guillotine, semi-starvation, proclamations, cockades, plumes, swords, carmagnoles, it's all gone on too long! Nobody knows any more what it's all about! We've seen too much, we've seen too many of these great patriots raised up for us to worship only for them to be hurled from your Tarpeian Rock – Necker, Mirabeau, La Fayette, Bailly, Pétion, Manuel and all the rest of them. How do we know you're not preparing the same fate for your new heroes? . . . Nobody knows any more!'

'Name them, Citizen Blaise! Name them! These heroes we're preparing to sacrifice!' Gamelin's tone of voice recalled the print-dealer to a sense of prudence.

'I'm a Republican and a patriot,' he replied, putting his hand over his heart. 'I'm as good a Republican as you, I'm as patriotic as you, Citizen Évariste Gamelin. I do not suspect your good citizenship nor do I accuse you of opportunism. But do not forget that my good citizenship and my devotion to the public cause are proved by my deeds. As for what I believe: I believe in giving my confidence to any person who is capable of serving the country. I doff my hat to men such as Marat, such as Robespierre, who are elevated to the dangerous honour of legislative power. I am ready to support them as far as my poor means allow and to give them the humble assistance of a good citizen. The Committees can bear witness to my zeal and devotion. In conjunction with true patriots, I've supplied oats and fodder to our brave cavalry and boots for our soldiers. Only today, I've had sixty cattle sent from Vernon to the army of the Midi through countryside infested with brigands and alive with messengers of Pitt and Condé. I do not talk, I act.'

Gamelin calmly put his water-colours back into his portfolio, tied the string and put it under his arm.

Through clenched teeth he forced out the words:

'It is a strange contradiction to help our soldiers carry the flag of liberty across the world and yet betray that liberty in one's own home by trying to arouse discontent and alarm in one of its defenders. Good day to you, Citizen Blaise.'

Aflame with love and with anger, Gamelin turned before he entered the alley alongside the Oratoire to look up at the window-sill with red carnations.

He had no doubts about the future of his country. Against the unpatriotic sentiments expressed by Jean Blaise he set his faith in the Revolution. Yet he had to admit that the print-dealer's assertions appeared reasonable to the extent that the people were no longer as interested in events as they had been. It was only too obvious that the enthusiasm of the early days had been replaced by a widespread indifference; that never again would one see the huge crowds of 1789, never again the thousands united in heart, mind and soul who had thronged thick in 1790 around the altar, to commemorate the Fall of the Bastille. But that simply meant that good citizens must redouble their zeal and boldness, must reawaken the people from their apathy, summoning them to choose between liberty and death.

Thus Gamelin deliberated, and the thought of Élodie upheld his courage.

Reaching the Quais, he saw above the setting sun dark heavy clouds which gleamed like mountains of glowing lava; all the roofs of the city were bathed in golden light; all the window panes flashed dazzlingly. And Gamelin thought of the Titans forging Dike, the city of brass, out of the burning debris of worlds past and gone.

Without possessing a scrap of bread for his mother or himself, he walked in a dream of being seated at a table, laden with food, which would be endless since it would encompass the whole world and at which there would be room for all regenerated mankind. In the meantime, he persuaded himself, his country like a good mother would feed her faithful child. Forcing the gibes of the print-dealer from his mind, he convinced himself that his idea of a pack of Revolutionary playing-cards was both a good one and a new one and that he was carrying a fortune in the portfolio under his arm. 'Desmahis will engrave them,' he told himself. 'We'll publish this new patriotic game by ourselves and we'll be sure to sell ten thousand a month at twenty sols a pack.'

And, impatient to realize his project, he turned and hurried along the Quai de la Ferraille, where Desmahis lodged above a glazier's shop.

There the glazier's wife informed Gamelin that Desmahis was not in, which did not greatly surprise the artist since he knew his friend's dissipated, vagabond nature and never ceased to marvel that a man with so little perseverance was able to produce so many engravings so finely done. Gamelin decided to wait for a while. The glazier's wife offered him a chair. She was in a bad temper and grumbled about the poor state of business despite everybody saying that the Revolution, by breaking windows, was making the fortune of glaziers.

Night began to fall: giving up waiting, Gamelin took his leave. Whilst crossing the Pont-Neuf, he saw coming along the Quai des Morfondus, carrying torches and driving back the crowds, a mounted detachment of the National Guard escorting, with a great clattering of their sabres, a cart in which a man was being driven slowly to the guillotine – a man nobody knew, some *ci-devant* aristocrat, the first to be condemned by the new Revolutionary Tribunal. He could be glimpsed now and then between the Guards' hats, seated facing the rear of the cart, his hands tied behind his back, his bare head swaying. The executioner was standing beside him, leaning against the rail of the cart. The passers-by, who had now formed a large crowd of onlookers, were telling each other he was probably one of those who had been trying to starve people, and they stood watching indifferently. As he came closer, Gamelin suddenly recognized Desmahis amongst them. He was trying to push his way through the crowd to run across the Quai in front of the procession. Gamelin called out and grasped him by the shoulder; Desmahis turned his head.

He was a young sturdily built, handsome man. At the Academy of Arts they had used to say that Desmahis possessed the head of Bacchus and the body of Hercules. His friends had called him 'Barbaroux' on account of his resemblance to that deputy of the people.

'Wait,' Gamelin said. 'I've something important to say to you.'

'Don't bother me now!' Desmahis replied roughly.

And, watching for an opportunity to cross quickly, he muttered over his shoulder:

'I was following a girl, a marvellous creature, in a straw hat, a milliner's assistant, fair hair right down her back; this damned cart got in the way . . . She'll be at the other end of the bridge by now.'

Gamelin tried again to hold him back, swearing that the matter was of great importance.

But Desmahis had already slipped across in between horses, guards, sabres and torches, and was fast in pursuit of the young girl from the milliner's shop.

IV

It was ten o'clock in the morning. The light of the April sunshine glistened on the wet leaves of the trees. The air, freshened by the previous night's storm, smelt deliciously sweet. The solitude's gentle stillness was broken only at long intervals by a horseman passing along the Allée des Veuves. On a wooden bench beside a thatched cottage in this shady Allée, Évariste sat waiting for Élodie. Since the day their hands had met over her embroidery and their breath had touched each other's cheeks, he had not returned to the *Amour Peintre*. For an entire week his proud stoicism and his timidity, which was becoming more and more pronounced, had kept him away from Élodie. He had written her a grave, seriously ardent letter, in which he had explained his grievances against the Citizen Blaise, and, making no mention of his love and concealing his sadness, had announced his determination never to return to the print-dealer's shop, a determination he was maintaining with a firmness greater than was likely to be approved by a woman in love.

Contentious by nature, Élodie's first instinct was always to defend her property under all circumstances, and she had now set about winning back her lover with all possible speed. She had first considered going to see him in his studio at the Place de Thionville. But, knowing his touchiness and judging from his letter that he was both hurt and angry, she was frightened lest his bitterness be turned against her as well as her father, and he would decide not to see her again also. She thought it better therefore to arrange a sentimental, romantic rendezvous with him, one which he could not well refuse and at which she would have ample time to charm and cajole him, since the solitude of the meeting-place would conspire to help her fascinate and conquer him.

At that time, little thatched cottages, built by shrewd architects to flatter the rustically inclined tastes of city people, were to be found in all the pseudo-English gardens and along all the fashionable country walks. The owner of this particular thatched cottage, La Belle Lilloise, had made it into a café, and to enhance its rustic charm had had it built on top of the artistically imitated remains of a ruined castle. And, as if a thatched cottage on a ruined castle were not enough to attract sensitive-natured customers, he had erected a tomb beside it beneath a weeping willow: a column surmounted by a funeral urn bearing the inscription: 'Cleonice to her faithful Azor'. Cottages, ruins, tombs: on the brink of its own extinction, the aristocracy had erected in its ancestral parks these symbols of poverty, decadence and death. And now the patriotic citizens took their pleasures – drinking, dancing, making love – in sham thatched cottages, in the shade of sham ruins, and amongst sham tombs; citizens and aristocrats, all were loving disciples of Rousseau and of Nature, all throbbed to the same pulse of philosophic sensitivity.

Having arrived at the rendez-vous before the appointed time, Évariste sat waiting, measuring the time by the beating of his heart as if it were the pendulum of a clock. A patrol passed, conducting a convoy of prisoners. Ten minutes later, a woman dressed entirely in pink, the fashionable bouquet of flowers in her hand and accompanied by a gallant in a three-cornered hat, red coat, striped waistcoat and breeches, slipped into the cottage, both looking so like the ladies and gentlemen of the old régime it made one think, like the Citizen Blaise, that there must be something in mankind which Revolutions will never change.

A few more moments passed and an old woman appeared from the direction of Rueil or Saint-Cloud, carrying before her in her outstretched arms a cylindrical box painted in bright colours, and sat on the bench beside Gamelin. She put her box down in front of her and he saw that the lid had a revolving needle fixed to it. The poor woman played a lottery game for the little children who came to the gardens. She also sold an old-fashioned sweetmeat which had once been called 'forget-me-not', but whether this name had conveyed too much the importune ideas of unhappiness and retribution or whether it had been abandoned by chance, the 'forget-me-nots' were now called 'pleasures'.

The old woman wiped the sweat from her forehead with the corner of her apron and gave vent to complaints against heaven, accusing God of injustice for having made life so hard for His creatures. Her man kept a tavern on the river bank at Saint-Cloud, and she came up every day to the Champs-Élysées, whirling her rattle and shouting: 'Pleasures for sale, mesdames!' And with all this work they could not earn enough to support them in their old age.

Seeing the young man on the bench disposed to sympathize with her, she expounded at great length the cause of her misfortunes. It was the Republic which, by robbing the wealthy, was taking the bread out of the mouths of the poor. And there was no use hoping for a better state of affairs. She knew, on the contrary, from many signs that things would only get worse. At Nanterre, a woman had given birth to a baby with the head of a serpent; lightning had struck the church at Rueil and melted the cross on the steeple; a werewolf had been seen in the woods at Chaville; masked men were poisoning water supplies and throwing powder into the air which spread diseases . . .

Évariste saw Élodie jumping out of a carriage. He ran towards her. The young woman's eyes were shining beneath the faint shadow of her straw hat; her lips, as red as the carnations she held in her hand, were smiling. A scarf of black silk, crossed between her breasts, was tied behind her back. The quick movements of her knees could be discerned beneath her yellow gown and on her feet were a pair of low-heeled shoes. Her hips were almost entirely free, for the Revolution had released the waists of its citizenesses; her skirts, however, still flaired out below the loins, concealed the curves of her legs only by exaggerating them and veiled the reality only by dilating its likeness.

He wanted to speak but could not find words, and reproached himself for this inadequacy which was preferred by

Élodie to the most eloquent of welcomes. She noticed also and took it to be a good sign that he had tied his cravate with more than usual care. She gave him her hand.

'I wanted to see you to have a talk with you,' she said. 'I haven't replied to your letter: it upset me; it didn't sound like you. It would have been far nicer if you had written it more naturally. As it is, it would be an injustice to your character and your commonsense to conclude that you don't want to return to the *Amour Peintre* just because you had a trifling argument there about politics with a man much older than yourself. Rest assured you need have no fear that my father will receive you ill when you visit us again. You do not know him: he will remember neither what he said to you nor what you replied. I don't say there is any great bond of sympathy between you both; but he bears no malice. I tell you frankly, he doesn't concern himself much over you . . . nor over me. He thinks only of his own affairs and his own pleasures.'

She led the way towards the shrubberies around the cottage, where he followed her with some distaste, knowing them to be the meeting-place for quick love affairs and paid assignments. She chose the most secluded table.

'What a lot of things I've got to talk to you about, Évariste! Friendship has its rights: you'll allow me to use them? I'll speak mostly about you . . . and a little about myself, if you don't mind.'

The landlord having brought a carafe and some glasses, she poured the lemonade into the glasses herself, like a good housewife; then she told him about her childhood, she spoke of her mother's beauty, which she loved to extol from filial piety and as the origin of her own beauty; she boasted of the vigour of her grandparents, for she was proud of her bourgeois blood. She told how, having lost this adored mother when she was sixteen, she had lived without anyone to love or rely on. She painted herself as she was, passionate, sensitive, courageous, and she added:

'Évariste, when I was a girl I spent too many melancholy and lonely years not to know the value of a heart like yours, and I warn you I will not willingly or easily give up a sympathy on which I believed I could rely and which was dear to me.'

Évariste looked at her tenderly:

'Can it be, Élodie, that I am not unimportant to you? May I believe . . .'

He stopped, fearing to say too much and thereby take advantage of so trusting a friendship.

She held out to him a little confiding hand that half peeped out of the long narrow sleeve with its lace frillings. Her bosom rose and fell with long-drawn sighs.

'Credit me, Évariste, with all the feelings you would like me to have for you, and you will not be mistaken about how my heart truly feels.'

'Élodie, Élodie, what you've just said, will you still repeat it when you know . . .'

He hesitated.

She lowered her eyes.

He concluded very softly:

'. . . that I love you?'

On hearing these last few words, she blushed: out of pleasure. And, whilst her eyes expressed a voluptuous tenderness, there flickered in spite of herself about one corner of her lips a quizzical smile. She was thinking:

And he believes it was he was the first to declare himself! . . . and he's frightened he's perhaps upset me! . . .

And she said to him fondly:

'You'd never seen, my dear, that I loved you?'

They felt as if they alone existed in all the world. In his exaltation Évariste raised his eyes to the sky gloriously blue and full of light:

'Look, the sky is watching us! It is good and kind and adorable, like you, my beloved. It has your sparkling brightness, your softness, your smile.'

He felt himself one with all nature, he associated it with his joy, with his triumph. To his eyes it was in order to celebrate their betrothal that the chestnut blossoms were alight like flaming candles and the poplars blazed on high like gigantic torches.

He exulted in his strength and his power. She, with her

gentler and also finer nature, more supple and more pliable, knew that her weakness was her strength and, as soon as he was conquered, submitted herself to him; now that she had him under her domination, she acknowledged in him the master, the hero, the god, and burned to obey, to admire and to offer herself. Under the shade of the shrubbery, he gave her a long, ardent kiss beneath which she bent back her head and, in Évariste's arms, she felt all her flesh soften and melt like warmed wax.

For a long time they talked on and on about themselves, everything else forgotten. Évariste was full of vague, elevated ideas, which threw Élodie into ecstasies. Élodie spoke of ordinary things, practical and personal. Then, when she judged there would be no advantage to her in staying longer, she stood up with a decisive movement, gave him the three red carnations from her balcony and jumped lightly back into the cabriolet which had brought her. It was a hired carriage, painted yellow, hung very high on its wheels, and it certainly had nothing of the ordinary about it, nor the coachman either. But Gamelin was not accustomed to hiring carriages, nor were those with whom he mixed. And at the sight of her being whirled away on those great wheels, he had a shrinking feeling in his heart and was assailed by a presentiment of overwhelming sorrow: by a kind of mental hallucination, it seemed to him that that hired carriage was carrying Élodie away from him far beyond the present world of everyday things towards a rich and joyous city, towards abodes of luxury and pleasure which he would never be able to enter.

The carriage disappeared. Évariste's disturbed mind gradually grew calmer: but a dull anguish remained and he felt that the hours of tenderness and forgetfulness, which he had just experienced, he would never know again.

He passed by the Champs-Élysées, where women in bright dresses were sitting on wooden chairs, talking or sewing, while their children played under the trees. A woman selling 'pleasures', though the box she carried was shaped like a drum, recalled to him the old woman with her box in the Allée des Veuves, and it seemed as if a whole epoch of his life had passed away between his meeting with this one and that one. He crossed the Place de la Révolution.* In the Tuileries Gardens he heard the distant roar of many voices, that tremendous sound of men all shouting together, so familiar in the great early days of the Revolution but which its enemies pretended would never be heard again. He hastened his steps as the roar grew louder and louder, reached the Rue Honoré and found it thronged with a crowd of men and women shouting: 'Vive la République! Vive la Liberté!' The walls of the gardens, the windows, the balconies, the roofs were packed with spectators waving their hats and handkerchiefs. Preceded by a sapper who was clearing a way for the procession, and surrounded by municipal officers, National Guards, gunners, gendarmes, hussars, there was advancing slowly, borne above the heads of the citizens, a man with a morose complexion, his forehead encircled with a crown of oak leaves, his body enveloped in an old green indoor coat with an ermine collar. The women were throwing him flowers. As he was carried along he darted all around him the piercing look of his jaundiced eyes, as if, in that enthusiastic multitude, he was still seeking out enemies of the people to denounce, traitors to punish. As he went by, Gamelin took off his hat, and joining his voice to a hundred thousand others, shouted:

'Vive Marat!'

Like the personification of Fate itself, the conquering hero entered the Hall of the Convention. Whilst the crowd slowly dispersed, Gamelin sat on a stone post in the Rue Honoré, pressing his hand over his heart to contain its wild beating. What he had just seen had filled him with an emotion unearthly in its blazing enthusiasm.

He venerated, he worshipped Marat who, sick, feverish and devoured by ulcers, was exhausting the last remnants of his strength in the service of the Republic, and who, in his poor house, open to all, always welcomed Gamelin with open arms, always spoke to him afire with enthusiasm about public affairs, sometimes questioned him about the plans of scoundrels. So now Gamelin was rejoicing that the enemies of 'The Friend of the People', in plotting his downfall had achieved

63

his triumph; he blessed the Revolutionary Tribunal which, in acquitting the Friend of the People, had given back to the Convention the most vehement, the most uncompromising of its legislators: In his mind he saw again that head burning with fever, garlanded with the civic crown, those features alive with intransigent pride and pitiless love, that powerful face, worn and ravaged, that clenched mouth, that broad chest, the agony-racked strength of this man who from up on his living chariot of triumph had seemed to be saying to his fellow-citizens: 'Follow my example! Be you all patriots to the death!'

The street was deserted, invaded by the shadows of the approaching night; the lamp-lighter passed with hand-lantern and pole, and Gamelin murmured:

'To the death!'

V

At nine o'clock in the morning Évariste found Élodie waiting for him on a bench in the Luxembourg Gardens.

Ever since they had exchanged their vows of love a month ago they had seen each other every day, either at the *Amour Peintre* or at the studio in the Place de Thionville. Yet the tenderness of their intimacy had a certain reserve about it, imposed by the serious and virtuous young lover, who, though ready to make his dear mistress his own before the law or with God alone for witness, according as circumstances demanded, was prepared to do so only in public and in the full light of day. Élodie knew quite well that this resolution was all that was honourable; but, despairing of a marriage which everything made impossible and refusing to brave social conventions, she secretly hoped for a liaison which could be kept hidden until time had given it respectability. She thought she would one day overcome the scruples of her too respectable lover and not wanting to delay any longer certain necessary revelations about her past, she had asked him to come for an hour's talk with her in the deserted gardens, near the Carthusian convent.

She gave him a tender, open-hearted look, took his hand, sat him on the bench beside her and spoke to him choosing her words carefully:

'I respect you too much, Évariste, to hide anything from you. I think I am worthy of you but I would not be if I did not tell you everything. Hear me and be my judge. I have nothing base nor vile to reproach myself with, nothing selfish even. I have been weak and credulous ... Take into account, dear friend, the difficult circumstances I was in. You know them; I lost my mother; I was left in the care of a young father who thought only of his own amusement and couldn't be bothered

65

with me. I was sensitive; by nature I was open and generous. I'd plenty of common sense as well. But in the past I have let myself be ruled by my feelings and not by my reason. I know, also, it would be the same today if the two were not now more in harmony, and I would give myself to you, Évariste, completely and forever!'

She explained herself clearly and firmly. Her words were prepared; for a long time she had resolved to make her confession, because she was open-hearted, because it pleased her to imitate Rousseau, and because she told herself with reason: 'Some day Évariste will find out secrets which I'm not the only one to know: it will be best and to my credit to tell him of my own free will what he would one day discover to my shame.' And, being naturally tender-hearted and easily led, she did not feel she was much to blame herself and this made her confession the easier; she certainly intended, as well, to tell only the minimum necessary.

'Ah, dear Évariste,' she sighed, 'Why could we not have met in those days when I was alone, forsaken . . .'

Évariste had taken literally Élodie's request that he should be her judge. Inclined by nature and his literary proclivities to indulge in private judgements, he prepared himself to receive Élodie's confessions.

As she hesitated, he indicated he was waiting for her to proceed.

She said very simply:

'A young man, who showed me a few of the good among the many bad qualities he possesses, found I attracted him a little and courted me with a perseverance surprising in such a person: he was full of the charm of youth and the idol of many attractive women who made no effort to hide their adoration from him. It was neither his good looks nor his youthful charm that appealed to me . . . He knew how to touch my heart by tokens of love and I believed that he truly loved me. He was passionate and yet so tender. I asked nothing more binding than his love, and his love was fickle. I blame only myself; this is my confession I'm making, not his. I am not complaining about him, for he is now a complete stranger to me. That I swear to you, Évariste! He is now to me as if he had never existed!'

She was silent. Évariste made no reply. He crossed his arms; in his eyes was a fixed, sombre look. He was thinking of both of them: of Élodie, his mistress, and of Julie, his sister. Julie too had listened to a lover, but, he thought, unlike the unfortunate Élodie she had let herself be carried away, not by the mistakes of an over-sensitive heart, but in order to find luxury and pleasure far away from those who loved her. His rigid morality had condemned his sister and was now ready to condemn his mistress.

Élodie continued, her voice very low:

'I had read so much philosophy; I believed men were naturally honest. My misfortune was to have met a lover who had not studied in the same school of Nature and morality, and whom class prejudice, ambition, self-love, and a false sense of honour had made selfish and treacherous.'

Her carefully calculated words produced their desired effect. Gamelin's eyes softened. He asked:

'Who was your seducer? Do I know him?'

'You do not know him.'

'Tell me his name.'

She had foreseen this and was determined not to tell it. She gave her reasons.

'I beg you, spare me that. For both our sakes. I've already said too much.'

And, as he insisted:

'For the sake of our love, which is more sacred to me than anything else, I will tell you nothing more precise about this ... stranger. I refuse to give you the least shadow for your jealousy to exaggerate. I will not bring this unimportant ghost back to haunt us both. And I am most certainly not going to acquaint you with this man's name when I have forgotten him.'

Gamelin insisted she surrendered to him the name of her seducer: that was the term he persisted in using, for to him there was no doubt that Élodie had been seduced, deceived, taken advantage of. He did not even conceive that it could

67

possibly have been otherwise, that she had obeyed the desire, the irresistible desire, of her own flesh and blood; he did not conceive that this tender, voluptuous creature, this lovely victim, had offered herself; it was necessary, to satisfy his ideal, that she had been taken by force or by guile, ravished, unable to turn to anyone for help. He questioned her in guarded terms, but with a sharp, embarrassing insistency. He asked her how this liaison had begun, if it had been long or short, tranquil or troubled, and how it had been broken off. And he came back unceasingly to the means this man had used to seduce her, as if these must unquestionably have been strange and outrageous. Everything he asked proved in vain. With a gently, beseeching stubbornness, she remained silent, her mouth compressed and her eyes full of tears.

Yet, when Évariste asked where this man was now, she replied:

'He has left the kingdom.'

She quickly corrected herself:

'... France.'

'An émigré!' Gamelin exclaimed.

She looked at him, speechless, at the same time reassured and dismayed to see him create for himself a truth which conformed with his political passions, and give of his own volition a Jacobin twist to his jealousy.

In actual fact Élodie's lover was a lawyer's under-clerk, a very pretty little lad, an angelic guttersnipe, whom she had adored and whose memory after three years still made her body thrill. He had always been on the look-out for rich, old women: he left Élodie for a lady of wide experience who rewarded his merits. After the abolition of offices, he had been given a post in the Mairie of Paris, and was now a sansculotte dragoon and the kept lover of a *ci-devant* aristocrat.

'An aristocrat! An émigré!' repeated Gamelin, whom she took good care not to undeceive, having never wished him to know the whole truth. 'And he shamefully abandoned you?'

She nodded her head.

He pressed her to his heart.

'Dearest victim of tyrannical corruption, I will avenge this infamy for you by my love. But, by heavens, if ever I meet him, I shall now know him!'

She turned her head away, saddened and amused, and disappointed, all at the same time. She would have preferred him wiser in matters of love, more natural, more brutal. She felt he pardoned so quickly only because his imagination was cold and the secrets she had just revealed to him awoke in him none of those mental images which torture the sensually inclined, and that indeed he only saw in this seduction a moral and social fact.

They had risen and were following the green paths of the garden. He told her that he esteemed her all the more because of the wrong she had suffered. Élodie felt that that was more than she required but, such as he was, she loved him, and she admired the artistic genius she saw so brilliantly in him.

As they came out of the Luxembourg Gardens, they met great crowds in the Rue de l'Égalité and all around the Théâtre des Nations, which did not at all surprise them: since, for several days, great excitement had been agitating the most patriotic Sections; everybody was denouncing the Orléans faction and the accomplices of Brissot who were plotting, it was said, the fall of Paris and the massacre of all Republicans. And Gamelin himself, only a short time ago, had signed a petition from the Commune demanding the expulsion of the Twenty-one.

Just before they passed under the arcade which joined the theatre to the neighbouring house, they had to make their way through a group of citizens clad in their carmagnoles who were being harangued, from up on the gallery, by a young soldier, looking in his helmet of panther-skin as handsome as the Eros of Praxiteles. This attractive-looking soldier was accusing the Friend of the People of laziness. He was saying:

'You are sleeping, Marat, and the Federalists are forging chains for us!'

No sooner had Élodie seen who it was than she said quickly:
'Come, Évariste!'

The crowd, she said, was frightening her and she was afraid of fainting in the crush.

They parted in the Place de la Nation, swearing their eternal love to each other.

That morning, very early, the Citizen Brotteaux had made the Citizeness Gamelin the magnificent gift of a capon. It would have been imprudent on his part to say how he had come by it: for he had been given it by a certain lady of the market at the Pointe Eustache, whose letters he occasionally wrote for her, and it was well known that the ladies of the market cherished Royalist sympathies and were in touch by correspondence with the émigrés. The Citizeness Gamelin had accepted the capon with deep gratitude. Such things were scarcely ever seen now; food of all kinds became more expensive every day. The people feared a famine: everybody said that that was what the aristocrats wanted, and that the food-grabbers were preparing for it.

Invited to eat his share of the capon at the midday meal, the Citizen Brotteaux duly appeared and congratulated his hostess on the rich aroma of her cooking. For indeed the artist's studio was filled with the smell of a savoury meat soup.

'You are a true gentleman, monsieur,' replied the good lady. 'As an appetizer for your capon, I've made some vegetable soup with a slice of bacon and a big beef bone. There's nothing gives soup a flavour better than a marrow bone.'

'A praiseworthy maxim, citizeness,' replied old Brotteaux. 'And you will do wisely, if tomorrow, and the next day, and all the rest of the week, you put this precious bone back into the pot, so that it will continue to flavour it. The wise woman of Panzoust used to do that: she made a soup of green cabbages with a rind of bacon and an old *savorados*. That is what they call the tasty and succulent medullary bone in her country, which is also my country.'

'This lady you speak of, monsieur,' the Citizeness Gamelin put in, 'wasn't she a little on the careful side, making the same bone last so long?'

'She did not live on a grand scale,' Brotteaux replied. 'She was poor, even though she was a prophetess.'

At that moment Évariste Gamelin came in, still deeply

affected by the confession he had just heard and promising himself he would discover the identity of Élodie's seducer, so that he might wreak on him the vengeance of the Republic and of himself.

After the usual politenesses, the Citizen Brotteaux resumed the thread of his discourse:

'Those who make a trade out of foretelling the future rarely grow rich. Their attempts to deceive are too easily found out and arouse detestation. And yet it would be necessary to detest them much, much more if they foretold the future correctly. For a man's life would become intolerable, if he knew what was going to happen to him. He would be made aware of future evils, and would suffer their agonies in advance, while he would get no joy of present blessings since he would know how they would end. Ignorance is the necessary condition of human happiness, and it has to be admitted that on the whole mankind observes that condition well. We are almost entirely ignorant of ourselves; absolutely of others. In ignorance, we find our bliss; in illusions, our happiness.'

The Citizeness Gamelin put the soup on the table, said the *Benedicite,* seated her son and her guest, and began to eat standing up, declining the chair which Brotteaux offered her next to him, since, she said, she knew what courtesy required of her.

VI

Ten o'clock in the morning. Not a breath of air. It was the hottest July anyone had known. In the narrow Rue de Jérusalem about a hundred citizens of the Section were queuing at the baker's door, under the watchful eyes of four National Guards standing at ease smoking their pipes.

The Convention had decreed the *maximum*: hence corn and flour had instantly disappeared. Like the Israelites in the desert, the people had to get up before dawn if they wanted to eat. All these people, tightly packed together beneath a sky of molten lead, whose heat made the foulness in the gutters steam and spread everywhere the stench of dirty, sweating humanity, all of them, men, women and children, were pushing each other, insulting each other, giving each other looks of hate, disgust, interest, desire or indifference. They had learnt, through bitter experience, that there was not enough bread for everybody: so the last to arrive were always trying to push to the front; those who had to move back were always complaining, losing their tempers and vainly claiming their disregarded rights. The women savagely jabbed with their elbows and pushed with their bosoms to keep their place or gain a better one. When the pressure became too suffocating, shouts always arose: 'Stop pushing!' And everybody would protest that it was someone else pushing them.

To avoid these daily disorders, the officials appointed by the Section had had the idea of attaching a rope to the baker's door for each person to take hold of in an orderly line; but hands too close together would meet each other on the rope and a fight would follow. Whoever lost hold, could never regain it. Those malevolently or mischievously inclined would cut it, and so the idea had to be abandoned.

In this particular queue, some were suffocating, some believed themselves dying, some made jokes, some flung obscene remarks, some hurled abuse at the aristocrats and the Federalists, the authors of all evil. When a dog went by, the wits hailed it by the name of Pitt. Occasionally a loud slap resounded, the hand of a citizeness meeting the cheek of someone attempting to be over familiar; while, pressed hard against by her neighbour, a young servant girl, with her eyes half-shut and her mouth half-open, kept gasping softly. Any word, any gesture, any attitude likely to arouse the broad humour of the ordinary amiable Frenchman, would cause a group of young ruffians to strike up the *Ça ira*, regardless of the protests of an old Jacobin indignant that an obscenely equivocal meaning should be attached to a refrain which expressed the Republican faith in a future of justice and happiness.

A bill-sticker appeared, his ladder under his arm to post up a proclamation by the Commune on a blank wall opposite the baker's shop, rationing the supplies of butcher's meat. Passers-by stopped to read the notice, still sticky with paste. An old woman selling cabbages, with a basketful of them on her back, called out in her loud, cracked voice:

'No more good meat for the likes of us! We'll have to make do with the guts!'

Suddenly there came from a sewer such a strong stench that several people were taken sick. A woman was found to be so ill she was handed over in a faint to two National Guards who carried her a few paces to a pump and put her head under it. Everybody held their noses; grumbling growls arose; ghastly and alarming rumours passed from one person to the next. People began asking each other whether some animal was buried there, or even some poisonous substance placed by some ill-disposed person, or more likely still some victim of the September massacres, an aristocrat or a priest, left in some neighbouring cellar.

'Is that where they put them then?'

'They left them everywhere!'

'It must be one of those prisoners from the Châtelet. On the

2nd September I saw three hundred of them piled up in a heap on the Pont au Change.'

The Parisians feared the vengeance of these aristocrats who, though dead, could still poison them.

Évariste Gamelin joined the queue, wanting to spare his old mother the fatigue of a long wait. His neighbour, the Citizen Brotteaux, accompanied him, tranquil, smiling, his Lucretius in the wide pocket of his coat.

The good old fellow enjoyed the sight around him, saying it was like a scene of low life worthy of the brush of a modern Téniers.

'These street-porters and good wives, are more amusingly quaint than the Greeks and Romans so dear to our artists now-adays. For myself, I've always favoured the Flemish manner.'

What he was too tactful and polite to mention was that he himself had once possessed a gallery full of Dutch masters equalled only by Monsieur Choiseul's collection in number and excellence.

'There is no beauty except in the Antique,' replied Gamelin, 'and in what is inspired by it: but I grant you those scenes of low-life by Téniers, Steen or Ostade are far better than the frills and fripperies of Watteau, Boucher or Van Loo: they make humanity look ugly but they do not degrade it like a Baudouin or a Fragonard.'

A street-hawker passed, shouting:

'*Bulletin of the Revolutionary Tribunal!* . . . list of the con-demned!'

'It's not enough, just one Revolutionary Tribunal', said Gamelin. 'There should be one in each town . . . no, even more, one in every village, in every hamlet. Every father of a family, every citizen, should constitute themselves judges. It's nothing less than parricide to show mercy when our country is threatened by the cannons of the enemy and the daggers of traitors. Think of it! Lyons, Marseilles, Bordeaux in revolt, insurrection in Corsica, the Vendée in flames, Mayence and Valenciennes in the hands of the enemy, treason everywhere – in the countryside, in the towns, in the camps, treason seated on the very benches of the National Convention, treason even in the councils of war of our generals!... Only the guillotine can save our country!'

'I've no objection, fundamentally, to the guillotine,' replied old Brotteaux. 'Nature is my only guide and teacher and she has certainly never given me evidence to believe that a man's life has any value; indeed, on the contrary, she shows in many ways that it has none. The sole destiny of all living beings seems only to become the fodder of other living beings fated also to the same end. Murder is a law of nature: consequently the death-penalty is lawful, provided it is exercised neither from virtuous nor judicial motives, but from necessity or in order to gain some profit from it. However, I must have perverse instincts, since the sight of blood is repugnant to me, a fault of character which all my philosophy has not yet been able to rectify.'

'Republicans are sensitive and humane,' Gamelin pursued. 'It's only the despots who believe the death penalty is a natural attribute of authority. One day the sovereign people will abolish it. Robespierre was against, and so were all good patriots; a law to abolish it cannot come too soon. But that won't be possible until the last enemy of the Republic has perished beneath the sword of justice.'

By now there were a number of late-comers behind Gamelin and Brotteaux, amongst them being several women from the Section: one a handsome buxom tricoteuse, wearing sabots and a kerchief and with a sword dangling from a shoulder belt; another a fair-haired, pretty girl in a worn little shawl looking very nervous; still another was a young mother, thin and pale, giving suck to a sickly-looking infant.

Unable to get more milk, the baby was trying to scream, but his cries were weak and his sobs choking gasps. He was pitifully small with a pallid and unhealthy skin and inflamed eyes; his mother kept gazing at him with sad, anxious eyes.

'He is very young,' said Gamelin, turning to look at the unfortunate child pressed wailing against his back amongst the packed crowd of late arrivals.

'He is six months old, the poor little darling!... His father is away with the army; he is one of the men who drove back the Austrians at Condé. His name is Dumonteil (Michel), a draper's assistant by trade. He enlisted at a booth they'd put up in front of the Hôtel de Ville. The poor boy wanted to defend his countty and to see the world. He writes to me telling me to be patient. But how d'you think I can feed Paul . . . that's what we call him . . . when I can't feed myself?'

'We'll be here for another hour at least,' exclaimed the pretty, fair-haired girl, 'and this evening we'll have to go through the same ceremony all over again outside the grocer's. You risk your life just to get three eggs and a quarter pound of butter.'

'Butter,' the Citizeness Dumonteil sighed. 'It's three months since I saw any!'

And a chorus of women's voices rose, bewailing the scarcity and cost of food, cursing the émigrés and consigning to the guillotine the *commissaires* of the Sections who gave shameless hussies fine table fowl and four-pound loaves of bread in return for their shameful services. Alarming stories swept round of cattle drowned in the Seine, of sacks of flour emptied in the sewers, of loaves of bread thrown into the latrines . . . It was all being done by the Royalists, the Rolandists, the Brissotins, who were determined to exterminate the people of Paris.

Suddenly the pretty, fair-haired girl with the tattered shawl burst out shrieking as if her skirts were on fire, for she started shaking them violently and turning out her pockets, proclaiming to all and sundry that her purse had been stolen.

The announcement of such a theft caused a wave of deep indignation to sweep through this crowd of common people, who had pulled down the fine houses in the Faubourg Saint-Germain, who had invaded the Tuileries, without taking away a thing, ordinary working men and women who would have had no compunction in burning down the Palace of Versailles itself, but would have considered their honour lost if they had stolen even so much as a pin. The young hooligans in the queue greeted the pretty girl's loss with vulgar jokes but these were immediately put a stop to by the outburst of public indignation. There was talk of hanging the thief from the nearest lamp-post. An investigation began in which everybody spoke at once and nobody was prepared to listen to a reason. The big tricoteuse, pointing to an old man suspected of being a defrocked monk, swore it was the 'Capuchin' who was the thief. The crowd, immediately persuaded, began shouting for his death.

The old man, so speedily denounced by the public spite, was standing very humbly in front of the Citizen Brotteaux. There was no denying he had all the appearance of a *ci-devant* monk. He had a venerable enough air, though it obviously bore evidence of the sufferings he had endured from the violence of the crowd and of the memories of the horrors of the September days. The fear on his face encouraged the suspicions of the crowd which is always ready to believe that only the guilty dread its judgments, as though the reckless haste with which it comes to them was not sufficient to terrify the most innocent.

Brotteaux had made it a rule never to oppose himself to popular feeling, above all when it showed itself at its most illogical and cruel, because, at such moments, he would say to himself, the voice of the people was the voice of God. But Brotteaux now proved inconsistent: he asserted that this man, whether Capuchin or not, could not have robbed the citizeness, since he had never for one single moment gone anywhere near her.

The crowd concluded that any one who defended the thief must be his accomplice, and now it was proposed to treat the two of them in the same violent manner, and, when Gamelin offered himself as a guarantor for Brotteaux, the wiseacres in the crowd proposed sending him along with the other two to the Section's headquarters.

But the pretty girl suddenly cried out joyfully that she had found her purse. The crowd immediately turned on her and, with a storm of hisses, threatened her with a public whipping, like a nun.

'Monsieur,' said the monk to Brotteaux, 'I thank you for defending me. My name is of no importance, but I owe it you to tell you that it is Louis de Longuemare. I am indeed a religious, but not a Capuchin, as these women have said. There is a world of difference, since I am a monk of the Order of Barnabites, which gave countless doctors and saints to the Church. Some people believe our Order originated with St Charles Borromeo: in actual fact, we must consider the apostle St Paul as our true founder since our arms bear his monogram. I have been forced to leave my convent, now the headquarters of the Section Pont-Neuf, and to wear secular dress.'

'Father,' Brotteaux replied, examining Monsieur de Longuemare's shabby old servant's coat, 'your dress bears sufficient witness that you have not forgotten your vocation: to look at it, one would think you had reformed your Order rather than abandoned it. What is more, it is obviously the goodness of your heart that impels you to expose yourself in these austere garments to the insults of this ungodly mob.'

'I cannot very well dress in the fashion, as if I were a gay n'er-do-well!'

'Father, what I am saying about your attire is to pay tribute to your character and to put you on your guard against the risks you are running.'

'Monsieur, you would, on the contrary, do better to encourage me to confess my faith. For I'm only too ready to fear danger. I have abandoned my monk's habit, monsieur, which is itself a form of apostasy. The last thing I wished was to desert the Convent where God had granted me for so many years the grace of a peaceful and retired life. I obtained permission to stay on there, and I continued to occupy my cell while they turned the church and the cloisters into some sort of town hall which they call the Section headquarters. I saw, monsieur, I actually saw them hack away the holy symbols. I saw the name of the Apostle Paul covered by a convict's cap. Sometimes I was present at the meetings of the Section and I heard amazing errors propounded. In the end I left that profaned place and have since lived, on a pension of a hundred pistoles allowed me by the Assembly, in a stable which was empty because the army had requisitioned the horses. I celebrate Mass there every day for a few of the faithful who come to bear witness to the eternal Church of Christ.'

'As for me, Father,' Brotteaux replied, 'if you care to know my name, it is Brotteaux and in former times I was what you would call a Publican.'

'Monsieur,' answered Father Longuemare, 'the example of St Matthew taught me that one can learn from a Publican.'

'You are too kind, Father.'

Gamelin interrupted: 'Citizen Brotteaux, you surely can't help admiring the qualities of these people. See how everybody here was prepared to lose his place in the queue to punish the thief. Although they're victims of such poverty and misery, their integrity is such that they cannot tolerate any form of dishonesty.'

'It certainly must be admitted,' agreed Brotteaux, 'that in their desire to hang the thief, these people were ready to do violence to the good Father here. Their greed, and their selfish determination to safeguard their own interests, were sufficient motives: by attacking one of them, the thief threatened all of them: self-preservation demanded his punishment . . . At the same time it's not improbable that most of these working men and women are honest enough and keep their hands off other people's property. They've had these sentiments inculcated into them since infancy by their fathers and mothers, who smacked their bottoms soundly and injected the virtues into them through their backsides.'

Gamelin did not conceal from his old neighbour that he considered such language unworthy of a philosopher.

'Man,' he said, 'is naturally good. God has planted the seed of virtue in the hearts of all men.'

Old Brotteaux was a sceptic and found in his atheism a sufficient satisfaction.

'I know this much, Citizen Gamelin, that while you are a revolutionary in the things of this world, you're a conservative, a reactionary even, where heaven is concerned. Robespierre and Marat are just the same. As for me. I find it odd that, though Frenchmen aren't prepared to put up with a mortal king, they insist on holding on to an immortal tyrant who is far more ferocious and despotic. For what is the Bastille or even the *Chambre Ardente* compared with hell-fire? Humanity models its gods on its tyrants and you reject the original yet preserve the copy.'

'Oh, citizen!' Gamelin protested. 'Aren't you ashamed to talk in such a way? How can you compare the dark gods born of fear and ignorance, with the Creator of Nature? Belief in a benevolent God is a moral necessity. The Supreme Being is the source of all virtue and a man cannot be a good Republican if he doesn't believe in God. Robespierre understood this, for, as we all remember, he had the bust of the philosopher Helvetius removed from the Hall of the Jacobins because he had preached atheism ... I hope, at least, Citizen Brotteaux, that when the Republic establishes the worship of Reason, you will not withhold your acceptance of so wise a religion?'

'I love reason, but my love does not make me a fanatic,' Brotteaux answered. 'Reason is our guide, a light to show us our way; but if you make a divinity of it, it will blind you and lead you into crime.' And, standing in the street gutter, he proceeded to develop this thesis, just as he had been used to do seated in one of Baron d'Holbach's gilt armchairs, which, as he was fond of saying, were the seats of natural philosophy.

'Jean-Jacques Rousseau,' he continued, 'who was not without talent, especially in music, was a young rascal who professed to derive his morality from Nature while all the time he had got it from the dogmas of Calvin. Nature teaches us to prey on one another and gives us examples of all the crimes and vices which the social state tries to correct or conceal. We ought to love virtue; but it is well to realize that we ought to only because it is a convenient expedient invented by men in order that they may live comfortably together. What we call morality is simply and solely a desperate enterprise, a forlorn hope on the part of our fellow men to reverse the order of the Universe, which is constant strife and murder, blind, ceaseless and implacable. All is self-destruction, and the more I think of it, the more I am convinced that the Universe is mad. Theologians and philosophers, who make God the creator of Nature and the architect of the Universe, reveal Him to us as an illogical and unbalanced Being. They declare He is benevolent because they are afraid of Him, but they are forced to admit the truth that His ways are vicious and beyond understanding. They attribute a malignity to Him seldom to be found in any human being. And that is how they get human beings to worship Him. For our miserable species would never lavish worship on a just and benevolent God from whom they had nothing to fear; they would only feel an empty and thankless gratitude for their benefits. Without purgatory and hell, your God would indeed be a useless creature.'

'Monsieur,' said Father Longuemare, 'do not talk about nature. You do not know what it is.'

'Come now, I know it as well as you, Father.'

'You cannot know it, because you deny religion, and religion alone teaches us what nature is, and how its original goodness was made evil. However, you must not expect me to answer you. God has granted me neither the eloquence nor the intellect to refute your errors. I would be afraid, by my inadequate defence, to give you occasion to blaspheme and more cause to harden your heart. I wish very deeply I could help you; yet the only result of my unworthy efforts might be to . . .'

The discussion was curtailed by loud shouts from the front of the queue to warn the long line of famished citizens that the baker was opening his doors. The queue began to move forward, very, very slowly. A National Guard on duty admitted the customers one by one. The baker, his wife and young son superintended the sale, assisted by two Civil Commissaries. These, with a tricoloured band around the left arm, made sure that the purchasers belonged to the Section and were given their proper share proportionate to the number of mouths to be fed.

The Citizen Brotteaux made the pursuit of pleasure the one and only aim of his life, believing that reason and the senses could justify no other, in the absence of a God to give subjective values any objective criteria. Accordingly, since he found the artist's opinions somewhat too fanatical and the monk's too simple, this wise man, intent on matching his behaviour with his opinions and on relieving the tedium of waiting, took out from the bulging pocket of his puce-coloured coat his Lucretius, now as always his faithful solace, companion and comforter. The binding of red morocco was worn by much use and the Citizen Brotteaux had wisely removed the coat of arms that had once embellished it. He opened the book at the passage where the poet and philosopher, wishing to cure men of the useless and troublesome passion of love, surprises a woman enfolded in the arms of her servant women in a state which would offend the sensibilities of any lover. The Citizen Brotteaux read these verses, not without continually casting surreptitious glances at the golden down on the back of the neck of the pretty girl in front of him and breathing voluptuously the smell of the moist skin of this little scullery wench. The poet Lucretius was a wise man, but he fished in select waters; his disciple Brotteaux cast his net more widely.

So he read on, taking a couple of steps forward every quarter of an hour. His ear, soothed by the grave cadences of the Latin poet, was deaf to the women's strident complaints about the price of bread, sugar, coffee, and candles and soup. In this calm and composed mood, he reached the threshold of the baker's shop. Behind him, Évariste Gamelin could see over his head the gilt cornsheaf attached to the iron grating that filled the fanlight above the door.

When Gamelin's turn came to enter the shop, he found the hampers and baskets all empty; the baker handed him the last scrap of bread left, a piece which did not weigh two pounds. Évariste paid his money and the gate was slammed behind him, for fear the people would riot and take the place by storm.

But such a fear was baseless: these poor people, trained to obey both by their former oppressors and by their new liberators, slunk away with downcast heads and dragging feet.

When he reached the corner of the street, Gamelin saw the Citizeness Dumonteil seated on a stone post, her little baby in her arms. She was sitting quite still; her face was empty of all colour and her tearless eyes seemed to see nothing. The baby was sucking its mother's finger greedily. Gamelin stood for a while in front of her, ashamed and hesitant. She appeared not to see him.

He stammered something, and then, pulling out his pocket knife, a clasp-knife with a horn handle, he cut his loaf in two and put half of it on the young mother's knees. She looked up at him in astonishment; but he had quickly turned the corner of the street.

Arriving home, Évariste found his mother sitting by the window darning socks. With a little laugh he put what was left of the bread into her hand.

'Dear mother, you'll have to forgive me. I was so tired standing waiting in the heat, and as I hobbled back here I began taking a bite every now and then. So I'm afraid there's scarcely even your half left.' And as he spoke, he pretended to brush crumbs from his coat.

VII

THE Citizeness Gamelin, using a very old-fashioned expression, had declared that by eating chestnuts they would become chestnuts. As a matter of fact, on that day, 13th July, she and her son made their midday meal of a basinful of chestnut porridge. As they were finishing this austere repast, the door was pushed open and immediately the room was full of the presence and the perfume of the lady who entered. Évariste recognized her: she was Citizeness Rochemaure. Assuming she had mistaken the door and was intending to visit the Citizen Brotteaux, her friend from former days, he was about to direct her to the *ci-devant* aristocrat's garret, or perhaps summon Brotteaux and so spare such an elegant lady the trouble of climbing a mill-ladder; but she at once made it clear that it was the Citizen Gamelin and none other whom she had come to see by announcing she was pleased to find him at home and was his servant to command.

They were not entirely strangers, having met occasionally in David's studio, at the Assembly Hall, at the Jacobin's at Venua's restaurant. She had been struck by his good looks, his youth and his interesting ambience.

Wearing a hat beribboned like a toy trumpet adorned with strips of paper and beplumed like the cockade of an ambassadorial deputy, the Citizeness Rochemaure was wigged, rouged, love-patched, musk-scented, yet beneath it all the flesh was still young and firm: these extreme artifices of fashion served only to reveal frantic efforts to seize every moment of pleasure from life, the feverish intensity of these terrible days whose tomorrows were forever uncertain. Her close-fitting bodice, with wide facings and large basques all glittering with steel buttons, was blood-red, and it was hard to say whether she sported the colours of the victim or of the executioner, so

84

aristocratic, and at the same time so revolutionary, was her attire. She was accompanied by a young officer, a dragoon.

With a long, mother-of-pearl cane in her hand, she made a tour of the studio; a tall, beautiful woman, full bosomed and generously proportioned, she kept lifting her gold lorgnette to her grey eyes to examine more closely the artist's canvases, smiling, exclaiming, reacting effusively to the artist's handsome looks, flattering him in order to be flattered.

'What is that most moving and beautiful painting, the one showing a lovely, kind-faced lady bending over a sick young man?' asked the citeness.

Gamelin told her it was meant to represent *Orestes being tended by his sister Electra*, and that, if he had been able to finish it, it might have proved the least unsatisfactory of his works.

He went on to explain:

'The subject is taken from the *Orestes* of Euripides. I read a translation made many years ago and there was a scene in it that filled me with admiration – the scene where the young Electra, supporting her brother's head on his bed of pain, wipes his face and mouth, holds back his long hair and entreats the brother she loves to hear what she has to tell him while the Furies are silent . . . As I read and re-read this translation, I felt as though something, some mist or fog, were coming between me and the true Greek meaning. It seemed to me as though the style of the original Greek must be different, more taut, more nervous. I was so keen to discover the precise meaning, I went to Professor Gail, who was Professor of Greek at the *Collège de France* (this was in 1791) and begged him to translate the scene for me word by word. He did so, and I realized that the ancient Greeks were much more simple and homely than people believe. For instance, Electra says to Orestes: "Dear brother, how glad I was to see you were sleeping! Shall I help you up?" And Orestes answers: "Yes, help me, take me in your arms, wipe my mouth and face, hold back the hair from over my eyes for it blinds me" . . . My mind full of the simple strength of these clear, vivid words, I sketched the picture you see there, citeness.'

The artist, who usually spoke little of his works, became

eloquent over this one. Encouraged by the obvious interest of the Citizeness Rochemaure, who continued lifting her lorgnette as an indication of her attention, he went on:

'Hennequin painted the madness of Orestes in a masterly manner. But surely it is the grief of Orestes that appeals to us even more poignantly than his madness. His devotion as a son, his obedience to a sacred obligation, drove him to commit his terrible deed – a crime which the gods found it possible to pardon, but which men could never forgive. In order that he might revenge outraged justice, he had repudiated Nature, made himself into a monster, torn from his heart all mercy and pity. Yet his spirit remained unbroken beneath the burden of his dreadful, yet innocent, crime . . . That is what I wanted to show in my painting of brother and sister.' He walked over to the canvas, and the look he gave it was one not lacking in satisfaction.

'Parts of it,' he said, 'are almost complete; the head and arms of Orestes, for instance . . .'

'Its composition is admirable . . . And Orestes makes me think of you, Citizen Gamelin.'

'You think there is a resemblance?' asked the artist, smiling his grave smile.

She took the chair Gamelin offered her. The young dragoon stood beside her, his hand on the back of her chair. That was something which revealed clearly the Revolution was an accomplished fact, for under the *ancien régime* no man would ever in company have touched the seat occupied by a lady, not even with so much as the tip of his finger. In those days a gentleman had been severely trained in the rules of politeness, sometimes quite difficult rules, and had been taught that a scrupulous restraint in public adds a peculiar zest and sweetness to the familiarities of the privacy of the boudoir, and that it is first necessary to experience that zest and sweetness before one is able to lose one's awe and respect for a woman.

Louise Masche de Rochemaure, daughter of a lieutenant of the King's hunt, widow of a *procureur*, and, for twenty years, the faithful mistress of the financier Brotteaux des Ilettes, had taken enthusiastically to the new ideas. She had been seen, in

July 1790, digging the soil of the Champ de Mars. Her inclination to be on the winning side had carried her smoothly from the Feuillant to the Girondins and to the Mountain, though at the same time a spirit of compromise, a passion to be liked, and a certain genius for intrigue kept her still in touch with the aristocrats and the counter-revolutionaries. She was a very gregarious person, frequenting coffee-houses, theatres, fashionable cafés, gaming-rooms, salons, newspaper offices and the antechambers of the Committees. The Revolution afforded her novelties, diversions, smiles, pleasures, business ventures, profitable speculations. Combining political intrigue with amorous adventure, playing the harp, drawing landscapes, singing love songs, dancing Greek dances, giving suppers, entertaining smart women such as the Comtesse de Beaufort and the actress Descoings, sitting up all night at *trente et un* and *biribi* or playing *la rouge et la noire*, she still found time for kindnesses to old friends. Inquisitive, tireless, empty-headed, frivolous, knowing man but nothing of men, as indifferent to the opinions she supported as to those she felt she should repudiate, understanding absolutely nothing of what was happening in France, yet showing herself enterprising, tough and brimful of an audacity based on ignorance of danger and an unlimited confidence in the power of her charms.

The soldier accompanying her was in the flower of his youth. A brass helmet, bordered with panther skin and flaming red chenille, shaded the face of a young cherubim and from its tip there streamed down his back a long and awe-inspiring mane of hair. His red jacket, in the form of a waist-coat, scarcely reached to his waist, so not to hide the elegant curve of his back. To his belt was attached an enormous sabre, the hilt the beak of a splendid eagle. His flapped breeches of sky blue moulded the fine muscles of his legs and were braided on the thighs with rich arabesques of a darker blue. He had the appearance of a dancer dressed for some daring, warlike role, in *Achilles at Scyros* or *Alexander's Wedding Feast* in a costume designed by some pupil of David intent on accentuating every line of the human body.

Gamelin vaguely remembered meeting him somewhere. It

was indeed the soldier he had seen a fortnight before haranguing the crowd from the arcades of the Théâtre de la Nation.

The Citizeness Rochemaure introduced him:

'The Citizen Henry, member of the Revolutionary Committee for the Section of the Rights of Man.'

She kept him always at her heels, a mirror of gallantry and a living certificate of her patriotism.

The citizeness congratulated Gamelin on his talents and asked if he would be willing to design a card for a fashionable milliner, a protégée of hers. He would, of course, choose an appropriate subject, a woman trying on a scarf in front of a cheval-glass for instance, a young workwoman carrying a hat-box under her arm.

She had heard Fragonard *fils*, young Ducis, as well as a certain Prudhomme mentioned as competent to execute a small matter of this sort; but she preferred to address herself to the Citizen Évariste Gamelin. All the same, she made no definite offer and it was obvious she had mentioned the commission merely to start the conversation. She had in fact come for something very different. She wanted the Citizen Gamelin to do her a favour: knowing he was acquainted with the Citizen Marat, she had come to ask him to introduce her to the Citizen Marat, with whom she wished to have a chat.

Gamelin replied that he was far too insignificant a person to present her to Marat, not that there was any need for anyone to introduce her; Marat, though overwhelmed with affairs, was not the inaccessible man he was said to be.

And Gamelin added:

'He will receive you, citizeness, if you are in distress: for his great heart makes him available to the unfortunate, and compassionate to all who suffer. He will receive you if you have some revelation to make him concerning the public safety: he has consecrated his life to unmasking traitors.'

The Citizeness Rochemaure replied that she would be happy to salute in Marat an illustrious citizen, who had rendered great services to his country, who was capable of rendering even greater, and that she wished to put this great legislator in touch with some well-meaning men, some philanthropists, favoured by fortune and capable of furnishing him with new means of satisfying his ardent love for humanity.

'It is desirable,' she added, 'to make the wealthy contribute to the public prosperity.'

The citizeness had, in fact, promised the banker Morhardt to arrange for him to dine with Marat.

Morhardt, a Swiss, like the Friend of the People, had joined with several deputies of the Convention, Julien (of Toulouse), Delaunay (of Angers), and the ex-capuchin Chabot, to speculate in the shares of the *Compagnie des Indes*. The game, very simple, was to bring down their price to 650 livres by proposing confiscatory motions in the Convention, buy the greatest possible number at this figure, and then, by proposing motions of a reassuring nature, push the price up again and unload the shares at 4000 or 5000 livres. But Chabot, Julien, Delaunay had become too well-known at this little game. People were suspecting the same game of Lacroix, Fabre d'Églantine, and even Danton. The man behind it all, the Baron de Batz, was on the look-out for new accomplices in the Convention and had advised the banker Morhardt to see Marat.

This idea of the counter-revolutionary speculators was not so strange as it might at first seem. Such people always try to ally themselves with those in power at the moment, and the power of Marat through his popularity, his pen and his character, was formidable. The Girondists were on the wane; the Dantonists, tempest-battered, no longer had the power to govern. Robespierre, the idol of the people, was jealously careful of his image of incorruptibility, suspicious and unapproachable. Marat was the man to get around, the man whose goodwill needed securing against the day when he would be dictator; and this was what everything – his popularity, his ambition, his eagerness to use extreme measures – indicated he would become. And after all, perhaps Marat might re-establish order, finance, prosperity. Several times he had risen to oppose the frenzied agitators who tried to outdo him in their fanaticism; for some time now he had been denouncing the demagogues almost as much as the moderates.

Having incited the people to pillage the monopolists and hang them in their own shops, he was now exhorting the citizens to show calm and prudence. He was becoming a man capable of governing.

Despite certain rumours spread about him, as they were against all the other leaders of the Revolution, these financial sharks did not believe he could be corrupted, but they knew him to be vain and credulous, and they hoped to win him over by flattery, and still more by their condescending friendship which they considered the most seductive form of flattery when offered by men such as themselves. They counted, thanks to him, on manipulating all the securities they wished to buy and sell, and making him serve their interests whilst believing himself to be acting solely for the public good.

A great fixer of assignations, although she was still young enough for love-affairs of her own, the Citizeness Rochemaure had now given herself the commission of bringing together the legislator-journalist and the banker, and in her extravagant imagination she already had the man of the cellars, his hands still red with the blood of the September massacres, taking part in the game of the financiers whose agent she was, flung by his own naïve temperament into this world she so loved of speculators, monopolists, contractors, foreign emissaries, gamblers and light women.

She insisted that Citizen Gamelin took her to the Friend of the People, who lived nearby, in the Rue des Cordeliers near the church. After making some little resistance, the artist yielded to the citizeness's wishes.

The dragoon, Henry, was invited to accompany them, but refused, pleading his wish to remain uninvolved, even with the Citizen Marat, who, no doubt, had rendered services to the Republic, but who was now weakening: had he not, in his newsheet, counselled the people of Paris to practise resignation?

And young Henry, in a melodious voice, with long sighs, deplored the fate of the Republic, betrayed by the men in whom she had put her trust: Danton rejecting the idea of a tax on the rich, Robespierre opposing the permanence of the

Sections, Marat whose pusillanimous counsels were paralysing the enthusiasm of the citizens.

'Oh!' he exclaimed. 'How weak such men seem besides Leclerc and Jacques Roux! . . . Roux! Leclerc! They are the true friends of the people!'

Gamelin heard nothing of these remarks, which would have roused his indignation: he had gone into the next room to put on his blue coat.

'How proud you must be of your son,' the Citizeness Rochemaure said to the Citizeness Gamelin. 'His talents and his character are outstanding.'

The Citizeness Gamelin seized the opportunity to give a good account of her son, without boasting of him too much before such a high-born lady, as she had been taught since childhood that the first duty the lowly born owe to the great is humility. She was prone to self-pity, not without cause, and found relief in any opportunity to air her grievances. She would dwell at length on the hardship of her life to any whom she thought capable of relieving them, and Madame de Rochemaure appeared to her to be such a person. She therefore made the most of such a propitious moment and, hardly stopping to take breath, related the distressful story of a mother and son dying of starvation. Nobody bought paintings any more: the Revolution had killed business completely. Food was scarce and beyond their means . . .

And the good woman poured out her lamentations with all the garrulity her thick lips and her halting tongue were capable of, to get them all out before her son, whose pride would not approve such complaints, should reappear. She was intent on arousing as quickly as she could the concern of a lady whom she judged to be rich and influential in her son's future. And she felt that Évariste's handsome looks would help her in that they would touch the heart of any well-born lady.

The Citizeness Rochemaure did indeed prove tenderhearted; she was much moved to think of the sufferings of Évariste and his mother and began planning to alleviate them. She would get the rich men among her friends to buy the young artist's paintings.

With a smile, she said, 'There is still money in France, but it is playing hide and seek.'

An even better thought came to her: now that there was no future for artists, she would obtain a position for Évariste in Morhardt's bank or with the brothers Perregaux, or a post as a clerk with one of the army contractors.

Then, on further reflection, she decided that such positions were not suitable for such a man; and she exclaimed that she had found the solution:

'There are a number of magistrates* still to be appointed to sit on the Revolutionary Tribunal. A magistrate is just the position for your son. I have several friends on the Committee for Public Safety. I know the elder Robespierre; his brother frequently comes to supper at my house. I'll speak to them. I'll get them to have a word with Montane, Dumas and Fouquier.'

The Citizeness Gamelin, overwhelmed with gratitude, put a finger to her mouth: Évariste was coming back into the room.

Accompanied by the Citizeness Rochemaure, he descended the gloomy staircase, its wooden steps thick with the dirt of ages.

On the Pont-Neuf, where the sun, already low down, was lengthening the long shadow of the pedestal on which had stood the *Cheval de Bronze* but which was now gay with the National colours, a crowd of men and women was standing about in little groups listening to citizens who were speaking in low voices. The crowd, looking dismayed and appalled, stood in silence broken at intervals by groans and cries of anger. Many were beginning to hasten towards the Rue de Thionville, formerly the Rue Dauphine; Gamelin made his way into one of these groups, and heard that Marat had just been assassinated.

Little by little the news was confirmed in detail: he had been murdered in his bath, by a girl who had come on purpose from Caen to commit the crime.

Some believed she had escaped: but most said that she had been arrested.

There they all stood, like a flock of lost sheep. Sadly they were thinking: 'Marat is no longer here to guide us, the sensitive, humane, kind-hearted Marat. Marat who was never mistaken, who saw through everything, who dared reveal everything!... What are we to do? What will become of us? We've lost our counsellor, our champion, our friend.' They knew whence had come the blow, and who it was that had guided that girl's arm.

'Marat has been struck down by the hands of criminals,' they groaned. 'His death will be the signal for the slaughter of all true patriots.'

Differing reports were circulating about the circumstances of the tragedy and of the last words of the victim. Ceaseless questions were being asked about the murderess, but all anyone knew was that she was a young woman sent by those traitors, the Federalists. Uttering fearsome threats, the citizens had already condemned the culprit to fitting punishments: this monster of iniquity must be scourged, broken on the wheel, torn limb from limb. They racked their brains to think of fresh tortures.

An armed troop of National Guards appeared dragging a determined-looking man to the Section headquarters. His clothes were torn and blood was streaming down his colourless face. He had been heard saying that Marat had deserved his fate through continually provoking people to pillage and massacre, and the Guards had had the greatest difficulty in rescuing him from the fury of the people. Outstretched arms pointed their fingers at him as being the accomplice of the assassin and threats of death were hurled at him as he was led by.

Gamelin stood stupefied with grief. His eyes burned so that his tears dried on his eyelids. His sorrow was the sorrow of a son and mingled with it was concern for his country at the loss of this hero of the people. His heart ached and he thought:

'First Le Peltier, then Bourdon, and now Marat!... Now I see the ordained fate of patriots: massacred on the Champ de Mars, at Nancy, in Paris, they will perish, everyone of them.' And he thought of the traitor, Wimpfen, who only a short time ago had marched on Paris at the head of a horde of sixty thousand Royalists and who would have put that heroic city to fire and the sword if he had not been stopped at Vernon by the brave patriots.

And how many dangers lay ahead, how many acts of treason, which only Marat's wisdom and vigilance could have revealed and foiled!

Who would know now how to denounce Custine idling time away and refusing to relieve Valenciennes, Biron dawdling in the Lower Vendée and letting Saumur be taken and Nantes besieged, Dillon betraying his country in the Argonne? ...

Meanwhile, all around him, louder every moment, rose the sinister roar of many voices:

'Marat is dead! Killed by the aristocrats!'

And as he turned, his heart heavy with grief, with hate and with love, to go to pay his last homage before the body of the martyr of liberty, an old peasant woman, wearing a Limousin coif, stopped him and asked if this Monsieur Marat who had been assassinated was not Monsieur le Curé Mara, from Saint-Pierre-de-Queyroix.

VIII

THE evening of the Festival was bright and calm, and Élodie, her arm in Évariste's, was strolling with him around the Champ de la Fédération. Workmen were hastily completing the erection of columns, statues, temples, a 'Mountain', symbolic Altar of the Nation. Other huge symbolic figures, Hercules brandishing his club and representing the people, Nature suckling the Universe from her inexhaustible breasts, were rising up at a moment's notice in this capital city as it lay, full of famine and fear, awaiting the dread sound of the Austrian cannon on the road from Meaux. La Vendée was making up for being checked at Nantes by a series of astounding victories. A ring of fire, flame and hate was encircling the great city of the Revolution.

And while she waited, she was preparing, as if she were the sovereign head of a vast empire, this superb welcome for the Deputies from the Primary Assemblies which had accepted the Constitution. Federalism was being rejected; the Republic, one and indivisible, would now inevitably conquer all its enemies.

Évariste gestured with his arm to the vast crowd:

'It was here,' he exclaimed, 'that that scoundrel Bailly, on the 17th July, 1791, ordered the people to be shot down at the foot of the Altar of the Nation! Passavant, a grenadier, was a witness of the massacre. He returned to his house, tore his uniform off, and shouted: ''I swore an oath to die for Liberty. Liberty is no more, and so I die.'' And he blew his brains out.'

As the peaceful citizens were examining the preparations for the Festival, one could see that their faces revealed as complete a lack of joy in life as their lives were joyless: to them the greatest of events became as insignificant and as dull as they felt themselves to be. Couple after couple passed by, their children running in front, or held by the hand or carried, looking as unprepossessing as their parents and with as an unhappy a future before them: children who would in due time beget children as wretched in spirit and appearance as they themselves. Yet, every now and then, there would pass a young girl, slender, fair and desirable, arousing in young men a not ignoble desire to possess her, and stirring in old men regrets for ecstasy not seized and now forever past.

Near the École Militaire, Évariste pointed out to Élodie the Egyptian statues designed by David from Roman models of the Augustan age, and they overheard an old Parisian, with powdered hair, exclaiming to himself:

'You'd think you were on the banks of the Nile!'

Élodie had not seen her lover for three days, and during that time serious things had been happening at the *Amour Peintre*. The Citizen Blaise had been denounced to the Committee of General Safety for defrauding the army of supplies. Fortunately for him, the print-dealer was well known in his Section. The Committee of Surveillance of the *Section des Piques* had stood guarantor of his patriotism to the Committee of General Safety and had fully justified his conduct.

After she had related all this with emotion, she added:

'Everything is all right now, but for a moment I thought the worst might happen. It looked as if my father would be put in prison. A few hours more and I would have come to you, Évariste, to get your influential friends to intervene on his behalf.'

Évariste made no reply. Élodie far from realized the true meaning of his silence.

They walked on, hand in hand, along the banks of Seine. Their talk was the tender platitudes of the romantic Julie and Saint-Preux; for Rousseau had also given them the colours with which to paint and embellish their love.

The Government had miraculously caused abundance to reign for one day in the starving city. A fair had been set up beside the Seine in the Place des Invalides: stalls were busy selling sausages, saveloys, chitterlings, hams covered with laurel leaves, Nanterre cakes, gingerbread, pancakes, loaves weighing four pounds, lemonade and wine. There were also booths selling patriotic songs, cockades, tricolour ribands, purses, and all sorts of cheap trinkets. Stopping in front of the display of an inferior jeweller, Évariste picked out a silver ring with Marat's head in relief on it. He put it on Élodie's finger.

Gamelin arrived, that evening, at the house in the Rue de L'Arbre Sec, where the Citizeness Rochemaure lived, in response to an urgent summons. He was shown into her bedroom where he found her reclining on a chaise-longue in an alluring state of undress.

While the citizeness's attitude revealed a voluptuous languor, all about her lay the evidence of her accomplishments, her diversions, her talents: a harp next to an open harpsichord; a guitar lying on an armchair, an embroidering frame with a square of satin stretched on it, a half-finished miniature, papers and books on a table; a library with books scattered as if by a beautiful hand as eager to know as to feel. She gave him that hand to kiss and said:

'Welcome, Citizen Magistrate! ... This very day Robespierre's brother had given me an excellent letter to give to President Herman in your favour. It goes something like this: "I bring to your notice the Citizen Gamelin who is to be commended for his talents and his patriotism. I feel it my duty to make known to you a patriot of high principles, and a revolutionary of unswerving integrity. I trust you will not neglect this opportunity to be of use to a Republican..." I took the letter myself immediately to President Herman who received me with the most cordial politeness and signed your nomination without a moment's delay. You are in.'

Gamelin stood silent, and then said:

'Citizeness, although I have not a scrap of bread to give my mother, I swear on my honour that my only reasons for accepting the duty of a magistrate are to serve the Republic and exterminate her enemies.'

The citizeness considered his gratitude cold and his compliment frigid. She suspected Gamelin lacked manners. But she loved youth too much not to pardon him a little boorishness. Gamelin was handsome, and that was enough merit for her. 'He can be moulded,' she thought to herself. And she invited him to come along to the suppers she gave each evening after the theatre.

'You will meet men of wit and talent at my house: Elleviou, Talma, the Citizen Vigée who turns out *bouts-rimés* with a marvellous facility. The Citizen François read us his *Pamela*, which is being rehearsed at the Théâtre de la Nation at the moment. Its style is elegant and pure, as is everything that comes from the Citizen François' pen. It is a moving play: we were all in tears. The young Citizeness Lange is taking the part of Pamela.'

'I agree with your judgement, citizeness,' Gamelin replied. 'But there is little national about the Théâtre de la Nation. And it must be annoying to the Citizen François that his works should be performed on the stage degraded by the contemptible verses of Laya: people have not forgotten the scandal of his *L'Ami des Lois* . . .'

'Citizen Gamelin, you can say what you like about Laya; he is no friend of mine.'

It was by no means out of the goodness of her heart that the citizeness had used her influence to get Gamelin appointed to a much sought-after position: after what she had done and might yet still do for him, she counted on binding him closely to her, and so securing for herself a friend at 'court' against the day when she might need one, for she was now sending many letters abroad as well as at home, and such a correspondence was always suspect.

'Do you go to the theatre often, citizen?'

At that moment, the dragoon, Henry looking more attractive than the youthful Bathyllus, came into the room. Two enormous pistols hung from his belt.

He kissed the beautiful citizeness's hand, as she said to him:

'There, look at him: the Citizen Évariste Gamelin, on whose behalf I have just spent the entire day at the Committee of General Safety, and who does not even know how to thank me. Scold him!'

'Oh, citizeness!' exclaimed the soldier. 'So you have just

been seeing that disgraceful sight: our legislators at the Tuileries! Why must the representative of a free people have to sit beneath the panelled ceiling of a despot? Why should the same lights that once revealed the plot of the Capet* and the orgies of Antoinette shine today down upon the deliberations of our legislators? It is enough to make Nature herself shudder with disgust!'

'Congratulate the Citizen Gamelin,' she replied. 'He has been appointed as a magistrate on the Revolutionary Tribunal.'

'My compliments, citizen!' Henry said. 'I'm happy to see a man of your character invested with that power. To tell the truth, though, I haven't much confidence in this mechanical justice created by the moderates in the Convention in this happy-go-lucky Nemesis which spares conspirators, pardons traitors, hardly dares lay a finger on the Federalists and fears to put the Austrian woman on trial. No, it's not the men on Revolutionary Tribunal who will save the Republic. It's they who are the guilty ones. In the desperate situation we're in, they're the ones who have blocked up the torrent of popular justice!'

'Henry,' said the Citizeness Rochemaure, 'hand me those smelling salts . . .'

When he arrived home, Gamelin found his mother and old Brotteaux playing piquet by the light of a smoky candle. The old citizeness was shamelessly calling a bid of 'Kings'.

When she heard her son had been made a magistrate, she kissed him, overcome with happiness at the thought of the honour it was for both of them and that it would mean they would henceforth never lack food.

'I am happy and proud to be the mother of a magistrate,' she said. 'Justice is the most beautiful and most necessary of things: without justice, the weak would be ceaselessly oppressed. And I know you will give good judgments, my Évariste: for ever since you were a child, I've never known you to be anything but just and kind-hearted. You could never abide wrongdoing and you were always most passionately against all forms of violence. You have always pitied the un-

fortunate and that's the finest quality a magistrate can have
... But, tell me, Évariste, how d'you have to dress for this
great Tribunal?'

Gamelin told her that the judges wore a hat with black
plumes, but that the magistrates had no special costume and
simply wore their everyday clothes.

'It would be better,' the citizeness replied, 'for them to wear
a wig and gown: it would inspire more respect for them.
Although you do dress yourself most carelessly, you are a fine-
looking man and you give distinction to your clothes: but
most men need to wear something special to make them look
important: it would be better if the magistrates had wigs and
gowns.'

The citizeness had heard it said that the duties of a magistrate carried a remuneration, and she did not refrain from
asking whether it was enough to live comfortably on, for a
magistrate in her opinion should cut a figure in the world.

She learnt with satisfaction that every magistrate received
an allowance of eighteen livres for each sitting and that the
enormous number of crimes against the safety of the State
obliged them to sit very frequently.

Old Brotteaux gathered together the cards, stood up and
said to Gamelin:

'Citizen, you have been invested with a high and most formidable office. I congratulate you on giving your scrupulous
integrity to a Tribunal more firm and less fallible perhaps than
any other, because it searches out the good from the evil, not
at all merely as absolute values in themselves, but only in their
relation to objective interests and obvious emotional atti-
tudes. You will have to weigh the balance between love and
hate, which is something which can only be done intuitively,
and not between truth and error, since to do that is an im-
possibility for the weak mind of man. If you give judgments
from the intuitions of your heart, you will run no risk of making
mistakes, since your verdict will be good in so far as it satisfies
the high and sacred standards of your scrupulous respect for
law. But, at the same time, if I were your President, I would do
as Bridoie used to: I would submit everything to a throw of
the dice. In matters of justice, that is still the surest method.'

IX

ÉVARISTE GAMELIN began his duties on September 14th, when the reorganization of the Tribunal had been completed. Henceforth it was to be divided into four sections, each consisting of fifteen magistrates. The prisons were overflowing and the Public Prosecutor was working eighteen hours a day. Defeat in the field, revolt in the provinces: the Convention intended to have one remedy for everything: Terror. Blood would have blood.

The first act of the new magistrate was to pay a formal visit to President Herman, and was charmed by his affable conversation and dignified courtesy. A friend and compatriot of Robespierre, whose sentiments he shared, he appeared to be a man of moderate views, governed by the humane outlook for which Dupaty and Beccaria will always be remembered and which the new judges conspicuously lacked. He approved of the greater leniency shown by the abolition of torture and of ignominious and cruel forms of punishment. He rejoiced to see the death-penalty, until recently so recklessly imposed for the most trifling offences, being inflicted less frequently and only for the worst of crimes. For his part, the President agreed with Robespierre and would gladly have had it abolished completely, except, of course, for cases endangering public safety. He would certainly regard any judge who did not impose the death penalty for crimes against national security as having committed treason against the State.

All his colleagues were of the same opinion: the old monarchical idea of reasons of State still inspired the Revolutionary Tribunal. Its judges were moulded by eight centuries of absolute power, and it was by the principle of divine right that the Tribunal even now tried and sentenced the enemies of Liberty.

On the same day Évariste Gamelin presented himself before the Public Prosecutor, the Citizen Fouquier, who received him in his office where he worked with his clerk of the court. He was a strongly built man, with a loud voice and the eyes of a cat, who bore on his wide, pale, pock-marked face evidence of the ravages which a sedentary existence and an indoor life leave on a vigorous constitution made for the open air and strenuous exercise. Mountains of paper towered around him like the walls of a sepulchre, and he was obviously happily at home amid those piles of terrible documents which seemed prepared to bury him alive. His conversation was that of a hard-working magistrate, devoted to his duties, oblivious to everything beyond the circle of his official functions. His hot breath smelt of the spirits he took to keep him going but which did not seem to affect his head, so lucid were his completely commonplace remarks.

He lived in a small apartment in the Palais de Justice with his young wife, who had given him twin boys. His wife, an aunt Henriette and the maid-servant Pélagie made up his entire household. He was kind and considerate to his womenfolk. Briefly, he was an excellent family man and an excellent Public Prosecutor, though without much initiative and completely lacking in imagination.

Gamelin could not help noticing, not without some displeasure, how greatly these magistrates of the new order resembled those of the old régime. And that, in fact, was what they were: Herman had held office as Advocate-General to the Council of Artois; Fouquier was a former *procureur* at the Châtelet. They had retained their previous characteristics. But Gamelin believed in Revolutionary regeneration.

Leaving the Public Prosecutor's office, he went along the gallery of the Palais and stopped before the little shops where all sorts of objects were artistically displayed for sale. At the Citizeness Ténot's stall he leafed through various historical, political and philosophical works: *The Chains of Slavery*; *An Essay on Despotism*; *The Crimes of Queens*. 'Splendid!' he thought. 'These are true Republican books!' And he asked the woman if she sold many of them. She shook her head:

'People only buy songs and romances.'

She took a duodecimo volume from a drawer.

'Here's something good,' she said.

Évariste read the title: *The Undressed Nun.*

In front of the next stall he found Philippe Desmahis, flamboyantly magnificent amongst the Citizeness Saint-Jorre's perfumes, powders and sachets, and assuring that beautiful tradeswoman that he loved her, that he would paint her portrait and that she must come to the Tuileries Gardens that evening to discuss it. He was very handsome. His words were as persuasive as his eyes. The Citizeness Saint-Jorre stood, her eyes lowered, listening in silence, only too prepared to believe him.

In order to find out all he could about the terrible powers with which he had been invested, the new magistrate decided to attend a meeting of the Tribunal as an ordinary member of the public. He made his way up the staircase where a large crowd was seated as if in an amphitheatre and pushed his way through into the ancient hall of the Parliament of Paris.

Everybody seemed prepared to suffocate just to watch the trial of some general or other. For, as Brotteaux was fond of saying: 'The Convention follows the example of the King of England and puts defeated generals on trial, in the absence of traitorous generals who take good care to avoid being brought to trial. Which does not mean,' Brotteaux used to add, 'that a defeated general is necessarily a criminal, since there must be such a one in every battle. But there is nothing like condemning a general to death to encourage the others . . .'

The Tribunal had already passed sentence on several: obstinate, empty-headed soldiers with the brains of sparrows in the skulls of oxen. The one now before the Tribunal scarcely knew more of the battles and sieges he had commanded than the magistrates who were questioning him: defence and prosecution were losing themselves in aims, objectives, munitions, attacks and counter-attacks. But the crowd of citizens trying to follow this obscure and interminable argument could only see behind this half-witted soldier the torn bleeding bodies of thousands of their fellow-countrymen who had died for the Republic; and, vocally, gesticulatingly, they were urging the magistrates, sitting quietly on their bench, to deliver their verdict like a hammer-blow against the enemies of the Republic.

Évariste was convinced of one thing; what they had to attack in this miserable creature were those two dread monsters which were tearing the nation apart: revolt and defeat. What did it really matter whether this soldier was innocent or guilty! With the Vendée in open revolt, with Toulon surrendering to the enemy, with the Army of the Rhine retreating before the victors of Mayence, with the English and the Dutch now masters of Valenciennes and the Army of the North at their mercy, it was imperative to teach these generals of the Republic to conquer or to die. At the sight of this witless old nincompoop losing himself down there among his maps, just as he had done far away on the plains of Northern France, Gamelin, to prevent himself shouting out 'Death!' with the crowd, went out of the hall as quietly as he could.

At the opening meeting of the reorganized Section, the new magistrate was complimented by President Olivier who made him swear on the old High Altar of the Barnabites, now the Altar of the Nation, to wipe from his heart, in the sacred name of humanity, every human weakness.

Gamelin, his hand raised, invoked as witness of his oath the august spirit of Marat, whose bust had just been placed against a pillar of the former church, opposite the bust of Le Peltier.

This was greeted by some applause, mixed with murmurs of protest. The assembly was in an excited mood. At the entrance to the nave some members of the Section armed with pikes began shouting.

'It is anti-Republican,' the President ruled, 'to carry arms into a meeting of free citizens'.

And he ordered all muskets and pikes to be deposited immediately in the erstwhile sacristy.

A hunchback with staring eyes and snarling lips, the Citizen Beauvisage of the Committee of Vigilance, went up into the pulpit which had now become the speakers' tribune and was surmounted by a red bonnet.

'The generals are betraying us' he said, 'and are surrendering our armies to the enemy. The Imperialists are pushing forward their cavalry around Péronne and Saint-Quentin. Toulon has been handed over to the English who are landing fourteen thousand men there. The enemies of the Republic are at work in the very heart of the Convention itself. Here, in Paris, countless plots are being hatched to free the Austrian woman. Now, this very moment, while I am speaking, it is being rumoured that her son, the Capet brat, has escaped from the Temple and is being carried in triumph to Saint-Cloud by those who would like to put him on the throne of that tyrant his father. The high cost of food, the increasing worthlessness of assignats are the result of the machinations of agents of foreign powers, here in Paris, beneath our very eyes. I call upon our fellow citizen, the new magistrate, in the name of public safety, to show no mercy to conspirators and traitors.'

As he stepped down from the tribune shouts arose in the audience of : 'Down with the Revolutionary Tribunals. Down with the Moderates!'

A stout, red-faced man, the Citizen Dupont *aîné*, a joiner living in the Place de Thionville, mounted the tribune and said he wished to ask the new magistrate a question. He demanded to know what attitude Gamelin intended to take up in the matter of the Brissotins and the Widow Capet.

Gamelin was timid and unpractised in public speaking. But indignation aroused him to eloquence. His face gone pale, he rose and said in a voice of suppressed emotion:

'I am a magistrate. I am responsible only to my conscience. Any undertaking I might give you would be against my duty, which is to speak in this court and hold my peace elsewhere. From henceforth, I shall not know you. Judgment is mine, not yours. I know neither friends nor enemies.'

The meeting, composed like all meetings of different types and subject to sudden and unforseen changes of mood, approved this declaration. But the Citizen Dupont returned to the charge; he had not forgiven Gamelin for obtaining a position he had coveted himself.

'I understand,' he went on, 'I even approve the new magistrate's scruples. It is said he is a patriot; it is for him to examine his conscience and decide whether it permits him to sit on this Tribunal which was intended to destroy the enemies of the Republic but which now appears resolved to spare them. These are circumstances with which any good citizen is bound to repudiate all complicity. Is it not now being asserted that several magistrates sitting on this Tribunal have allowed themselves to be bribed, and that the President Montané himself altered the rulings of the court to save the head of the woman Corday?'

At these words the whole hall reverberated with loud applause. The vaults were still echoing with the noise when Fortuné Trubert mounted the tribune. He had become thinner than ever during the past few months. His face was white and his cheekbones seemed on the verge of piercing the skin; his eyes had a vacant look under their inflamed eyelids.

'Citizens,' he began, in a weak, breathless voice that yet had a strange penetrating quality, 'we cannot accuse the Revolutionary Tribunal without at the same time accusing the Convention and the Committee of Public Safety from which it derives its powers. The Citizen Beauvisage has alarmed us by reminding us that the President Montané interfered with the course of justice in favour of a criminal. Why did he not add, to relieve our fears, that Montané has since, on the denunciation of the Public Prosecutor, been dismissed from his office and thrown into prison? . . . Is it impossible for us to watch over the public safety without casting suspicion upon everybody? Is there no wisdom, no integrity, left in the Convention? Are not Robespierre, Couthon, Saint-Just honest men? Have you not noticed the fact that the most violent language is used by those individuals who have never been known to fight for the Republic? Their words and their speeches do more harm than good. I say, citizens, less talk and more work. It is with cannon and gun, and not with shouting, that France will be saved. Half of the cellars of this Section have still not yet been dug up. Many citizens still possess considerable quantities of bronze. Need we remind those citizens who are more wealthy than most, that gifts are the best guarantee of their patriotism? Need we recommend to their generosity the wives and daughters of our soldiers who are covering themselves with glory? One of these soldiers, the Hussar Pommier (Augustin), formerly a wine merchant's assistant in the Rue de Jérusalem, when he was watering his troop's horses, just before Condé on the tenth of last month, was attacked by six Austrian cavalrymen. He killed two of them and took the other four prisoners. I ask this Section to put on record that Pommier (Augustin) has done and acted as a dutiful son of the Republic'.

This speech was applauded and the members dispersed amidst cries of 'Vive la République'.

Left alone in the nave with Trubert, Gamelin shook his hand warmly. He thanked him for his speech and asked how he was keeping.

'I? Oh, very well! Very well!' Trubert replied, coughing and spitting blood into his handkerchief. 'The Republic has many enemies within, as well as without, and there is a considerable number of them in our own Section. It is not with loud talk, but with laws and the power to enforce them that Empires are founded ... Good-night, Gamelin ... I have some letters to write.'

And with his handkerchief pressed to his lips, he disappeared into the erstwhile sacristy.

Overnight the Widow Gamelin had assumed a fine air of importance. From henceforth her cockade was always fastened securely on her hood, in keeping with her sudden adoption of Republican haughtiness and of the dignified bearing appropriate to the mother of a magistrate of the State.

Her inborn veneration for the law, her child-like admiration for the judges gown and cassock, her awe for those to whom God delegates this divine right of life or death, all these feelings made her now regard her son, whom till yesterday she had thought of as little more than a child, as a worshipful, holy and august being. To her simple mind the continuity of the concept of justice through all the changes of the Revolution was a conviction as strong as the conviction of the legislators of the Convention regarding the continuity of the conception of the State under different systems of government, and so the Revolutionary Tribunal appeared to her every bit as majestic as any of the time-honoured jurisdictions she had been taught to revere.

The attitude of the Citizen Brotteaux to the young magistrate was a mixture of surprised interest and reluctant deference. His views about the continuity of justice under successive governments were the same as the Widow Gamelin's in that, in complete contradiction to that lady's attitude, his scorn for Revolutionary Tribunals was equalled only by his contempt for the judicial courts of the old régime. Not daring to express his opinions openly yet unable to keep himself from saying nothing, he wove a knot of innuendoes which Gamelin unravelled sufficiently to suspect the lack of patriotism that lay behind them.

'The noble Tribunal upon which you are soon to be seated,' Brotteaux said to him on one occasion, 'was instituted by the French Senate for the security of the Republic, and it was certainly a magnanimous gesture on the part of our lawmakers to set up such a court to try our enemies. I recognize its generosity, but doubt its wisdom. It seems to me they would have done better to have killed off quickly and secretly the more irreconcilable of their enemies and won over the others by gifts and promises. A Tribunal such as yours kills off people slowly and inspires too little fear to achieve any good. It has to consider its first duty to be to set an example. The harm it does is to unite all in whom it inspires fear, and makes out of a diverse crowd of contradictory interests and passions, a powerful party capable of effective, united action. You inspire terror, and it is terror more than courage that turns people into heroes. I pray, citizen, you may not one day see the terrible progeny of your Terror arrayed against you!'

The engraver Desmahis found time, although occupied that week by an affair with a prostitute from the Palais-

Égalité, a brown-haired giantress named Flora, to congratulate his friend and to inform him that his appointment was a great compliment to the world of art.

Élodie herself – who without realizing it detested everything revolutionary and dreaded official duties as the most dangerous of rivals – even the tender Élodie was impressed by the glamour attached to a magistrate whose word could mean life or death. In addition, her loving heart was filled with satisfaction by other fortunate results that followed upon Évariste's promotion as a magistrate; her father, the Citizen Blaise, went out of his way to call at the studio in the Place de Thionville and embraced the young magistrate affectionately and respectfully.

Like all the anti-revolutionaries, he had a great respect for the authorities established by the Republic, and ever since his being denounced for fraud in his supplies to the army, he had gone in wholesome fear of the Revolutionary Tribunal. He felt complete security was impossible for a man like himself, so much in the public eye and involved in so many business transactions. The Citizen Gamelin, therefore, appeared suddenly to be a friend worth cultivating. After all, they were both good citizens and on the side of justice.

He shook the painter-magistrate's hand warmly, declaring himself to be his true friend and a true patriot, a well-wisher of the arts and liberty. Gamelin pressed the hand now so generously offered.

'Citizen Évariste Gamelin,' the Citizen Blaise continued, 'as my friend and as a talented artist, you must accompany me tomorrow on a couple of days' excursion through the countryside. You can make some drawings and we can enjoy a good talk.'

Several times a year the print-dealer was in the habit of making a two or three days' excursion of this kind in the company of artists who made drawings, suggested by him, of landscapes and ruins. He had a quick sense of what would please the public, and these little expeditions always resulted in some picturesque sketches which were then finished off at home and cleverly engraved. Prints in red or colours were struck off from these, and resulted in a good profit for the Citizen Blaise. He had over-doors and panels executed from the same sketches and these sold as well or better than the decorative work of Hubert Robert.

On this occasion he intended the Citizen Gamelin to make naturalistic sketches of buildings, so greatly had the magistrate's office increased for him the young artist's importance. Two other artists were to accompany the party: the engraver Desmahis, who drew well, and an almost unknown person named Philippe Dubois, who was an excellent designer in the style of Robert. As was the custom, the Citizeness Élodie and her friend the Citizeness Hasard accompanied the party. And, expert at combining pleasure with profit, Jean Blaise had also invited the Citizeness Thévenin, an actress at the Vaudeville, reputed to be on the friendliest terms with him.

X

CLAD in a black-cocked hat, scarlet waistcoat, doeskin breeches and yellow-topped boots, the Citizen Blaise rapped with the handle of his riding whip at Gamelin's studio door at seven o'clock the following Saturday morning. The Citizeness Gamelin was in the studio making polite conversation with the Citizen Brotteaux, while he was standing knotting his high white cravate in front of a scrap of a mirror.

The Citizeness Gamelin greeted him: 'I trust you will have an enjoyable journey, Monsieur Blaise! Since you're going to paint landscapes, why don't you take Monsieur Brotteaux with you? He, too, is an artist.'

'Indeed!' Jean Blaise replied. 'Will you come with us, Citizen Brotteaux?'

Being of a sociable nature and fond of enjoying himself, Brotteaux accepted the invitation, after being assured he would not be intruding.

The Citizeness Élodie arrived, having climbed the four staircases in order to embrace the Widow Gamelin, whom she called her dear mother. Dressed in white from head to foot, she smelt of lavender.

An old travelling berline, with two horses, its hood lowered, stood waiting in the square. Rose Thévenin sat in the back with Julienne Hasard. Élodie had given precedence to the actress and seated herself on the left, putting the thin Julienne between them both. Brotteaux seated himself at the back, facing the Citizeness Hasard, with Évariste opposite Élodie. As for Philippe Desmahis, he placed his athletic frame on the seat next to the coachman whom he astonished by informing him that in certain American countries trees flowered with chitterlings and sausages.

The Citizen Blaise, an excellent rider, was mounted on his

own horse and rode in front to avoid the dust thrown up by the berline.

As the wheels clattered along the road out of Paris, the travellers forgot their cares; and, at the sight of the fields, of the trees and the sky, gay and pleasant thoughts filled their minds. Élodie decided that she had been born to rear chickens, helped by Évariste, who would become the mayor of a little village beside a river, near a wood. The elm trees bordering the road flew by as they raced along. As they entered villages, the peasants' dogs hurled themselves along beside the carriage, barking at the legs of the horses, and a large spaniel lying in the middle of the road got out of the way reluctantly. Fowls scattered and fled; geese in huddled groups waddled slowly to safety. Children, their faces fresh as the morning, gazed at the passing coach. The day was hot and cloudless; the earth parched and thirsting for rain. They stopped just outside Villejuif and walked through the little town. Desmahis entered a fruiterers to buy some cherries for the ladies who were feeling the heat uncomfortably. The shopkeeper was a pretty woman, and Desmahis appeared reluctant to emerge. Philippe Dubois shouted to him, using the nickname his friends always gave him:

'Hi, there, Barbaroux! . . . Barbaroux!'

At the sound of this detested name, the passers-by stopped and faces appeared at every window. Then, when they saw a handsome young man come out of the shop, his coat flung open, his neckerchief flying loose over his broad chest and carrying his coat and a basket of cherries on the end of a stick over his shoulder, a gang of sans-culottes rushed at him and seized violent hold of him. Ignoring his indignant protests they would have dragged him to the Hôtel de Ville, if old Brotteaux, Gamelin and the three young women had not testified that the citizen was named Philippe Desmahis, a copperplate engraver and a good Jacobin. Even then the suspect was made to show his *carte de civisme* which luckily he had in his pocket, for he was very careless over such things. Thus he escaped from the hands of these patriotic villagers with nothing worse than the loss of one of his lace ruffles, which had been torn off. But this was a comparative trifle, and he even received the apologies of the National Guards, who had been the most savage in their handling of him but who now wanted, as recompense, to carry him in triumph to the Hôtel de Ville.

A free man once more, and with the Citizenesses Élodie, Rose and Julienne fussing around him, Desmahis looked at Philippe Dubois – he did not like the man and suspected him of deliberately playing a practical joke – and said with a wry smile, towering head and shoulders above him:

'Dubois, if you ever call me Barbaroux again I'll call you Brissot. He's a little fat man with a foolish face, greasy hair, oily skin and clammy hands. Everybody will have no doubt at all that you are that scoundrel Brissot, the enemy of the people. All good Republicans will be filled with horror and loathing at the sight of you, and will hang you from the nearest lamppost. Do you understand me?'

The Citizen Blaise, who had been watering his horse, announced that he had arranged the matter satisfactorily, though it was quite clear to all that it had been arranged without him.

The company got in again and as they drove on across the Plain of Longjumeau, Desmahis informed the coachman that it was in this very place that several inhabitants from the moon had once landed, very like frogs in shape and colour, only much, much bigger. Philippe Dubois, who was a pupil of Regnault, had been to Rome where he had seen Raphael's tapestries, which he maintained were unsurpassable. He admired the colouring of Correggio, the drawing of Domenichino, the invention of Caracci, but considered the paintings of Pompeio Battoni incomparable with regard to style. He had met Monsieur Menageot and Madame Le Brun in Rome but as they had both declared themselves against the Revolution, the less said of them the better. However, he spoke highly of Angelica Kauffmann, whose taste was refined and who had an excellent knowledge of the Antique.

Gamelin deplored the prematurely rapid decline of the belated flowering of French painting, since it dated only from Lesner, Claude and Poussin and corresponded with the decline of the Italian and Flemish schools. He attributed this to the decay in manners and to the Academy which reflected social opinion too much in matters of art. However, the Academy had now happily been abolished and under the influence of new canons of taste, David and his school were creating an art worthy of a free people. Without a trace of envy, Gamelin assigned first place among the young painters to Hennequin and Topino-Lebrun. Philippe Dubois indicated his preference for his own master Regnault to David, and based his hopes for the future of painting upon that rising artist Gérard.

Meanwhile, Élodie was complimenting the Citizeness Thévenin on her red velvet toque and white gown. The actress repaid the compliment by congratulating her two companions on their dresses and advised them how to do better still; the art, she said, lay in avoiding ornaments and trimmings.

'A woman can never be dressed too simply,' she declared. 'You can see this on the stage where the costumes are made so that every pose is appreciated. That is their true beauty and they need no embellishments.'

'You are right, my dear' Élodie replied. 'But there is nothing more expensive in a dress than simplicity. It's not always through bad taste that we add frills and furbelows. Sometimes it's to save money.'

There followed a lively discussion about the autumn fashions – completely plain, tight-waisted dresses.

'So many women put themselves at a disadvantage by following the fashion!' Rose Thévenin declared. 'Every woman should study her own figure'.

Gamelin joined in:

'The only beauty in a dress lies in having the draperies follow the lines of the figure and fall in folds. Cutting and sewing only make a dress hideous.'

These sentiments, more suited to a treatise by Winkelmann than to a man speaking to Parisiennes, met with the scorn they deserved: they were completely ignored.

'For this winter' Élodie observed, 'they are making quilted dresses of taffeta and muslin in the Lapland style, and coats *à la Zuline*, loose waisted and opening over a stomacher *à la Turque*.'

'Horrible, cheap things,' the actress interrupted. 'You can get them ready-made. I have a little seamstress whose work is positively angelic. I'll send her to visit you, my dear.'

So they chattered on lightly, eagerly discussing and appraising various fine fabrics – striped taffeta, china-silk, muslin, gauze, nankeen.

And to old Brotteaux, as he listened to them, there came pensive, pleasant thoughts of these veils which hide the charms of women's bodies and how they are forever changing – how they last for a few years only, to be renewed eternally like the flowers of the field. And his eyes, as they gazed back and forth from these three beautiful women to the cornflowers and the poppies among the wheat, were wet with smiling tears.

They arrived at Orangis about nine o'clock and halted in front of the inn, *L'Auberge de la Cloche*, where the Poitrines, man and wife, offered accommodation for man and beast. The Citizen Blaise, all disorder in his dress now repaired, helped the citizenesses to alight. After ordering lunch for midday, they all set off, preceded by a village lad carrying their paint-boxes, drawing-boards, easels and parasols, to the meadow near the confluence of the Orge and the Yvette, where there was a charming view over the green plain of Longjumeau bounded by the Seine and the forest of Sainte-Geneviève.

Jean Blaise, the leader of this troop of artists, was exchanging humorous anecdotes with the *ci-devant* aristocrat, stories that inconsequentially passed from Verboquet the open-handed, to Catherine Cuissot the pedlar, from the demoiselles Chandron to the fortune-teller Galichet, as well as to characters of later days such as Cadet-Rouselle and Madame Angot.

Évariste, seeing a band of harvesters binding their sheaves, was moved by a sudden love of Nature; tears filled his eyes and his heart became overwhelmed with a feeling of content and concord with all things. Desmahis, on the other hand, was busy blowing the light down from the dandelions on to the hair of the citizenesses. All three, as town girls always do, loved gathering posies, and they were busy in the meadows plucking the mullein, whose blossom, the campanula, grows close to the stem, little blue bells hanging one above the other, together with the slender twigs of the scented vervain and all the wild flowers of late summer – wallwort, mint, dyer's weed, milfoil. Rousseau had made botany the fashion among townswomen, so all three knew the name and meaning of every flower. The delicate petals, drooping for lack of moisture, wilted in Élodie's hand and fell about her feet, and she sighed:

'Poor flowers, they are dying already!'

All eventually set to work and attempted to express nature as each of them saw her; but all saw her through the eyes of the master who had influenced them. Philippe Dubois quickly sketched a deserted farm in the style of Hubert Robert, including a clump of storm-battered trees and the dried-up bed of a stream. There on the banks of the Yvette, Évariste Gamelin found a landscape by Poussin waiting for him to sketch. Philippe Desmahis discovered a pigeon-cote to render in the picturesque style of Callot and Duplessis. Old Brotteaux, who self-mockingly prided himself on his imitations of the Flemish school, was soon engaged in drawing a cow with infinite care. Élodie was sketching a peasant's hut, while her friend Julienne, who was a colourist's daughter, was using her palette. A crowd of children swarmed round her, watching her paint, and at intervals she would tell them scoldingly to get out of her light, calling them pestering little flies and giving them lollipops. The Citizeness Thévenin picked out the pretty ones, washed their faces, kissed them and twined flowers in their hair. She held them to her with an air of gentle sadness, because she had never known the joys of motherhood, and also to increase her charms by a show of tender sentiment and to give herself practice in the art of posing and grouping.

She was the only member of the party neither sketching nor painting. So she passed the time partially by learning her part in a play but still more by entertaining her companions, moving gracefully from one to another with her book in her hand, an entrancing, charming creature. Women said of her: 'No complexion, no figure, no voice, no nothing.' Yet she gave life, colour and harmony wherever she went. Faded yet beautiful, tired but indefatigable, she was the life and soul of the expedition. Sad, gay, sensitive, quick-tempered, tolerant, yet with a tongue like a polished rapier, vain yet modest, honourable when most dishonourable, wholly delightful: and if Rose Thévenin was accorded no acclaim for triumphant success, if she was not worshipped as a goddess, it was because she had been born out of her time in a Paris which lacked incense and altars for the Graces. Élodie herself, who pulled a face whenever she spoke of her and always referred to her as 'my stepmother', nevertheless always succumbed to her charms whenever she was with her.

The play she was rehearsing at the Théâtre Feydeau was *Les Visitandines*, and Rose was full of self-congratulation at having been given a part full of 'naturalness'. This was the quality she always aimed at and always achieved.

'Shan't we be seeing Pamela, then?' inquired Desmahis.

The Théâtre de la Nation had been closed and the actors sent off to the Madelonettes and to Pélagie.

'And that's what you call liberty?' Rose Thévenin demanded, opening her beautiful eyes wide in indignant protest.

'The actors and actresses of the Théâtre de la Nation are aristocrats, and *Pamela* tends to make people regret the privileges of the old nobility.'

'Gentlemen,' said Rose Thévenin, 'are you prepared only to listen to those who flatter you?'

As midday approached everybody began to feel hungry and the little group walked back to the inn.

Évariste attached himself to Élodie and smilingly recalled memories of their first meetings:

'Two young birds had fallen from their nests on the roof down on to your window-sill. You looked after the little creatures. One of them lived and later flew away. The other one died in the nest of cotton-wool you had made him. I remember you said: "That was the one I loved best." You were wearing a red bow in your hair that day, Élodie.'

A little behind the others, Philippe Dubois and Brotteaux were talking about Rome, which they had both visited,

Brotteaux in 1772 and Dubois during the last days of the Academy. Brotteaux had never forgotten the Princess Mondragone, to whom he would have poured out his complaints but for the Count Altieri who followed her everywhere like her shadow. Philippe Dubois made a point of recalling that he had been invited to dine with Cardinal de Bernis and found him to be a most obliging host.

'Yes, I knew him,' Brotteaux said, 'and it is quite without boasting that I can add that I was one of his most intimate friends for a time: he had a taste for low society but he was an amiable companion, and, in spite of his tendency to exaggerate, there was more sound philosophy in his little finger than in the heads of all you Jacobins who are determined to make us virtuous by Government decrees. I truly prefer our simple-minded God-eaters* who neither know what they're saying nor what they're doing, to your mad law-menders, who take it upon themselves to send us to the guillotine to force us to become good and wise and worshippers of some Supreme Being who has created them in His likeness. In the old days I used to have Mass said in the Chapel at Les Ilettes by a poor devil of a Curé who used to shout when he'd had a drop too much: "No criticism of sinners, if you please! Unworthy as we are, we priests make our living out of sinners!" I think you must agree that that purveyor of prayers had sound ideas. We should adopt his principles and govern men as they are and not as what we'd like them to be.'

Rose Thévenin had come closer to the old man to listen to what he was saying. She knew he had lived in the grand style and the thought of this made her sentimentalize the *ci-devant* aristocrat's present poverty, which she considered the less humiliating since it was not his fault but the result of general causes. She saw him, with a mixture of curiosity and respect, as a surviving example of those generous, wealthy aristocrats about whom her older theatrical friends spoke with deep regret. Also, the old man in his puce-coloured coat, so worn yet so well cared for, pleased her by his amiable manner.

'Monsieur Brotteaux,' she said to him, 'we know how in days gone by, on moonlit nights in a noble park, you would wander in the shade of myrtle groves with actresses and dancers to the music of distant flutes and violins . . . They were more beautiful, your goddesses of the Opéra and the Comédie-Française, weren't they, than we poor little National actresses of today?'

'Not one iota, mademoiselle,' Brotteaux replied. 'Believe me, if anyone such as you had been known in those days, she would have moved alone (not that she would have wished such solitude), in the park which you are kind enough to describe so flatteringly . . .'

The Hôtel de la Cloche was quite a rustic inn. A branch of holly hung over the large wagon doors which opened on to a courtyard where poultry pecked about in the damp soil. On the far side stood the house, two storeys crowned by a high-pitched tiled roof and whose walls were almost hidden under old, climbing rose-trees covered with roses. To the right, pruned fruit trees showed their tops above the low garden wall. To the left was the stable, with a manger outside and a barn supported by wooden beams. A ladder leant against the wall of a shed full of agricultural implements and stumps of trees. A white cock kept an eye on his hens from the top of a broken-down cabriolet. Beyond the barn were the cow sheds, in front of which a dunghill rose in mountainous grandeur. As they entered, a girl, as broad as she was high and with straw-coloured hair was busy turning it over with a pitchfork. The liquid manure filled her wooden shoes and bathed her bare feet, her heels rising every now and then out of her shoes, as yellow as saffron. Her petticoat was kilted and revealed the filth on her enormous calves and thick ankles. Philippe Desmahis was staring at her, amusedly astonished at this whimsical example of Nature's oddness, when the landlord called out

'Now then, Tronche, my lass! Go and fetch some water!'

She turned her head, revealing a red face and a huge mouth with a proportionately huge tooth missing. Nothing less than a bull's horn had been needed to cause such a gap in that powerful jaw. She stood there grinning, pitchfork on her shoulder. Her sleeves were rolled back and her arms, as thick as any other woman's thighs, shone in the sun.

The table was laid in the farm kitchen, where a brace of fowl, almost done to a turn, was roasting under the hood of an open fireplace, above which were hung, by way of ornament, a few old fowling pieces. The bare, whitewashed room, almost twenty feet long, was lit only by panes of greenish glass in the door and by one window, framed in roses, beside which the grandmother sat turning her spinning-wheel. She wore a coif and a lace frilling in the fashion of the Regency. The distaff was gripped by her twisted, earth-stained fingers, and she made no attempt to drive away the flies which clustered around her eyelids. Long, long ago, as a child in her mother's arms, she had seen Louis XIV pass by in his coach.

Sixty years ago she had made the journey to Paris. In a quavering sing-song voice she told the tale to the three young women standing before her, how she had seen the Hôtel de Ville, the Tuileries and the Samaritaine, and how, as she was crossing the Pont-Royal, a barge laden with apples for the Marché du Mail had broken apart, how the apples had floated with the current and how the river had become red with rosy-cheeked fruit.

She had heard of the changes that had taken place lately in the kingdom, and in particular of the bickering there was between the priests who had taken the oath and those who refused to. She knew also there had been wars and famines and signs in the sky. She did not believe the King was dead. His escape had been arranged, she was convinced, by way of a subterranean passage, and they had substituted a man of the common people to be given to the executioner.

In his wicker cradle at the old woman's feet, Jeannot, the latest of the Poitrines, was cutting his teeth. The Citizeness Thévenin lifted up the cradle and smiled at the baby, who moaned feebly, exhausted by feverish convulsions. The child must have been very ill, because they had sent for the doctor, the Citizen Pelleport, who, being a deputy-substitute to the Convention, naturally would require no payment.

An innkeeper's daughter herself, the Citizeness Thévenin was in her element; not satisfied with the farm girl's washing of the plates and dishes, she gave them an extra wipe, and an extra polish to the knives and forks. Whilst the Citizeness Poitrine was busy attending to the soup, which, as a good cook should, she tasted occasionally, Élodie busied herself slicing a four-pound loaf, hot from the oven. When he saw what she was doing, Gamelin said to her:

'I read a book a few days ago by some young German whose name I've forgotten. There was a beautiful young girl in it called Charlotte, who was busy cutting the bread like you are, Élodie, and she was doing it so gracefully and charmingly that when he saw her the young Werther fell in love with her.'

'Did they get married?' asked Élodie.

'No,' Évariste answered. 'It all ended with the violent death of Werther.'

As they were hungry they ate well, but the food was indifferent. Jean Blaise complained bitterly. He was a great man for his food and always insisted upon eating well; his gluttony no doubt arising from the general scarcity. In every household the Revolution had emptied the cooking-pot. Ordinary citizens had to go without. Clever ones such as Jean Blaise, who made huge profits amidst the wretched poverty around him, were able to go to the food shops where they stuffed themselves as full as they could. Brotteaux, on the other hand, who was living on chestnuts and bread-crusts in this year II of liberty, was able to remember the days when he had dined at Grimod de la Reynière's at the end of the Champs-Élysées. Eager to win the reputation of an accomplished gourmet he reeled off, as he sat there eating Citizeness Poitrine's bacon and cabbage, a list of exotic kitchen recipes and a string of wide gastronomic maxims. When Gamelin protested that a good Republican scorns the pleasures of the table, the old aristocrat, always the lover of antiquity, made the young spartan a present of the true recipe for the famous old black broth.

After dinner, Jean Blaise, who never forgot business, set his group of artists making studies and sketches of the inn, whose dilapidated condition appeared to him quite romantic. Whilst Desmahis and Dubois were sketching the cowsheds, the girl Tronche came out to feed the pigs. At that moment, the doctor, the Citizen Pelleport, who had been giving his professional services to the Poitrine baby, appeared at the farmhouse door. He walked over to the artists, and, after complimenting them on their talents which he said were an honour to the entire nation, he pointed to Tronche in the midst of her pigs.

'You see that creature,' he said. 'Well, she's not one girl, she's two girls. I speak professionally, you understand. I was so amazed at the extraordinary size of her bone structure that I examined her, and I discovered she had most of her bones in duplicate: in both thighs she's got two femurs welded together, in each shoulder she has a double humerus. Some of her muscles are also duplicated. In my opinion, it's a case of a pair of twins associated or rather mixed-up together. An interesting phenomenon. I informed Monsieur Saint-Hilaire of the facts and he thanked me. That, citizens, is a monster which you see before you. They call her here "the girl Tronche". They should call her "the girls Tronches". For there are two of them. Nature produces these freaks . . . Well, good evening, citizens; we shall be having a storm tonight . . .'

After supper by candlelight, the Blaise Academy moved out into the courtyard where they were joined by a son and daughter of the house in a game of blindman's bluff, which all the younger people played with the hectic energy proper to the high spirits of youth and not on account of the uncertain, precarious times in which they were living. When it had become quite dark, Jean Blaise proposed they played children's games in the farm kitchen. Élodie suggested the game of 'Hunt the heart' and everybody agreed. Under Élodie's instructions, Philippe Desmahis sketched seven hearts in chalk on pieces of furniture, on the doors and on the walls, one less than the number of players, for old Brotteaux had obligingly joined in. They then danced round in a ring singing '*La Tour, prends garde!*' and at a sign from Élodie each ran to put their hand on a heart. Gamelin, in his awkward absent-mindedness, was too late to find one not taken and had to pay a forfeit, the little knife he had bought for six sous at the fair at St Germain and with which he had cut the loaf for the starving mother. The game continued and one after the other Blaise, Élodie, Brotteaux and Rose Thévenin failed in turn – a ring, a reticule, a little morocco-bound book, a bracelet. The forfeits were then raffled on Élodie's lap, and each had to redeem their property by showing their social accomplishments – by singing a song or reciting a poem. Brotteaux chose the speech of the patron saint of France in the first canto of the *Pucelle*:

> '*Je suis Denis et saint de mon métier,*
> *J'aime la Gaule, . . .*'

The Citizen Blaise, though far less well-read, replied spontaneously with Richemond's riposte:

> '*Monsieur le Saint, ce n'était pas la peine*
> *D'abandonner le celeste domaine.*'

Everybody at that time was reading and re-reading with delight the masterpiece of the French Ariosto; the most grave of men smiled over the loves of Jeanne and Dunois, at the adventures of Agnes and Monrose and the exploits of the winged ass. Every man of culture knew by heart the best parts of this amusing yet philosophical poem. Évariste Gamelin himself, austere as he was, recited the descent of Grisbourdon into hell quite fervently, when he recovered his knife from Élodie's lap. Without any accompaniment, the Citizeness Thévenin sang Nina's ballad:

> '*Quand le bien-aimé reviendra*'.

Desmahis sang to the tune of *La Faridondaine*:

> '*Quelques-uns prirent le cochon*
> *De ce bon saint Antoine*
> *Et lui mettant un capuchon*
> *Ils en firent un moine*
> *Il n'en coûtait que la façon . . .*'

Notwithstanding this, Desmahis was in a thoughtful mood. He was, for the moment, ardently in love with the three women he had been playing forfeits with, and was throwing at each in turn burning glances of vibrant appeal. He was in love with Rose Thévenin for the graceful movement of her supple body, her clever acting, her teasing eyes, and her voice that went straight to a man's heart; he was in love with Élodie because he recognized instincively her strong personality and kind sense of humour; he was in love with Julienne Hasard, in spite of her colourless hair, pale eyelashes, freckles and flat chest, because, like Dunois in Voltaire's *Pucelle*, he was always generously prepared to give a token of love to the least attractive – the more so, in this instance, because she appeared at the moment to be the most neglected, and so the most amenable to his advances. Being without any trace of vanity, he was never certain these would be found acceptable; equally he was never certain they would not be found so. He never missed the opportunity, therefore, of making them and taking a chance. Seizing the opportunities offered during the game of forfeits, he had made some tender speeches to Rose Thévenin, who did not appear displeased but who could hardly say much in return under the jealous eyes of the Citizen Jean Blaise. He spoke more warmly still to the Citizeness Élodie, whom he knew to be in love with Gamelin, but he was not so demanding as to require one woman all for himself. Élodie could never care for him; but she was obviously not being successful in her attempts to hide the fact that she considered him quite a handsome fellow. Finally, he whispered his most ardent words into the ear of the Citizeness Hasard, who received them with a look of bewildered stupefaction, which could have meant either abject submission or chill indifference. Desmahis, however, did not conclude she was indifferent.

The inn possessed only two bedrooms, both on the first floor and opening on to the same passage. The one on the left, the better of the two, boasted a flowered wallpaper and a mirror the size of a man's hand, whose gilt frame had been tarnished by generations of flies ever since the days when Louis XIV had been a child. In it, beneath sprigged muslin curtains, stood two beds with down pillows, sheets and counterpanes. This room was allotted to the three citizenesses.

When the hour came to retire, Desmahis and the Citizeness Hasard, each with a bedroom candlestick in their hand, bade each other good-night in the passage. A note quickly passed from the amorous engraver to the painter's daughter, begging her when everybody was asleep to come to him in the garret above the citizenesses' room.

During the day, he had shown judicious foresight and made a careful study of the lie of the land, exploring the garret which he had found full of old chests and trunks, together with strings of onions and apples and pears left there to ripen with swarms of wasps crawling over them. He had happened even to notice an old trestle-bed, now unused as far as he could see, with a palliasse all ripped and flea-infested.

Across the passage, facing the citizenesses' room was another of much more modest dimensions where the men of the party were to sleep, in what comfort they could. The sybarite, Brotteaux, however, took himself off to sleep in the hay in the barn. Jean Blaise somehow simply disappeared. Dubois and Gamelin were quickly asleep and as soon as silence, like a stagnant pool, had enveloped the house, the engraver arose and crept up the wooden staircase, which creaked under his bare feet. The garret door stood half open. From inside there came the warm, acrid, stifling smell of rotting fruit. On the rickety trestle-bed, fast asleep, with her mouth wide open, her shift drawn up, and her legs wide apart, lay the girl Tronche. She was enormous. Through the garret window, the moonlight bathed her skin with silver and azure: skin which between flecks of dirt and slivers of manure, shone with the freshness of youth. Desmahis threw himself upon her; she woke with a start, crying out with fright. But, as soon as she understood what he wanted of her, she lay back reassured, and, showing no sign of surprise or unwillingness, paetended to be still plunged in a half-sleep, which, relieving her of any scruples in the matter, allowed her a certain pleasure . . .

Desmahis returned to his room, where he fell into a deep, peaceful sleep until daybreak.

Late the next day, after a final spell of work, the itinerant Academy took the road back to Paris. When Jean Blaise paid their host in assignats, the Citizen Poitrine complained bitterly at the absence nowadays of what he called 'square-money', and said he'd light a fine candle for any rogue who'd bring the 'yellow boys' back again.

He offered the citizenesses all the flowers they wished, and at his command the girl Tronche climbed a ladder in her sabots and kilted skirts, thus revealing a fine view of her noble, mud-bespattered legs, and effortlessly began to cut blossoms from the climbing roses on the wall. From her huge hands showers, torrents, avalanches of flowers fell into the laps of Élodie, Julienne, and Rose Thévenin. The entire party, when they reached Paris at nightfall, carried armfuls home, and their sleeping and their awakening were filled with the perfume of their fragrance.

XI

On the morning of September 7th the Citizeness Rochemaure went to visit Gamelin, the new magistrate, in order to solicit his help on behalf of a friend who had been denounced as a suspect. On the stairs she met the *ci-devant* Brotteaux des Ilettes who had, in the happy days now past, been her lover. Brotteaux was on his way to deliver a gross of his dancing dolls to the toy merchant in the Rue de la Loi, and, to carry them more easily, he had tied them to the end of a pole, as street-hawkers do. His manners to women were always courteous, even to those towards whom long familiarity had made him indifferent, as could hardly fail to be the case with Madame de Rochemaure – unless indeed the added seasoning of betrayal, absence, unfaithfulness and obeseness proved an added appetizer to the fascination she had formerly held for him. Whether that was so or no, he greeted her now, on those sordid stairs with their cracked tiles, as chivalrously as he had ever done on the entrance steps at Les Ilettes, and begged her to do him the honour of entering his garret. She climbed the ladder quite nimbly and found herself under the sloping, wooden beams which supported the tiled roof pierced by one skylight. It was impossible to stand upright and she sat down on the only chair in the wretched place. After a brief glance around, she asked in a tone of surprise and sorrow:

'Is this where you live, Maurice? You must have little fear of anyone intruding on you. Only a devilish imp or a cat could find you here.'

'I am somewhat cramped,' the *ci-devant* wealthy aristocrat replied, 'and I do not deny that occasionally it rains on my bed. A trifling inconvenience. On fine nights I am able to see the moon, that symbol and confidant of lovers. For the moon, madame, ever since the world began has been invoked by lovers, and when full, with her pale, round face, she recalls to lovers the object of their desires.'

'I know,' the citizeness sighed.

'Of course, the same thing makes the cat create a fine row outside there in the gutter. But we must forgive love if it makes cats caterwaul on the tiles, considering how it fills the lives of men and women with betrayal and torment.'

Both of them had had the tact to speak as if they were friends who had parted only the night before, and though they had now become strangers to each other, their conversation was gracious and friendly.

Even so, Madame Rochemaure's thoughts appeared to be elsewhere. The Revolution had for a long time been a source of pleasure and profit to her. Lately, however, it had begun to cause her anxiety and disquietude. Her suppers were growing less joyous and brilliant; her music no longer charmed the clouds from sad faces; her tables were being forsaken by the most avid of punters. Many of her acquaintances, now under suspicion, had gone into hiding; her lover, the financier Morhardt, was under arrest, and it was on his behalf she had come to see the Magistrate Gamelin. She was a suspect herself. A posse of National Guards had searched her house, riffled the drawers of her cabinet, pulled up the floorboards, thrust bayonets into her mattresses. When they had found nothing, they had apologized and drunk her wine. But they had come dangerously close to finding her correspondence with Monsieur d'Expilby, an émigré. And certain friends her handsome protégé, Henry, had among the Jacobins, had warned her that he was beginning to endanger her own party by his violent language, which appeared too extravagent to be sincere.

With her elbows on her knees and her head resting on her cupped hands, she sat deep in thought. Then she turned to her old lover who was sitting on the palliasse and said:

'What do you think of it all, Maurice?'

'I think our new masters give a philosopher and an observer of life's passing show much to reflect upon and to laugh at. I also think it would be better for you, my dear, if you were out of France.'

'Maurice, what is going to happen to us?'

'You asked me that, Louise, one day when we were driving on the banks of the Cher, along the road to Les Ilettes. The horse had got out of control, do you remember, and was galloping off with us at a dangerous pace. But women were born inquisitive! And now today, for a second time, you want to know what is going to happen to us. Ask the fortune-tellers. I cannot see into the future, my dear. Even the soundest philosopher is little good at that. All things have an end. One can foresee only the possibilities. The victory of the Coalition and the allies entering Paris. They are not far off; but I doubt if they will get here. These soldiers of the Republic take their defeats with an invincible zest. Or it may be that Robespierre will marry Madame Royale* and make himself Protector of the Kingdom during the minority of Louis XVII.'

'Do you think so!' exclaimed the citizeness, overwhelmed with excitement at the thought of being privy to such a promising intrigue.

'Or again it may be,' Brotteaux continued, 'that the Vendée will triumph and restore the rule of the priests over a country heaped with ruins and piled with corpses. You cannot conceive, my dear, the iron influence the clergy still has over the masses of the foolish – I beg your pardon, I meant to say "of the faithful". A slip of the tongue. But, in my poor opinion, the most likely conclusion will be that the Revolutionary Tribunal will bring about its own destruction; it is making too many enemies. Its policy of Terror threatens too many, and they will unite and destroy it, and with it the whole idea of Republican government. I believe it was you who involved our young friend Gamelin in this Tribunal by obtaining him the position of a magistrate. He has a lively conscience; he will be implacable. The more I think of it, dear friend, the more I'm convinced that this Revolutionary Tribunal, set up to save the Republic, will end by destroying it. Like the King, the Convention has decided to have its *Grands Jours*, and to provide for its security by magistrates appointed by itself and dependent upon it. But how inferior are the Convention's *Grand Jours* to those of the monarchy! The determination of

129

the Revolutionary Tribunal to make everybody equal will quickly make it hateful and ridiculous. Did you know, Louise, that this Tribunal, which is about to put the Queen of France on trial, yesterday condemned to death a young servant girl for shouting ''Long live the Queen!'' She was convicted of malicious intent to destroy the Republic! Our judges, with their black hats and plumes, are modelling themselves on that William Shakespeare, so admired by Englishmen, who introduces crude buffoonery in the midst of his most tragic scenes.'

'Never mind, Maurice! Tell me, are you still as lucky with women as you used to be?'

'Alas!' Brotteaux replied. 'The doves fly to the bright new dove-cotes and alight no more on the old ruined tower.'

'You are still the same . . . good-bye, dear friend. Until we meet again.'

That same evening Henry, the dragoon, paid an uninvited visit to Madame Rochemaure and found her in the act of sealing a letter which he noticed was addressed to the Citizen Rauline at Vernon. The letter, he knew, was for England. Rauline received Madame de Rochemaure's correspondence from a postilion of the posting service and then sent them on to Dieppe by means of a fishwife. The captain of a fishing boat delivered them under cover of night to a British ship cruising off the coast. An émigré, Monsieur d'Expilly, received them in London and passed them on, if he thought advisable, to the Court of St James.

Henry was young and handsome; Achilles himself was not such a paragon of graceful youth and vigour when he donned the armour Ulysses offered him. But the Citizeness Rochemaure, once so captivated by the charms of the young hero of the Commune, now regarded him with suspicion. Her attitude had altered since the day she was told that the young dragoon had been denounced to the Jacobins for allowing his zeal to outrun his discretion, and she now feared he might compromise and ruin her. On his side, Henry did not feel that her changed attitude would break his heart; but he was annoyed at having fallen in her favour. He relied on her to meet various expenses in which the service of the Republic had involved him. Also, and by no means least, he knew to what extremities women will proceed, how they can turn in a moment from ardent love to cold indifference, how easily they can bring themselves to sacrifice what they once cherished and destroy what they once held dear. He had therefore begun to suspect that his fascinating mistress might one day have him thrown into prison in order to rid herself of him. Common prudence suggested he should attempt to regain his lost ascendancy and so he had come prepared to use all his charms upon her. He approached her, drew back, approached again, hovered over her, retreated at a run, all in the approved ballet fashion of seduction. Then he flung himself on to a chair and, in his irresistible voice, that voice which he knew went straight to women's hearts, he extolled the charms of Nature and solitude and finally with a lovelorn sigh proposed an excursion to Ermenonville.

Meanwhile she was fingering the strings of her harp, striking cords and gazing about her with an expression of bored impatience. Henry suddenly stood up and with a gesture of gloomy resolution informed her he was leaving to join the army and would be at Maubeuge in a few days.

Her nod of approval revealed neither scepticism nor surprise.

'You congratulate me on my decision?'

'Indeed I do.'

She was expecting the arrival of a new admirer who was much more to her taste and whom she hoped would prove much more useful, a contrast in every way to Henry. He was another Mirabeau, a Danton turned army contractor, a lion who spoke of pitching every patriot into the Seine, and she was on tenter-hooks, thinking she heard the bell ring every moment.

To hasten Henry's departure, she became silent, yawned, fingered the music score, and yawned again. Then, since he made no move to go, she said she had to go out and went into her dressing-room.

He called to her in a quivering voice:

'Farewell, Louise! . . . Shall I ever see you again?' – but his hands were searching in the open writing desk.

When he reached the street, he opened the letter addressed to the Citizen Rauline and read it with avid absorption. It conveyed indeed a confused picture of the state of public feeling in France. It spoke of the Queen, of the actress, Rose Thévenin, of the Revolutionary Tribunal, and included numerous comments made in confidence by the worthy Brotteaux des Ilettes.

Having read it to the end and returned it to his pocket, he stood hesitating for a moment; then, like a man who had made up his mind and says to himself 'let's get it over with', he turned and made his way to the Tuileries where he entered the antechamber of the Committee of General Safety.

The same day, at three o'clock in the afternoon, Évariste Gamelin was seated on the magistrates' bench with his fourteen colleagues, most of whom he knew, simple, honest, patriotic people – another painter like himself, a surgeon, a cobbler, a *ci-devant* marquis who had given ample proof of his patriotism, a printer, two or three small tradesmen, a cross-section of the inhabitants of Paris. There they sat, in their workman's blouse or their bourgeois coat, with their hair close-cut *à la Titus*, or fashioned *à la catogan*; with cocked hats tilted over their eyes, round hats on the back of their heads, or red caps of liberty down over their ears. Some were clad in coat, flapped waistcoat and breeches, as under the old régime, others wore the carmagnole and striped trousers of the sans-culottes. Their top-boots, buckled shoes and sabots presented every kind of masculine attire. Since they all had occupied their seats on several occasions already, they appeared to Gamelin very much at their ease and he envied them their unconcern. For himself, his heart was thumping, and there was a roaring noise in his ears, and he seemed to be seeing everything through a mist.

When the usher proclaimed the opening of the sitting of the Tribunal, three judges took their seats behind a green table on a small raised platform. They wore cockaded hats crowned with large black plumes and over their coats of office a heavy silver medal was hung on a tricolour riband. In front of them, at the foot of the platform, sat the Deputy Public Prosecutor who was similarly dressed. The clerk of the court was seated between the judges and the chair ready to be occupied by the prisoner. To Gamelin these men appeared different from their everyday aspect; they looked nobler, graver, more fearsome, although their manner was ordinary enough as they turned over papers, beckoned to an usher or leaned back to listen to a magistrate or an officer of the court.

Above the judges' heads hung the tablets recording the Rights of Man; to their right and their left, against the ancient walls, stood the busts of Marat and Le Peltier Saint-Fargeau. Facing the magistrates' bench, at the far end of the hall, rose the public gallery. The first row was filled with women, all of whom, young and old, wore the high coif with the pleated tuck hiding their cheeks; their bosoms, most of which, in the fashion of the day, revealed the fullness of the nursing mother, were covered with a crossed white kerchief or the round top of a blue apron. They sat with their folded arms resting on the rail of the tribune. Behind them, scattered among rising tiers of seats, were a mixture of citizens all dressed in the varied clothing which at that time gave such a picturesque character to every gathering. Near the doors, on the right, a space was reserved behind a barrier for the public to stand. The business before this particular section of the Tribunal had attracted the interest of only a few spectators, though doubtless the other Sections also sitting at the moment would be hearing more exciting cases.

This fact reassured Gamelin a little; as it was, his heart seemed likely to fail him, and if the day had been hotter he would almost certainly have fainted. His eyes took in the most trifling details of the scene around him: the cotton-wool in the ears of the *greffier* and a blot of ink on the Deputy Prosecutor's papers. As if through a magnifying glass he could see the capitals of the Gothic columns, sculptured at a time when all knowledge of the classical orders had been forgotten, with wreaths of nettle and holly. But wherever he looked, his eyes returned again and again to that fatal chair, old, covered with red Utrecht velvet, its seat worn and its arms blackened with use. At every door armed National Guards stood guard.

At last the accused was brought in, escorted by grenadiers, but with his arms unbound, as the law directed. He was a man of about fifty, thin, with a brown face, bald head, hollow cheeks and tight lips, dressed in an old-fashioned coat of bright red. Doubtless it was the fever which made his eyes glitter and gave his cheeks a shiny appearance of varnish. He sat down in the chair. He crossed his extraordinarily thin legs and clasped his huge knotted hands around his knees. His name was Marie-Adolphe Guillergues, and he was accused of misusing a supply of forage for the Republican army. The act of indictment listed numerous and serious charges against him, but of no single one of them was there any positive proof. Under examination Guillergues denied most of the charges and tried to dismiss the remainder as not being applicable to himself. He spoke eloquently, in a dry, precise manner, and gave the impression of being a dangerous man to do business with. He had an answer for everything. When the judge asked him an embarrassing question his face betrayed no reaction and his voice remained confident, but his hands, still clasped in front of him, kept twitching as if in agony. Gamelin was fascinated by this and whispered to the colleague next to him, an artist like himself:

'Watch his thumbs!'

The first witness for the prosecution alleged a number of most damaging facts. Those who followed him, however, appeared loath to testify against the prisoner. The Deputy Public Prosecutor spoke strongly but rather vaguely about specific charges. The advocate for the defence adopted a tone of bluff conviction of his client's innocence and so aroused a sympathy for the accused which he had failed to earn by his own efforts. The sitting was then suspended and the magistrates assembled in the room provided for their deliberations. After a confused and confusing discussion, they found themselves divided almost equally in their opinion. On the one side were the unemotional men of reason whom no feelings could move; on the other were those who let their feelings sway them, who could not be approached by argument, only by appeals to their hearts. These always voted guilty. They were the true, pure, unadulterated metal of the Revolution; their only thought was for the safety of the Republic and they cared less than nothing for anything else. Their attitude strongly impressed Gamelin who felt it was with them that his own sympathies lay.

'This Guillergues,' he thought, 'is a cunning rogue, a villain who has speculated with the forage intended for our cavalry. To acquit him would be to let a traitor escape, to betray our army.' And with the thought, Gamelin could see the Hussars of the Republican Army, mounted on under-nourished, stumbling horses, being cut to pieces by the enemy's sabres . . . "Yet supposing Guillergues was really innocent . . . ?'

Suddenly he recalled Jean Blaise, similarly suspected of misusing army supplies. There must be many others like Guillergues and Blaise, contriving disaster and the downfall of the Republic! An example had to be made. But supposing Guillergues were innocent . . . ?

'There is no proof,' Gamelin said aloud.

'There never is,' retorted the foreman, shrugging his shoulders; he was made of the true, pure metal!

Finally, there were found to be seven voting guilty and eight voting innocent.

They re-entered the hall and the sitting was resumed. The magistrates were required to give reasons for their verdict, and each spoke in turn facing the vacant chair. Some spoke at length, other confined themselves to one sentence; a couple babbled unintelligibly.

When Gamelin's turn came, he stood up and said:

'When considering a crime so great as stealing the sinews of victory from the defenders of our country, we need to be shown positive proof of guilt. We have not been shown any such proof.'

By a majority of votes the accused was declared not guilty.

Guillergues was brought in again and stood before his judges amid a murmur of sympathy from the spectators which gave him an indication of the nature of the verdict. He became a different man. His face lost its harshness, his lips relaxed. Now the impression he gave was that of a venerable and innocent man. The President read out the verdict in a voice filled with emotion; the audience burst into applause. The gendarme who had escorted Guillergues embraced him. The President summoned him on to the platform and also embraced him. Then the magistrates all kissed him. Gamelin's eyes were hot with tears.

Outside, the courtyard of the Palais, lit by the last rays of the setting sun, was packed with an excited, howling mob. The day before, the four Sections of the Tribunal had pronounced thirty sentences of death, and on the steps of the great staircase a crowd of tricoteuses were sitting waiting to see the tumbrils leave. But as he descended the steps among the mass of people, Gamelin saw nothing and heard nothing. He was overcome by his own act of justice and humanity, and full of self-congratulation at having recognized innocence when he saw it. All the while and smiling through her tears, Élodie stood waiting in the courtyard; she flung herself into his arms and lay there as if in a faint. When she had recovered, she said:

'Évariste! You're good, you're so noble, you're so generous! Listening to you in there, your voice was so gentle and so manly – it seemed as though it were going right through me like magnetic waves. I was electrified by it. I stared at you on your bench. I could see only you. And you, my dear, you never guessed I was there? I was in the gallery, in the second row, on the right. Oh, isn't it wonderful to have done something good! It was you who saved that poor man. Without you, he was done for. You've given him back to life, to all his beloved ones. At this very moment, he must be blessing you. Oh, Évariste, how happy and proud I am to be in love with you!'

Their arms around each other, pressed close together, they

walked through the streets feeling as though they were floating on air.

They were going to the *Amour Peintre*.

'Let's not go through the shop,' Élodie said when they reached the oratory.

She made him enter by the coach door and go up to her apartment with her. On the landing, she took a heavy iron key out of her reticule.

'You'd think it was a prison key,' she said. 'You are going to be my prisoner, Évariste.'

They passed through the dining-room and went into the girl's bedroom.

Évariste felt upon his lips the cool freshness of Élodie's lips. He held her to him, pressing closely. Her head thrown backwards, her eyes half-closed, her hair falling loose, her whole body ready to surrender, she escaped his hold and ran, as if running in her sleep, to push in the bolt on the door . . .

Night had long fallen when the Citizeness Blaise opened the door of her apartment for her lover and said to him softly in the darkness:

'Good-bye, my love! This is the time my father usually returns. If you hear any noise on the staircase, run back up quickly to the top floor and don't come down until you're quite sure there's no danger of being seen. To get the door on the street opened, knock three times on the concierge's window. Good-bye, dear heart! Good-bye, my soul!'*

When he found himself in the street, he saw the window of Élodie's room open slightly and a tiny hand pluck a red carnation which fell at his feet like a drop of blood.

XII

ONE evening when old Brotteaux arrived in the Rue de la Loi with a gross of dancing dolls for the toy merchant, Citizen Caillon, usually polite and quiet spoken, stood there stiff and unsmiling amongst his dolls and Punch and Judies and gave Brotteaux a far from generous welcome.

'You must be more careful, Citizen Brotteaux,' he began, 'far more careful! There is a time for laughing and a time for being serious. Jokes are sometimes taken seriously. A member of the Committee of Safety of the Section inspected my shop yesterday and when he saw your dancing dolls he declared they were anti-revolutionary.'

'It is you who are joking!' Brotteaux exclaimed.

'By no means, citizen, by no means. He said your little dolls insidiously mocked at the National representatives. In particular, you had caricatured Couthon, Saint-Just and Robespierre, and he seized the lot. It's a complete loss to me, to say nothing of the grave risk you've exposed me to.'

'But it's not possible! How could any sane man imagine these Harlequins, these Scaramouches, these Colins and Colinettes, which I've painted just as Boucher used to fifty years – how could any sane man take them to be parodies of Couthon and Saint-Just?'

'Its possible you did not do it deliberately and with malice, though a man so versatile as you is always to be distrusted. Nevertheless, it's a dangerous game to play. I'll give you an example how dangerous. Natoile, who runs that little outdoor theatre in the Champs-Élysées, was arrested the day before yesterday for anti-patriotism, just because he made Polichinelle poke fun at the Convention.'

'Now you listen to me,' Brotteaux said, lifting the cloth which covered his little dangling toys. 'Look at those masks and faces. Are they or are they not simply characters from plays and mimes? Just how could you let yourself be persuaded, Citizen Caillon, that I was making a mockery of the National Convention?.'

Brotteaux was completely taken aback. He had always made great allowance for human folly, but had never thought it could go so far as to suspect his Scaramouches. Repeatedly he protested his and their innocence; but the Citizen Caillon was adamant.

'Take your dolls away, Citizen Brotteaux. I have the highest esteem for you but I don't intend being blamed or getting into trouble on your account. I mean to remain a good citizen and to be treated as such. Good evening to you Citizen Brotteaux, and take your dolls away.'

The old man set out for home again, carrying his now suspect dolls over his shoulder at the end of the pole, mocked at by children who took him for the rat-poisoner. He felt in the depths of despair. He did not, certainly, depend entirely for a living upon his dolls; he sometimes used to paint portraits for young recruits starting for the army and wanting to leave their likeness behind for their sweetheart, charging them twenty sous a piece, and painting them under the archways of doors, or in one of the market halls among the darners and old-clothes menders. But these petty jobs took him much time and care, and he was not nearly so good at painting portraits as he was at making dancing dolls.

Sometimes, too, he acted as amanuensis for the market women, but this meant involving himself in Royalist plots and the risks were great. He recalled that another toy merchant, named Joly, lived in the Rue Neuve-des-Petits-Champs, near the former Place Vendôme and he decided to go and offer him the following day the merchandise which the frightened Caillon had rejected.

A drizzling rain began to fall. Fearing its effect on his marionettes, Brotteaux quickened his step. After he had crossed the Pont-Neuf and was turning the corner of the Place de Thionville, he saw by the light of a street lamp a thin old man sitting on a stone post, apparently exhausted with hunger and fatigue yet still preserving a certain venerable air. He wore a tattered overcoat, had no hat and appeared to be about sixty years of age. As he approached the poor wretch, Brotteaux recognized the Father Longuemare whom he had saved from hanging six months ago while they were both waiting in the queue at the baker's shop in the Rue de Jérusalem. Feeling himself responsible for the man as a result of the service he had done him, Brotteaux walked over to him and introduced himself as that Publican who had stood with him among the crowd on a day of great scarcity, and asked if he could be of some further use to him.

'You seem tired, Father. Try some of this cordial.' And Brotteaux took out a flask of brandy, from alongside his Lucretius in the pocket of his puce-coloured coat.

'Drink some, and I will assist you back to your house.'

Father Longuemare pushed away the flask and tried to get up, only to fall back again.

'Monsieur,' he said, weakly but firmly, 'for the last three months I've been living at Picpus. At five o'clock yesterday afternoon I was warned they were waiting at my lodgings to arrest me, so I did not return home. I have nowhere to go. I have been wandering the streets and am a little tired.'

'In that case, Father,' Brotteaux suggested, 'please do me the honour of sharing my garret.'

'Monsieur,' the Barnabite replied, 'you understand that I am a suspect.'

'So am I,' said Brotteaux, 'and, what is worse, my marionettes are, as well. There they lie, under that flimsy cloth, exposed to this fine rain that is chilling our bones. Yes, Father, I have to tell you that after being a Publican I now earn my living by making dancing dolls.'

Father Longuemare took hold of the hand which the *ci-devant* aristocrat extended to him and accepted his hospitality. Back in his garret, Brotteaux gave him a meal of bread, cheese and wine, the wine having been put out in the rain-gutter to keep cool – for was he not a sybarite?

His hunger appeased, Father Longuemare said:

'I ought to tell you of the circumstances that led me to flee from my home and left me where you found me on the point of death. When I was turned out from my cloister, I lived on the meagre allowance the Assembly permitted me. I gave lessons in Latin and Mathematics and wrote pamphlets on the present persecution of the Church in France. I even wrote a work of some length to prove that the Constitutional oath required of priests is subversive to ecclesiastical discipline. The increasingly severe measures of the Revolution deprived me of all my pupils, and I could no longer draw my pension because I did not possess the necessary certificate of citizenship. I went to claim it at the Hôtel de Ville, convinced that I was well entitled to it. Being a member of an order founded by the Apostle Paul himself, I have always prided myself on following his example, and on being a good French citizen and an upholder of all man-made laws which do not oppose the Divine laws. I presented my application for my certificate of citizenship to Monsieur Colin, the pork-butcher who is the municipal officer responsible for the issue of such certificates. He asked me my profession, I said I was a priest. He asked me if I was married, and when I said I was not, he told me that that was the worse for me. Finally, after numerous other questions, he asked if I had proved my citizenship on the 10th August, the 2nd September and the 31st May. He said that no certificate could be issued except to those who had given proof of their patriotism by registering on those three dates. Since I naturally could not give him a satisfactory answer, he said all that he could do was to take my name and address and promise a prompt inquiry into my case. He kept his word. As a result of his inquiry, two Commissioners of the Committee of General Safety of Picpus, with a band or armed men, arrived at my lodging during my absence to take me to prison. I do not even know of what crime I am accused. But you will agree that one can only have pity for Monsieur Colin, who must be sadly lacking in intelligence to hold it against a priest for not having displayed his patriotism on the 10th August, the 2nd September, and the 31st May. A man capable of such a thing is surely worthy of our pity.'

'I am in the same position. I have no certificate,' Brotteaux said. 'We both are suspects. But you are tired, Father. To bed, and we will discuss plans for your safety tomorrow.'

He gave the mattress to his guest and took the palliasse for himself; but in his humility the monk so pressingly demanded the latter, his wish had to be complied with; otherwise he would have slept on the bare floor.

Having completed these arrangements, Brotteaux blew out the candle to save tallow and as a wise precaution.

In the darkness the monk said, 'Monsieur, I thank you for what you are doing for me, though I realize it matters little to you whether I am grateful or not. Let God record it to your merit. That is what should be a matter of immediate consequence to you. But God sees no difference between what is simply the outcome of natural goodness and what is done for His glory. So I beg you, monsieur, to do for Him what you have been ready to do for me.'

'Father,' Brotteaux replied, 'do not concern yourself over such a matter nor feel yourself under any obligation to me whatever. What I am doing at this moment and the merit of which you exaggerate, I am not doing out of love: for though you may well be a lovable man, Father, I do not know you well enough to have any feelings for you. Nor is what I am doing out of humanity, for I am not as simple as Don Juan, to believe, like him, that humanity has certain rights, and such a prejudice, in a mind so free as his, grieves me. I do it simply out of that egoism which inspires all men's acts of generosity and self-sacrifice, by making us see ourselves in all who dwell in misery, by causing us to count our blessings, and by inciting us to help one who shares our common humanity, deluding us into believing that in helping him we are also helping ourselves. I do it also simply because I've nothing better to do: for life is so completely pointless, we have to seek desperately for distractions, and benevolence adds a certain flavour, of an insipid sort, for want of anything more savoury. Finally, I do it out of pride to make myself feel superior to you. Briefly, I do it calculatedly to show you what an atheist can do.'

'Do not slander yourself, monsieur,' said Father Longuemare. 'God has revealed to me, more than He has yet to you, the power of His grace, yet I am not as good a man as you, and am far your inferior in natural loving kindness. However, you must allow me one advantage over you. You say you cannot love me, because you do not know me. Yet, I, monsieur, not knowing you, love you better than myself: God demands that of me.'

Having spoke thus, Father Longuemare knelt on the floor, and, having said his prayers, lay down on his palliasse and fell peacefully asleep.

XIII

ÉVARISTE GAMELIN took his seat at the Tribunal for the second time. Before the sitting opened, he had discussed with his colleagues the news that had arrived that morning. Some of it was uncertain and some false; but what could be relied on as true was appalling. The armies of the Coalition, commanding all the roads had joined forces, La Vendée continued to gain victories, Lyons was in revolt, Toulon had surrendered to the English, who at that moment were landing fourteen thousand troops there.

For Gamelin and his colleagues these events were as much matters of domestic concern as events of world-wide interest. Their own fates were bound irrevocably with that of their country and its salvation meant their salvation. Their own interests and the nation's were so entwined that the latter dictated their opinions, emotions and conduct.

Seated on his bench, Gamelin was given a letter from Trubert, Secretary of the Committee of Defence; it informed him of his appointment as Commissioner of Supplies of Powder and Saltpetre:

You will excavate all the cellars in the Section in order to extract the substances necessary for the manufacture of gunpowder. The enemy may reach Paris tomorrow: it is essential that the soil of our country provides us with the means to repel our aggressors. I send you herewith instructions from the Convention regarding the treatment for saltpetre.   Fraternal greetings.

At that moment the accused was brought in. He was one of the last of the defeated generals whom the Convention was handing over to the Tribunal, and the most insignificant. Gamelin shuddered at the sight of him: it seemed as if he were seeing again the same soldier whom, as a spectator, he had

144

seen sentenced and sent to the guillotine three weeks ago. The man was the same, with his obstinate, self-opiniated air: the procedure was the same. His answers were given in a cunning brutal way, which robbed them of all conviction. His double-faced double-dealing and the accusation he brought against his subordinates made it difficult to remember he was attempting the honourable task of defending his good name and his life. Everything he said was questionable, every statement disputable, position of armies, total forces involved, munitions received, orders given or received, troops engaged: nothing could be known for certain. Nobody could make any sense of these confused, aimless, ridiculous manoeuvres which had ended in disaster, nobody, not even the advocate for the defence, for the prosecution, the accused himself, the judges or the magistrates; and the strange thing was that nobody would admit, even to himself, that all this was so. The judges amused themselves drawing plans and discussing problems of tactics and strategy; the accused continued to reveal his natural predilection for double-dealing.

The argument dragged on and on. And as it did, Gamelin kept seeing on the shattered roads of the North ammunition wagons stuck in the mud, cannons capsized in the ruts, and mile upon mile of broken defeated troops flying in disorder and continuously under attack on all sides from the enemy's cavalry. And he kept hearing from the vast host of betrayed men a mighty roar of accusation arising against this general. Darkness was falling when the hearing ended, and the sculptured head of Marat could be half-seen like a phantom above the President's head. Called upon to pronounce their verdict, the magistrates could not agree. Gamelin rose, and in a dull voice, as if the words were being forced from his throat, yet with deadly incisiveness, declared the accused guilty of treason against the Republic. A roar of approval arose from the crowd and caressed his youthful zeal. The sentence was read by the light of torches which shed a wavering pallid light on the accused's bony forehead which could be seen to be wet with sweat. Outside, on the steps thronged with the usual mob of cockaded harridans, Gamelin could hear his name, now becoming known to the habitual members of the crowd, being passed from mouth to mouth, and he was surrounded by a group of tricoteuses who, shaking their fists, demanded he obtain the head of the Queen.

The following day Évariste was called on to decide the fate of a poor woman, the Widow Meyrion. She used to go from house to house delivering bread, pushing a little hand-cart along the streets and carrying a wooden tally around her waist on which she cut notches with her knife to represent the number of loaves she delivered. She had earned eight sous a day. The Deputy Public Prosecutor appeared unusually vindictive towards this unfortunate creature, who, it appeared, had shouted 'Vive le Roi' on several occasions, had been heard to make anti-revolutionary remarks in the houses at which she called, and was accused of being involved in a plot to engineer the escape of the Queen. When questioned by the judge, she admitted the allegations against her; whether a simpleton or a fanatic, she professed the most extreme Royalist sentiments and counted herself lost.

The Revolutionary Tribunal, dedicated to Equality, prided itself on its impartiality and made a point of being as severe with porters and servant-girls as with aristocrats and financiers. Gamelin himself could not conceive a people's government acting otherwise. He would have judged it contemptible, an insult to the people, to exclude the people themselves from punishment; that would have appeared as if the people, so to speak, were unworthy of punishment. If reserved only for the aristocrats, the guillotine would have appeared to him as a sort of iniquitous privilege. Gamelin was beginning to turn punishment into a religious and mystical ideal, to give it a virtue and merit of its own. He was beginning to believe that society owes criminals their punishment and that to cheat them of it is to do them an injustice in depriving them of their rights. He declared the woman Meyrion guilty and worthy of the supreme penalty, regretting only that the fanatics, more guilty than her, who had been her accomplices, were not there to share her fate.

*

146

Almost every evening Évariste attended the Jacobin Club which met in the former chapel of the Dominicans, vulgarly known as the Jacobins, in the Rue Honoré. In a courtyard, where stood a tree of liberty, a poplar whose leaves rustled ceaselessly, the chapel, built in an inferior, clumsy style and surmounted by a heavy roof of tiles, had a bare gable pierced by a round window and an arched doorway, above which the National colours were flown on a flagstaff crowned with a cap of liberty. The Jacobins had appropriated the premises and taken the name given to the dispossessed monks, in the same way as had the Cordeliers and the Feuillants. Gamelin had once regularly attended the Cordeliers and at the Jacobins he missed the familiar sabots, carmagnoles and rallying cries of the Dantonists. At the Jacobins, Robespierre's club, an official reserve and bourgeois gravity were the accepted form. Marat, the Friend of the People, was no more, and since his death Évariste had followed the doctrines of Robespierre whose opinions ruled the Jacobins, and through them a thousand affiliated Jacobin clubs scattered all over France. During the reading of the minutes, his eyes wandered over the bare, gloomy walls, which, after having sheltered the spiritual sons of the arch-inquisitors.

There, without pomp or ceremony, sat the most powerful men in the country: men who ruled by the power of the spoken word. They ruled the city of Paris and dictated to the Convention itself the laws it made. These builders of the new order – so respectful of the rule of law that they continued to be Royalists in 1791 and would have wished to remain Royalists even after the King had been brought back, after his flight, from Varennes – so obstinate in their attachment to the Constitution, so determined to be friends of the old order even after the massacres of the Champ de Mars and never to become revolutionaries against the revolution, so contemptuous of popular feelings – these builders of the new order cherished in their dark and powerful souls a love of their country which had made them bring forth fourteen armies to defend it and to use the guillotine as the instrument of their reign of terror. Évariste sat lost in admiration of their singleness of mind, their vigilance, their reasoned dogmatism, their unsleeping suspicion, their meticulous administration, their supreme gifts in the art of governing, their remorseless sanity.

The public which formed the audience that day gave little sign of its presence, save a long-drawn low murmur, like the rustlings of the leaves of the tree of liberty outside.

For that day, the 11 Vendémiaire,* a young man with a receding forehead, piercing eyes, prominent nose, pointed chin, pock-marked face, and an air of cold self-possession, had slowly mounted the tribune. His hair was powdered white and he wore a blue coat that accentuated his slim figure. He carried himself with a precise distinction and walked with a light rhythmic movement that made some compare him derisively to a dancing-master and had caused others to nickname him the French Orpheus. Speaking in a clear voice, Robespierre delivered an eloquent, logical attack upon the enemies of the Republic. He dealt forcibly by means of uncompromising and metaphysical arguments with Brissot and his accomplices. He spoke at great length, his sentences flowing smoothly and harmoniously. Soaring into rarer spheres of philosophy, he hurled his thunderbolts at the base conspirators crawling on the ground.

Évariste listened and understood. Until now he had accused the Girondists of working for the restoration of the monarchy or the triumph of the Orléans faction and of planning the destruction of Paris, that heroic city which had freed France and would one day free the world. Now, through the voice of this wise man, he was discovering lighter and purer truths; he was comprehending a philosophy, a metaphysic, of revolution which raised his thoughts far above gross material happenings into a world of absolute certainties safe from all the subjective errors of the senses. In themselves things are involved and confused; facts are so complex it is difficult not to lose one's way amongst them. Robespierre simplified everything for him, revealing the good and the evil to him in simple, clear terms. Either Federalism or Centralization; Centralization meant unity and

148

safety; Federalism meant chaos and damnation. Gamelin tasted the mystical joy of a believer who has come to know the word that saves and the word that destroys. Henceforth the Revolutionary Tribunal, like the ecclesiastical tribunals of former times, would recognize crime as an absolute, definable in one word. And because he was by nature religious, Évariste received these revelations with an awed enthusiasm, his heart expanded and rejoiced at the thought that henceforth he possessed a symbolic means to discern between guilt and innocence. Oh, treasures of faith! Those who have faith, have need of nothing else!

The wise Robespierre enlightened him further regarding the perfidious intentions of those who favoured equality of property and partition of land, who were demanding the abolition of wealth and poverty and the establishment of a happy mediocrity for all. Misled by their specious arguments, Gamelin had originally approved of their aims, which he had considered to be in accordance with the principles of a true Republican. But Robespierre unmasked their machinations and convinced him that these men, ostensibly so disinterested, were working to undermine the Republic, that they were alarming the wealthy in order to arouse powerful and implacable enemies against the Republic. Once private property was threatened, the whole population would suddenly turn against the Republic, since those who possessed least, valued it the most. To alarm vested interests was to conspire against the Republic. These men, who were proposing a system of equality and common ownership of all goods, as being a worthy aim for all good citizens to secure universal happiness and justice, were in reality traitors more dangerous even than the Federalists.

But the greatest revelation given him by the wisdom of Robespierre concerned the crimes and infamies of atheism. Gamelin had never denied the existence of God; he was a deist and believed in a Providence which watches over mankind; but he admitted he had only a very vague conception of this Supreme Being and, being deeply attached to the principle of freedom of conscience, he was quite prepared to allow that right-thinking citizens might follow the example of Lamettrie, Boulanger, Baron d'Hollach, Lolande, Helvétius, the Citizen Dupis, and deny the existence of God, if at the same time they accepted a moral order and were able to find in themselves the resources necessary to lead a virtuous life. He had even felt sympathy for these atheists when he had seen them attacked and persecuted. Robespierre cleared his mind and opened his eyes. By his virtuous eloquence, the great man showed him the true character of atheism, its nature, its aims, its effects; he demonstrated how that doctrine, born in the salons and boudoirs of the aristocracy, was the most insidious invention which the enemies of the people have ever devised to demoralize and enslave the people; how it was a crime to deprive the unfortunate of the consoling thought of a benevolent Providence which would reward and compensate them, so rendering them easy victims of the vile passions that degrade and enslave men; how in short, the monarchical epicureanism of a Helvétius led to immorality, cruelty and every form of licentiousness. Now that Gamelin had heard these sentiments from the lips of a great man and a great citizen, he swore eternal enmity towards all atheists, especially when they carried the infection of a joyous and open heart, like old Brotteaux.

In the days which followed, Évariste had to give judgment, one after the other, upon a *ci-devant* aristocrat convicted of having destroyed grain in order to starve the people, three émigrés who had returned to foment civil war in France, two prostitutes fron the Palais-Égalité, and fourteen Breton conspirators, women, old men, adolescents, masters and servants. The evidence was incontrovertible, the law explicit. Among the guilty was a girl of twenty, in her young beauty a fascinatingly adorable figure when seen under the shadow of the fate awaiting her. Her golden hair was bound with a blue ribbon; her fine linen kerchief gave a glimpse of her neck, white and supple.

Évariste was consistent in his decision: death. And all the accused, with the exception of an old gardener, were sent to the guillotine.

The following week, Évariste and his Section mowed off the heads of forty-five men and eighteen women.

The judges of the Revolutionary Tribunal followed the principle as old as justice itself of drawing no distinction between men and women. President Montaré, moved by the bravery and beauty of Charlotte Corday, had indeed tried to save her by altering the procedure of her trial, but he had lost his seat as a result. Women, almost invariably, were shown no favour under examination, in strict accordance with the rule common to all tribunals. The magistrates feared them, distrusting their artfulness, their tendency to deception, their powers of seduction. Their determination and resolution equalled those of men and this encouraged the Tribunal to treat them equally. Most of the magistrates were men of mediocre sensuality and never allowed themselves to be affected by the prisoner being a woman. They condemned or acquitted as their conscience and their zeal dictated. The women almost always appeared before the Tribunal with their hair carefully arranged and dressed with as much elegance as their unfortunate conditions permitted. But few of them were young and fewer pretty. Prison and anxiety had withered them, the harsh light of the Assembly Hall betrayed their weariness and anguish, accentuating their pallid eyelids, their blotched, pimpled cheeks, their white, drawn lips. However, more than once the fatal chair had held a young girl, palely beautiful, over whose eyes the shadow of death had drawn like a voluptuous veil a liquid film of tears. At such a sight, which magistrates might not be affected, either by tenderness or by irritation? Which might not, in his secret, depraved heart, have imagined the sacred intimacies of the beautiful body before him, which represented to his morbid fancy at one and the same time the body of a living woman and the body of a dead woman? Which magistrate might not have gloated, with voluptuous yet ghoulish imaginings, over the atrocious plessure he felt in handing over to the executioner that beautiful, desirable body? Such possibilities, perhaps best not dwelt on, cannot be denied by anyone who knows mankind. Évariste Gamelin, as an artist cold and pedantic, could see beauty only in the Antique: it inspired his admiration rather than stirred his senses. His classical taste was so severe that he rarely found a woman who lived up to it; he was as insensible to the charms of a pretty face as he was to Fragonard's colouring and Boucher's figures. He had never known desire except when he was deeply in love.

Like most of his colleagues on the Tribunal, he considered women more dangerous than men. He hated the *ci-devant* princesses, creatures he imagined to himself in his horrified dreams as weaving plots in company with the Queen to assassinate good patriots; he hated even all those beautiful mistresses of financiers, philosophers and men of letters, guilty only of having enjoyed the pleasures of the senses and of the mind and of having lived at a time when to be alive had been very heaven. He hated them without admitting to himself his hate, and when he had to pass judgment on one of them, he condemned her with resentment, yet thoroughly convinced in himself that he was condemning her justly for the public good. And his honesty, his complete modesty, his cold intelligence, his devotion to his country, his very virtues themselves, pushed beneath the blade of the guillotine heads which might well have aroused his pity.

But how is this and what is the significance of this strange prodigy? Only yesterday it had been necessary to seek out the guilty, to force oneself to discover their hiding-places and to make them confess their crime. Today there is no longer the hunt with a pack of hounds, no longer the pursuit of a frightened prey: now from all sides come victims freely offering themselves. Aristocrats, virgins, soldiers, prostitutes flock to the Tribunal, dragging too slowly their own condemnation from the judges, claiming death as a right they are impatient to enjoy. This multitude which the zeal of the informers has crowded into the prisons, and wears out the lives of the Public Prosecutor and his assistants in bringing before the Tribunal, is not enough: punishment must also be provided for those who do not wish to wait. And so many others, still prouder and more impatient, begrudging their death to the judges and the executioner, take their lives themselves! The fury to kill inspires a fury to die. Here, in the Conciergerie, a young soldier, handsome, strong, and beloved; he has left in the prison an adorable girl who loves him and who has said to him: 'Live for me!' He wants neither to live for her nor for love nor for glory. He has lit his pipe with his writ of accusation. He is a Republican, breathing Liberty with every breath he takes, yet he turns Royalist so that he may die. The Tribunal tries its hardest to save him, but he proves the stronger; judges and magistrates are forced to let him have his way.

Évariste, naturally of an anxious and scrupulous turn of mind, became increasingly so as he learnt the lessons of the Jacobins and watched everybody becoming more suspicious, more alarmed. At night, as he walked the dark streets on his way to Élodie, he imagined a printing-press for forging assignats below every cellar grating; in the dark corners of every empty baker's hop he imagined mountains of hidden food fraudulently held back for a rise in prices; through the glittering windows of the restaurants he imagined he heard speculators plotting the ruin of his country as they quaffed bottles of Beaune and Chablis; in the evil-smelling alley-ways he could actually see prostitutes trampling under their feet the National cockade to the applauding shouts of elegant young scoundrels; he was coming to see conspirators and traitors everywhere he looked. And his thought became continually: 'Oh, Republic! Against so many secret or declared enemies, only one thing can help you! Saint Guillotine, save my country! . . .'

Élodie used to wait for him in her little blue bedroom above the *Amour Peintre*. To warn him he could come up, she used to put her little watering-can on the window-sill next to the pot of carnations. Nowadays his coming filled her with horror, he was appearing more and more to her to be something vilely monstrous: she feared him and adored him. All the night long, pressing ferociously against each other, the bloody-minded lover and the sensually mad girl made savage and silent love.

XIV

FATHER LONGUEMARE got up at dawn, and after sweeping the room went off to say his Mass in a little chapel in the Rue d'Enfer, served by a non-juring priest. There were thousands of similar retreats in Paris, where the rebellious clergy clandestinely gathered together little flocks of the faithful. The police of the Sections, though vigilant and suspicious, shut their eyes to these hidden folds from fear of exasperating the flocks and from some remnant of veneration for sacred things. The Barnabite bade farewell to his host who had great difficulty in persuading him to come back for dinner, and in the end only succeeded by promising that the food would be neither plentiful nor delicate.

Left to himself, Brotteaux lit a small earthenware stove; then, as he busied himself preparing the meal for the monk and the epicurean, he read his Lucretius and pondered on the human condition.

This wise man had never been surprised that miserable humans, foolish puppets at the mercy of the forces of Nature, should find themselves more often than not in absurd and painful situations; but where he failed in wisdom was in believing that the Revolutionaries were more foolish and more wicked than other men, thereby falling into the error of the ideologue. Nevertheless, he was by no means a pessimist and did not believe that life was wholly bad. He admired Nature in many ways, especially in its manifestation in the astronomological system and in the act of physical love, and so he adapted himself to the daily routine, pending the day, which could not now be far off, when he would no longer know fear or desire.

He carefully coloured some dancing dolls and made a Zerline which resembled Rose Thévenin. He liked the girl and his epicureanism highly approved of the arrangements of the atoms of which she was composed.

These tasks kept him occupied until the return of the Barnabite.

'Father,' he said as he opened the door for him, 'I told you, you remember, that our meal would be meagre. We have nothing but chestnuts. All the more reason, therefore, that they should be well cooked.'

'Chestnuts!' exclaimed Father Longuemare with a smile. 'There is no more delicious a dish. My father, monsieur, was a poor gentleman of the Limousin, whose entire estate consisted of a ruined pigeon-cote, an uncared-for orchard, and a clump of chestnut trees. He fed himself, his wife and his twelve children on big, green chestnuts, and we all grew up strong and sturdy. I was the youngest and the wildest; my father used to declare, by way of a joke, that he would have to send me to America to be a pirate . . . Ah, monsieur! How fragrant your chestnut soup smells! It takes me back to the table where my mother used to sit smiling, with her little ones all around her.'

The meal over, Brotteaux set off for Joly's, the toy merchant in the Rue Neuve-des-Petits-Champs, who took the dancing dolls which Caillon had rejected and ordered not just another gross of similar ones but two gross to begin with.

On reaching the former Rue Royale Brotteaux saw gleaming in the Place de la Révolution a steel triangle between the top of two upright beams: it was the guillotine. An immense crowd of joyfully curious spectators pressed round the scaffold awaiting the arrival of the laden tumbrils. Women were hawking Nanterre cakes on trays hung in front of them and shouting their wares; sellers of cooling drinks were ringing their little bells; an old man at the foot of the Statue of Liberty had put up a peep-show surmounted by a swing on which a monkey was playing antics. Underneath the scaffold, dogs were licking up yesterday's blood. Brotteaux turned back towards the Rue Honoré.

Back once more in his garret, where he found the Barnabite reading his breviary, he carefully wiped the table and arranged his colour-box on it together with the materials and tools on his trade.

'Father,' he said, 'if you should not consider the occupation unworthy of the sacred calling with which you are invested, I would ask you to help me make my marionettes. A worthy tradesman, Joly by name, has given me a rather large order this morning. Whilst I am painting these figures already constructed, you would be doing me a great service if you would cut out heads, arms, legs and bodies from the patterns here. You could not find better; they are modelled on Watteau and Boucher.'

'I agree with you, monsieur,' replied Longuemare. 'Watteau and Boucher were well equipped to create such baubles. It would have been more to their credit if they had confined themselves to such innocent figures. I shall be delighted to help you, but I fear I may not be expert enough.'

Father Longuemare was right to doubt his own skill; after several unsuccessful attempts, it was obvious that his genius did not lie in cutting out pretty shapes in thin cardboard with the point of a penknife. But when Brotteaux gave him, at his suggestion, some string and a bodkin, he proved himself very capable in endowing with movement the little creations he had failed to make, and in teaching them to dance. When trying them afterwards, he found he had a happy knack of making them execute three or four steps of a gavotte, and when they thus rewarded his pains, a smile would flicker on his stern lips.

Once, as he pulled the strings of a Scaramouche to a dance tune, he observed:

'Monsieur, this little travesty reminds me of an unusual story. It was in 1746, when I was completing my novitiate under the care of Father Magitot, an elderly man of great learning and austere morals. At that time, you may remember, dancing figures which had of course been intended to amuse children had come to exercise an extraordinary fascination over women and even over men, both young and old. Indeed, they were all the rage in Paris. The fashionable shops were full of them; they were to be found in the houses of people of quality, and it was nothing unusual to see some grave and reverend old gentleman dancing his doll in the street or in a public garden. Father Magitot's age, character and sacred calling did not avail to guard him against infection. Every time he saw anyone jumping his cardboard marionette, his fingers itched to be doing the same – an impatience that soon became almost intolerable.

'One day he was paying a visit, on an important matter involving the interests of the whole Order, to Monsieur Chauvel, advocate in the courts of Parliament, and he noticed one of these dancers hanging from the chimney piece. He had a terrific temptation to pull its string, but managed to resist it with a tremendous effort. But this frivolous ambition pursued him everywhere and gave him no peace. In his studies, in his meditations, in his prayers, at church, at chapter, in the confessional and in the pulpit, he was possessed by it. After days of unbearable agony of mind, he presented his extraordinary case before the General of the Order who happened fortunately to be in Paris at that time. He was an eminent ecclesiastic from Milan, a Doctor and a Prince of the Church. His advice to Father Magitot was to satisfy a craving which was innocent in its inception, importunate in its consequences and inordinate in its excesses, and which threatened to impose the gravest disorders in the soul which was afflicted by it. On the advice, or more strictly, on the order of the General, Father Magitot returned to Monsieur Chauvel's house, where the lawyer received him, as on the first occasion, in his study. There, seeing the dancing doll still in the same place, he ran excitedly to it and begged his host to do him the favour of allowing him to pull the string. The lawyer gave him permission most willingly, and informed him in confidence that sometimes he made Scaramouche (that was the doll's name) dance while he was preparing his briefs, and that, only the night before, he had practised modulating on Scaramouche's movements the peroration of his speech in defence of a woman falsely accused of poisoning her husband. Father Magitot seized the string tremblingly, and saw Scaramouche under his manipulation twitching madly like one possessed being exorcized.'

'Your story does not surprise me, Father,' Brotteaux said. 'One sees such obsessions. But it is not always cardboard figures that cause them.'

Father Longuemare, who was a man of religion, never talked about religion; Brotteaux was constantly talking about it. And, since he felt a bond of sympathy between himself and the Barnabite, it amused him to embarrass the monk and to disturb him with objections to various articles of the Christian faith. Once, when they were working together making Zerlines and Scaramouches, he remarked:

'When I consider the events which have brought us to our present condition, I doubt if I know which party has shown most madness in the general insanity. Sometimes I am greatly tempted to believe it was the monarchy.'

'Monsieur,' the monk replied, 'when God forsakes them, all men like Nebuchadnezzar lose their wits, but no man has been so fatal to the kingdom as the Abbé Fauchet, no man has ever fallen so deeply into ignorance and error as he. France must surely have greatly exasperated God that He should send her Monsieur l'Abbé Fauchet.'

It seems to me we have seen other wrong-doers than this unfortunate Fauchet.'

'Monsieur l'Abbé Grégoire was also a man full of malice.'

'And Brissot, and Danton, and Marat, and a hundred others. What have you to say about them, Father?'

'They were laymen, monsieur. The laity can never incur the same responsibility as the clergy. The evil they do does not have such universal repercussions.'

'And your God, Father? What have you to say about His behaviour towards this Revolution?'

'I do not understand you, monsieur.'

'Epicurus said: "God either wishes to prevent evil and cannot, or can and does not wish to, or cannot and does not wish to, or wishes to and can. If He wishes to and cannot, He is impotent; if He can and does not wish to, He is perverse; if He cannot and does not wish to, He is impotent and per-

verse; if He does wish to and can, then why doesn't He?"
Tell me that, Father!'

And Brotteaux threw a look of satisfaction at his companion.

'Monsieur,' replied the monk, 'there is nothing that
saddens me more than these difficulties you raise. When I
look into the reasoning of non-believers, it seems as though I
am looking at ants piling up a few blades of grass in an attempt
to dam back a torrent that sweeps down from the mountains.
Permit me not to argue with you. I would have too many
arguments and too little ability to present them. Besides, you
will find yourself refuted in the Abbé Guénée and twenty
others. I will only say that what you quote from Epicurus is
foolishness: for God is judged in it as if He were a man and
had a man's morals. Ah, well, monsieur, the unbelievers,
from Celsus down to Bayle and Voltaire, have deluded fools
with similar paradoxes.'

'Don't you see, Father,' Brotteaux replied, 'into what
errors your faith leads you? Not content with finding all
truth in your theology, you even refuse to find any in the
works of so many noble minds who think differently from
you.'

'You are completely mistaken, monsieur,' Longuemare
protested. 'On the contrary, I believe that nothing can be
altogether false in a man's thought. The atheists occupy the
lowest rung on the ladder of understanding; but even with
them, gleams of sense are to be found and flashes of truth, and,
even where the shadows are darkest, men possess a mind into
which God can put understanding: that was what happened
to Lucifer.'

'Well, monsieur,' Brotteaux said, 'I will not be so generous
and I swear to you that I don't find one atom of sense in all the
works of your theologians.'

At the same time he would repudiate any wish to attack
religion, considering it necessary for people; he only desired
that its ministers were philosophers instead of controversial-
ists. He deplored the fact that the Jacobins were for replacing
it with a newer and more malignant religion, the cult of
Liberty and Equality, of the Republic and the State. He had

noticed that religions are fiercest and most cruel in the vigour of their youth and that they grow milder as they grow older. He was anxious, therefore, to see Catholicism preserved, since though it had devoured many victims in its youth, it was now, burdened by the weight of years and an enfeebled appetite, content with roasting four or five heretics every hundred years.

'For the rest,' he added, 'I have always got on very well with your God-eaters and Christ-breeders. I used to keep a chaplain at Les Ilettes, where Mass was said every Sunday; all my guests used to come along to it. The philosophers were the most assiduous and the girls from the opera the most fervent. I was fortunate then and had numerous friends.'

'Friends!' exclaimed Father Longuemare. 'Friends! Do you really believe, monsieur, they liked you, all your philosophers and all your courtesans, who have degraded your soul so that God Himself would have difficulty in recognizing it as one of the temples He built for His glory?'

Father Longuemare continued to live another week with the Publican without being troubled. As far as possible he observed the discipline of his Order and every night at the canonical hours he would get up from his palliasse to kneel on the bare floor and recite his offices. Though they were both reduced to eating scraps, he duly observed fasts and abstinences. A smiling but pitiful spectator of these austerities, Brotteaux asked him one day:

'Do you really believe God finds any pleasure in seeing you endure cold and hunger like this?'

'God Himself,' the monk replied, 'gave us the example of suffering.'

On the ninth day after the Barnabite had come to share the philosopher's garret, Brotteaux went out at dusk to deliver his dancing dolls to Joly, the toy merchant of the Rue Neuve-des-Petits-Champs. He was on his way back, pleased at having sold them all, when, as he was crossing the former Place du Carrousel, a girl wearing a blue satin pelisse bordered with ermine, ran towards him limping, threw herself into his arms and held him in the embrace peculiar to suppliants from time immemorial.

She was trembling; it was even possible to feel the fast beat of her heart. Moved by her look of pathetic vulgarity, Brotteaux, veteran amateur of the theatre, thought how Mademoiselle Raucourt could have profited by seeing her.

She spoke breathlessly, lowering her voice for fear of being overheard by passers-by:

'Take me with you, citizen, and hide me, for pity's sake! . . . They are in my room in the Rue Fromenteau. As they were coming upstairs, I ran into Flora's room – next to mine – and jumped out of the window into the street. That's how I've sprained my foot . . . They were coming for me; they want to put me in prison and put me to death . . . Last week they put Virginie to death.'

Brotteaux understood well that she was talking of the delegates of the Revolutionary Committee of the Section or of the Commissaries of the Committee of General Safety. At that time, the Commune had a virtuous *procureur,* the Citizen Chaumette, who hunted down prostitutes as being the most deadly enemies of the Republic. He wanted to reform their morals. The young ladies of the Palais-Égalité, were, indeed, no great patriots. They regretted the old ways and did not always hide the fact. Several had been guillotined already as conspirators.

The Citizen Brotteaux asked her what she had done to bring down on her a warrant of arrest.

She swore that she had no idea, she had done nothing she could be blamed for.

'Well, then, my child,' Brotteaux told her, 'you are certainly not a suspect: you have nothing to fear. Go back to bed and leave me in peace.'

At that, she confessed everything:

'I tore out my cockade and I shouted: "Vive le Roi!"'

He took her along the deserted quais. Clinging to his arm, she continued:

'It's not that I liked him, the King; I never met him, you know, but he probably wasn't much different from other men.

But these lot are wicked. They are cruel to us poor girls. They torment me, annoy me, hurt me in every kind of way; they want to prevent me carrying on my trade. I have no other. You can be quite sure if I had, I wouldn't be doing what I do . . . What do they want? They're so hard on ordinary people, the milkman, the charcoalman, the water-carrier, the laundress. They won't be happy till they set all poor folks against them.'

He looked at her: she seemed only a child. She was no longer shaking with fear. She was almost smiling, as she limped along lightly beside him. He asked her her name. She replied that it was Athénaïs and that she was sixteen.

Brotteaux offered to see her safely to anywhere she wanted to go. She knew no one at all in Paris; but she had an aunt, a servant at Palaiseau, who would take her in.

Brotteaux made up his mind.

'Come along, my child,' he said to her.

And he led her away, leaning on his arm.

Back in his garret, he found Father Longuemare reading in his breviary.

He showed Athénaïs to him, holding her by the hand:

'Father, here is a girl from the Rue Fromenteau who has shouted "Vive le Roi!" The Revolutionary police are after her. She has nowhere to go. Will you allow her to spend the might here?'

Father Longuemare closed his breviary.

'If I understand you correctly,' he said, 'you are asking me, monsieur, if this young girl who is, like myself, threatened with a warrant for arrest, may for her secular salvation spend the night in the same room as I.'

'Yes, Father.'

'By what right should I object? Should I consider myself offended by her presence? Should I be so sure that I am of more value than she in the sight of God?'

He ensconced himself, for the night, in an old broken-down armchair, declaring he would sleep well in it. Athénaïs lay on the mattress. Brotteaux stretched himself on the palliasse and blew out the candle.

The hours and half-hours rang from the clocks of the churches: he slept not and heard the mingled breathing of the monk and the prostitute. The moon, symbol and witness of ancient loves, rose and poured into the garret a beam of silver which aureoled with light the fair hair, the golden eyelashes, the delicate nose and the curved red mouth of Athénaïs, asleep with her fists clenched.

'There lies,' he thought to himself, 'a terrible enemy indeed for the Republic.'

When Athénaïs awoke, it was day. The monk had disappeared. Brotteaux was reading his Lucretius under the skylight, learning from the Latin poet how to live without fear and without desire; and yet he was filled with a regret and an unease.

On opening her eyes, Athénaïs was stupefied to see above her head the roof-beams of a garret. Then she remembered, smiled at her preserver, and reaching out her arms caressed him with her pretty little dirty hands.

Sitting up on the mattress, she pointed to the dilapidated armchair in which the monk had passed the night.

'He has gone? ... He hasn't gone to denounce me, has he?'

'No, my child. You couldn't find anywhere a more honest person than that old madman.'

Athénaïs asked in what way the old man was mad; and, when Brotteaux told her it was religion, she reproached him gravely for saying such a thing and declared that men without religion were worse than beasts and that, for herself, she prayed to God often, hoping He would forgive her sins and receive her into His blessed mercy.

Then, noticing that Brotteaux was holding a book in his hand, she took it to be a book of the Mass and said:

'And there, you see, you say your prayers too! God will reward you for what you have done for me.'

Brotteaux told her the book was not a book of the Mass and that it had been written long before the Mass had been introduced into the world. She then thought it must be a *Key to Dreams* and asked if it contained an explanation of an extraordinary dream she had had. She could not read and had heard of only these two books.

Brotteaux replied that this book only explained the dream of life. Finding this beyond her, the pretty child did not try to understand it and gave her face a cursory wash in the earthenware pot which had replaced the silver basins Brotteaux had once been accustomed to. Then she arranged her hair before her host's shaving mirror with scrupulous care and gravity. Her slender white arms raised above her head, she made an occasional remark between long intervals:

'You ... You were rich once?'

'What makes you think that?'

'I don't know. But you *were*. And you were an aristocrat, I'm sure.'

From her pocket she took a little Holy Virgin made of silver in a round ivory shrine, a piece of sugar, some thread, scissors, a flint and steel, a few cases of needles and other odds and ends, and after selecting what she required, she sat down and began mending her skirt which had been torn in several places.

'For your own safety, child, put this in your cap!' Brotteaux told her, giving her a tricolour cockade.

'I will gladly, monsieur', she agreed. 'But it'll be for love of you and not for love of the Republic.'

When she was dressed and had made herself as presentable as possible, she took her skirts in both hands and dropped a curtsey as she had been taught to do in her village, saying as she did so:

'Monsieur, I am your most humble servant.'

Though she was ready to oblige her benefactor in any way he wished, she decided it was more becoming when he demanded nothing and that it would also become her better to offer nothing herself. It seemed to her a romantic way to part, and indeed what good manners required.

Brotteaux slipped a few assignats into her hand to pay her coach fare to Palaiseau. It was half of all he had, and although he had been famous for his lavish generosity to women, it was the first time he had ever made an equal partition of all he owned with any woman.

She asked him his name.

'I am called Maurice.'

He opened the garret door for her reluctantly.

'Good-bye, Athénaïs.'

She kissed him.

'Monsieur Maurice,' she said, 'when you think of me, if you ever do, think of me as Marthe. That is the name I was christened and the name they call me in my village . . . Good-bye and thank you . . . Your very humble servant, Monsieur Maurice.'

XV

THE prisons were full to bursting and must be emptied; the work of judging and judgment had to go on without rest or respite. Seated against the tapestried walls with their fasces and their red caps of liberty, the judges maintained the same gravity, the same awesome calm, as their Royal predecessors. The Public Prosecutor and his Deputies, worn out with fatigue, feverish with brandy and lack of sleep, could only shake off their exhaustion with a violent effort; their shattered health made them tragic figures. The magistrates, all so different in character and origins, educated or ignorant, generous or mean, gentle or violent, sincere or hypocritical, but all of them men who, knowing the Republic to be in danger, suffered or pretended to suffer the same anguish, to be afire with the same ardour; all were poised ready for atrocities primed by conscience or fear, and thus they formed one living organism, one single, unthinking, irritable mind, one single apocalyptic, bestial soul which could, by the mere exercise of its natural functions, produce a teeming progeny of death. By turn capriciously cruel or kind-hearted, they would, when momentarily overcome by a sudden pang of pity, acquit with tears in their eyes a prisoner whom only an hour before they would have mocked as they condemned him to the guillotine. As day followed day, the more impetuously they followed their impulses.

Judges and magistrates worked, feverish and half-asleep with exhaustion, distracted by the excited shouts of the sovereign people outside, threatened by the sans-culottes and tricoteuses who crowded the galleries and public enclosure, influenced by insane evidence, relying on the denunciations of madmen, in a poisonous atmosphere which dulled their brains, set their ears hammering and temples beating and covered their eyes with a veil of blood. Vague rumours were rife among the people of magistrates being bribed by the gold of the accused. To these, the magistrates replied as a body with indignant protests and merciless condemnations. They were, in fact, neither better not worse than their fellow men. Freedom from sin is more often than not a piece of good fortune rather than a virtue: any person who might have agreed to take their place would have acted as they did, and performed to the best of his mediocre soul their appalling tasks.

Antoinette, the Queen, so long awaited, sat at last in the fatal chair, in a black gown and the object of such concentrated hate that it was only the certainty of her fate which made the court observe the forms of law. To the mortally conclusive questions hurled at her she replied sometimes with the instinct of self-preservation, sometimes with her usual haughtiness, and once, owing to a hideous suggestion by one of her accusers, with the noble dignity of a mother. The witnesses against her confined themselves completely to venom and calumny; her defence witnesses were frozen with terror. The Tribunal, forcing itself to follow the rules of procedure, waited as patiently as it could till all the formalities were completed, before hurling against the nations of Europe the head of the Austrian-born Queen of France.

Three days after the execution of Marie Antoinette, Gamelin was called to the bedside of the Citizen Fortuné Trubert, who lay dying on a bed of sacks in the cell of an expelled Barnabite father, within thirty steps of the office where he had worn out his life. His white head was sunk deep in the pillow. His eyes, already almost sightless, turned their glassy pupils towards his visitor; his hot, dry hand grasped Évariste's and pressed it with unexpected strength. Three times in the last two days he had vomited blood. He tried to speak: his voice, hoarse and weak as a whisper at first, grew louder, deeper:

'Wattignies! Wattignies! ... Jourdan has encircled the enemy ... he has raised the blockage at Mauberge ... We have recaptured Marchiennes, *ça ira* ... *ça ira* ...'

167

And he smiled.

These were not dreams of a sick man, but a clear vision of events to be that flashed through a brain soon to be enveloped in eternal night. Trubert foresaw the outcome of the policy of terror. Where voluntary recruitment had failed, compulsion had succeeded in producing a strong disciplined army; in their terror the generals had realized the best thing for them was to be victorious. One final effort, and the Republic would be saved.

After half an hour of semi-consciousness, Fortuné Trubert's face, hollow and worn with disease, lighted up again and his hands moved.

He lifted his finger and pointed to the only piece of furniture in the room, a small, walnut desk. His voice was weak and breathless, but his mind still unclouded.

'My friend,' he said, 'like Eudamidas I leave my debts to you, my friend: three hundred and twenty livres ... the account is in that red book over there ... Adieu, Gamelin. Be vigilant. Watch over the defence of the Republic. *Ça ira.*'

The shadow of night was filling the cell. All that could be heard was the painful breathing of the dying man and the scratching of his hands on the sheet.

At midnight, he uttered some disconnected words:

'More saltpetre ... Get the guns delivered ... My health? Excellent! ... Pull down all the bells! ...

He died at 5 o'clock in the morning.

By order of the Section his body lay in state in the nave of the former church of the Barnabites, at the foot of the Altar of the Nation, on a camp bed covered with a tricolour flag and with his forehead encircled with a crown of oak leaves.

Twelve old men dressed in Roman togas, with palms in their hands, twelve young girls wearing long veils and holding flowers, stood round the funeral bed. At the feet of the dead man, two children each held an inverted torch. Évariste recognized one of them as his concierge's little daughter Joséphine, and in her childish gravity and her charming beauty she reminded him of those sculptured figures of Love and Death on Roman tombs.

The funeral procession made its way to the cemetery of Saint-André-des-Arts to the singing of the *Marseillaise* and the *Ça ira*.

As he placed his kiss of farewell on Fortuné Trubert's brow, Évariste wept. He wept for himself, envying him who reposed there, his task accomplished.

On returning home, he received notice that he was appointed a member of the General Council of the Commune. After standing as candidate for four months he had been elected unopposed, after several ballots, by some thirty voters. No one voted now; the Section meetings were deserted; the one thought of rich and poor was to avoid the performance of public duties. The most momentous events no longer aroused either enthusiasm or curiosity; the newspapers were never read. Out of the seven hundred thousand inhabitants of Paris, Évariste doubted whether even three or four thousand still maintained the old Republican spirit.

That same day the Twenty-one came up for trial.

Despite everything, despite their innocence or guilt of the misfortunes of the Republic, despite their vanity, ambition and impetuosity, despite their quickness to declare war and their feebleness in waging it, despite the fact that they were being hauled before the Tribunal simply for the example they had given, they were nonetheless the first and the most brilliant leaders of the Revolution, whose delight and glory they had once been. The judge, who will question them with biassed artfulness; the pale accuser, who as he sits there behind his little table is planning their dishonour and death; the magistrates who will soon put to nought all the attempts of the defence to save them; the people in the galleries who are overwhelming them with howls of insult and abuse, all of them, judge, magistrates and people, only yesterday applauded their eloquence, extolled their talents and their virtues. But they no longer remember.

Once Évariste had made Vergniaud his god, Brissot his oracle. But he had forgotten; if any trace of his former worship remained in his memory, it served only to increase their monstrosity in deceiving such fine citizens as himself.

On returning home after the sitting of the Tribunal, Gamelin heard heart-rending cries as he entered the house. It was the little Joséphine whom her mother was whipping for having played in the square with some urchins and dirtied the beautiful white dress which she had worn for the funeral of the Citizen Trubert.

XVI

HAVING for three months participated in the daily sacrifice to the State of victims, both illustrious and obscure, Évariste found a case all for himself; an accused against whom he had his own personal accusation.

Ever since he had sat on the Tribunal, he had watched eagerly, among the mass of culprits who appeared before him, for the man who had seduced Élodie. In his vivid imagination he had painted a portrait of this man, some of the details being indeed accurate. He pictured him as young, handsome, haughty, and had convinced himself that the man had fled to England. He believed he had now found him in a young émigré named Maubel who had come back to France, been denounced by an innkeeper and arrested at an inn at Passy. His case, like a thousand others, was presented by the Public Prosecutor, Fouquier-Tinville. Letters had been found on him which Fouquier-Tinville regarded as proof of a plot between Maubel and Pitt's agents, but which actually were only letters written to the émigré by a banking-house in London where he had deposited certain funds. Maubel, who was young and good-looking, seemed mainly interested in various love affairs. Evidence of some connection he had with Spain was found in his pocket-book. Spain was then at war with France, but actually these letters were only of a purely private nature, and if the court of preliminary inquiry had not registered a note of insufficient evidence on these scores, it was only on the grounds that justice should never be in too great a hurry to release a prisoner.

Gamelin had a report of Maubel's first interrogation and he was struck by what it revealed of the young man's character, which he considered fitted that of Élodie's betrayer. He then spent many hours in the private room of the clerk of the court, poring eagerly over the papers relating to the case. His suspicions received a remarkable confirmation on his discovering in an old note-book of the émigré the address of the *Amour Peintre*, together though with those of the *Singe Vert* and several other shops which sold prints and paintings. But when he was informed that in this same note-book had been found some red carnation petals carefully wrapped in a piece of silk, he remembered that the red carnation was Élodie's favourite flower, the one she had in the pot on her windowsill, wore in her hair, and, as he had good reason to know, gave as a love token, and his last doubts vanished. Convinced now that he was right, he resolved to question Élodie, though without letting her know the circumstances which had led him to discover the culprit.

As he climbed the stairs to his lodgings, he noticed even on the lower landing a strong smell of fruit, and on reaching the studio, he found Élodie helping the Citizeness Gamelin to make quince jam. Whilst the old housewife was kindling the stove and considering ways of saving fuel and moist sugar without spoiling the quality of the jam, the Citizeness Blaise, seated on a straw-bottomed chair, wearing an apron of brown holland and with her lap full of the golden fruit, was peeling the quinces, quartering them and throwing them into a shallow, copper basin. The strings of her coif were thrown back over her shoulders, the strands of her black hair coiled above her moist forehead; from her whole person there breathed an air of domestic charm and intimate grace which aroused gentle thoughts and tranquil desire.

Without moving from her chair, she gave her lover her beautiful smouldering look as of molten gold and said:

'You see, Évariste, we are working for you. You're going to have a delicious store of quince jelly for the winter which will do you good and make your heart joyful.'

But Gamelin went up to her and said quietly in her ear a name:

'Jacques Maubel . . .'

At the moment Combalot the cobbler showed his red nose

at the half-open door. He had brought some shoes he had repaired, together with the bill for them.

For fear of being taken for a bad citizen he always used the new calendar. The Citizeness Gamelin, who always examined her bills carefully, was all mixed up by the *Fructidors* and *Vendémiaires.*

She sighed:

'Jesus! They want to change everything – days, months, seasons, the sun and the moon! Dear God, what is this pair of shoes down here for the 8 Vendémiaire, Monsieur Combalot?'

'Citizeness, just have a look at your calendar and you'll understand it.'

She took the calendar down from the wall, glanced at it and turned her head away with a shudder.

'It doesn't look Christian!' she exclaimed in a shocked voice.

'Not only that, citizeness,' said the cobbler, 'but now we've only three Sundays in the month instead of four. And not only that: we'll soon have to change our ways of counting. There'll be no more *liards* and *demers*, everything'll be measured by distilled water.'

At these words, the Citizeness Gamelin her lips trembling, looked up at the ceiling and sighed:

'They're going too far!'

And, while she was lamenting, looking like one of the female saints in wayside shrines, a piece of coal began to smoke and, together with the stifling smell of the quinces, made the air in the studio unbreathable.

Élodie complained it was hurting her throat and asked for the window to be opened. As soon as the cobbler had left and the Citizeness Gamelin gone back to her stove, Évariste repeated the name in the ear of the Citizeness Blaise:

'Jacques Maubel.'

She looked at him as if a little surprised, and said very calmly as she went on cutting a quince in quarters:

'Well? . . . Jacques Maubel what? . . .'

'It was he.'

'Who?'

'The one you gave a red carnation to.'

She declared she did not know what he was talking about and asked him to explain himself.

'That aristocrat! That émigré! That scoundrel!'

She shrugged her shoulders and denied with the most candid air that she had ever known a Jacques Maubel.

And truly she had never known a man of that name.

She denied ever having given red carnatións to anyone but Évariste; but, on this point, her memory was perhaps not so good.

Évariste had had little experience of women and he was far from fully understanding Élodie's character; nevertheless he thought her quite capable of pretence and of deceiving a cleverer man than he.

'Why deny it?' he said. 'I know.'

She asserted again having known nobody named Maubel. And having finished peeling the quinces, she asked for some water to rinse her sticky fingers.

Gamelin brought her a basin of water.

As she washed her hands, she renewed her denials.

He repeated again that he knew, and, this time, she kept silent.

She did not see where her lover's question was leading and was a thousand miles from suspecting that this Maubel, whom she had never heard of, was to be brought before the Revolutionary Tribunal; she understood nothing of the suspicions which obsessed him, but she knew they were baseless. And for that reason, since she saw she had little hope of dissipating them, she had little wish to. She stopped defending herself from having known Maubel, preferring to leave her lover lost on a false trail, when at any moment, the least word might start him on the right one. Her little lawyer's clerk of former days, now become a handsome, patriotic dragoon, had since quarrelled with his aristocratic mistress. Whenever he met Élodie in the street, his eyes seemed to say: 'Come my beauty! I feel sure I'm ready to forgive you for having abandoned you and to take you back again.' So she made no further attempt to cure what she called her lover's whims; Gamelin remained convinced that Jacques Maubel was Élodie's seducer.

During the days that followed, the Tribunal devoted itself to crushing Federalism which, like a hydra, had threatened to devour Liberty. This meant busy days; and the magistrates, worn out with fatigue, despatched with as much haste as possible the case of the woman Roland, the instigator and accomplice of Brissot and his party.

Meanwhile Gamelin spent every morning in the room of the clerk of the court in order to hasten the Maubel trial. Some important pieces of evidence were at Bordeaux: he arranged for a Commissioner to be sent by post-coach to fetch them. At last they arrived.

The Deputy Public Prosecutor read them, made a grimace and said to Évariste:

'This isn't much use! There's nothing here any good! Just trifles! If we could only prove that this *ci-devant* Comte de Maubel ever went to England without a passport! . . .'

Gamelin finally succeeded. The young Maubel received his writ of accusation and was brought before the Revolutionary Tribunal on the 19 Brumaire.

From the first day of the sitting the President wore the gloomy and dreadful face he took care to assume for the hearing of cases in which the evidence was weak. The Deputy Prosecutor stroked his chin with the feather of his pen and affected the serenity of a conscience at ease. The clerk read out the writ of accusation: never yet had the court heard anything so shallow.

The President asked the accused if he had not been aware of the laws passed against the émigrés.

'I was aware of them and I observed them,' answered Maubel. 'I left France provided with the proper passports.'

He had satisfactory explanations to give for his reasons for going to England and for returning to France. His face was pleasant, with a frankness and confidence that impressed. The women in the gallery looked at the young man with favourable eyes. The prosecution maintained that he had gone to Spain when that nation was at war with France: he affirmed he had never left Bayonne during that period. One point only remained obscure. Among the papers he had thrown into the fire at the time of his arrest, only a few fragments had remained on which some words in Spanish had been deciphered together with the name of 'Nieves'.

On this subject Jacques Maubel refused to give any explanations. And, when the President told him that it was in his own interest to clear up the point, he replied that a man should not do always what was in his own interest.

Gamelin's only aim was to get Maubel convicted of a crime: three times he pressed the President to ask the accused to explain the dried carnation petals so carefully kept in his pocket book.

Maubel replied that he did not consider himself obliged to answer a question which had no concern with the case, since no letter had been found concealed with the petals.

The magistrates retired to the Hall of Deliberations, favourably impressed by the young man whose mysterious conduct appeared to be chiefly concerned to hide a lover's secret. This time the good patriots, feeling themselves the purest of the pure, would gladly have voted for acquittal. One of them, a *ci-devant* aristocrat, who had proved his loyalty to the Revolution said:

'Is it his birth that is being brought against him? I also had the misfortune to be born into the aristocracy.'

'Yes, but you left them,' Gamelin retorted, 'and he didn't.'

And he spoke with such vehemence against this conspirator, this agent of Pitt, this accomplice of Coburg, who had voyaged over land and sea in order to stir up the enemies of liberty: he demanded so forcibly this traitor's condemnation that he awoke the always restless impulsiveness, the old stern implacability of the patriotic magistrates.

One of them said to him, cynically:

'There are favours which cannot be refused between colleagues.'

The verdict of death was passed by a solid majority.

The condemned man heard his sentence with a quiet smile.

His eyes, which had been gazing unconcernedly about the hall, fell on Gamelin's face, and took on an expression of unutterable contempt.

Nobody applauded the sentence.

On being taken back to the Conciergerie, Jacques Maubel wrote a letter while awaiting the hour of execution which was to take place the same evening, by torchlight:

My dear sister, the Tribunal sends me to the scaffold, giving me the only joy I have been able to feel since the death of my beloved Nieves. They have taken from me the only thing I had left of her, a pomegranate flower, which they insisted on calling, I don't know why, a carnation.

I loved all beautiful things: in Paris, in happier times, I collected paintings and engravings which are now in a safe place and which will be delivered to you as soon as it is possible. I beg you, my dear sister, to keep them in memory of me.

He cut a lock from his hair, enclosed it in the letter, which he folded, and wrote on the back the address:

To the Citizeness Clemence Dezeimeries
        née Maubel
                La Réole

He gave all the money on him to the turnkey, begging him to see that this letter was despatched. Then he asked for a bottle of wine and drank it in little sips as he awaited the arrival of the tumbril . . .

After supper, Gamelin ran to the *Amour Peintre* and burst into the blue bedroom where every night Élodie was waiting for him.

'You are avenged,' he told her. 'Jacques Maubel is no more. The cart which was taking him to his death has passed under your windows, surrounded by torches.'

She understood:

'You miserable creature! It is you who have killed him, and he was not my lover! . . . I didn't know him . . . I'd never set eyes on him . . . What had he done? He was young, kind . . .

177

and innocent. And you have killed him! You monster! You wretched monster!'

She fell into a half-swoon. But, amid the shades of this faint death, she felt herself as if drowning in a strangely mixed flood of horror and ecstatic lust. Slowly she returned to consciousness, her eyes opened wide showing the whites and enlarged pupils, her breasts swelled up, her impatient hands groped for her lover. She pressed him to her as if choking the life out of him, she thrust her nails into his flesh, and with her bleeding lips she gave him the most silent, most forceful, most long, most painful and most delicious of kisses.

She gave him her love with her whole body, and the more he seemed to her terrible, cruel and atrocious, the more he seemed to her covered with the blood of his victims, the more she hungered and thirsted for him.

XVII

On the 24 Frimaire,* at ten in the morning, under a clear pink-blue sky that was melting the ice of the night, the Citizens Guénot and Delourmel, delegates of the Committee of General Safety, went to the Barnabites and asked to be taken to the Committee of Surveillance of the Section, in the capitular room, whose only occupant at that moment was the Citizen Beauvisage, who was busy piling logs on the fire. Owing to his short squat figure, they did not notice him at first.

In the cracked voice of hunchbacks, the Citizen Beauvisage begged the delegates to seat themselves and put himself entirely at their service.

Guénot then asked if he knew a *ci-devant* Monsieur des Ilettes, residing near the Pont-Neuf.

'He is an individual,' he added, 'whose arrest I am instructed to effect.'

And he produced the order from the Committee of General Safety.

Beauvisage, after searching in his memory for some time, replied that he knew no individual named des Ilettes, that the suspect in question might not be an inhabitant of his Section, since certain parts of other Sections met in the near neighbourhood of the Pont-Neuf; and that, if he did live in his Section, it must be under another name than that shown on the Committee's order; that, nevertheless, it would not be long before they discovered his whereabouts.

'Les us lose no time!' Guénot said. 'Our vigilance was aroused in this case by a letter from one of the man's accomplices which was intercepted and placed in the hands of the Committee a fortnight ago, but which the Citizen Lacroix took action upon only last evening. We are overwhelmed with business; denunciations are piling in on us from all sides, in such abundance one doesn't know which to attend to first.'

'It is the same with us,' replied Beauvisage proudly. 'Denunciations are flowing into the Committee of Vigilance of our Section. Some are made out of patriotism, some as a result of the bait of a hundred sols' reward. Lots of children denounce their own parents, just to get their inheritance the sooner.'

'This letter,' Guénot resumed, 'emanates from a *ci-devant* named Rochemaure, a woman who liked entertaining people at her house, where they played *biribi*, and it is addressed to a certain Citizen Rauline; but its intended recipient is really an émigré in the service of Pitt. I have brought it with me to read you the portion relating to this man des Ilettes.'

He drew the letter from his pocket.

'It begins with copious details about those members of the Convention who might, according to this woman, be won over by the offer of money or the promise of a remunerative post under a new government, more stable than the present. Then follows this passage:

I have just returned from visiting Monsieur des Ilettes, who lives near the Pont-Neuf in a garret where one has to be either a cat or an imp to reach him: he is reduced to earning a living by making marionettes. He is a man of sound judgement, for which reason I am transmitting to you, monsieur, the main points of his conversation. He does not believe the existing state of affairs will last long. Nor does he foresee it being ended by the victory of the Coalition, and events appear to justify his opinion; for as you are aware, monsieur, news from the front has been bad for some time now. He would seem rather to believe in the revolt of the poor, especially of the women of the lower classes who remain deeply attached still to their religion. He believes that the widespread alarm caused by the Revolutionary Tribunal will soon unite all France against the Jacobins. 'This Tribunal,' he said, jokingly, 'which imprisons the Queen of France and a baker, is like that William Shakespeare so admired by the English, etc. ...' He thinks it not impossible that Robespierre may marry Madame Royale, and have himself named Protector of the Kingdom.

I should be grateful to you, monsieur, if you would send me the sums owing to me, that is to say one thousand pounds sterling, by the way you are accustomed to, but on no account write to Monsieur Morbardt: he has just been arrested, put in prison, etc., etc.

'This Sieur des Ilettes makes marionettes, it seems,' Beauvisage said. 'That's a valuable clue . . . though there are many cheap trades like that carried on in the Section.'

'That reminds me,' said Delourmel, 'I promised to bring a doll home for my little daughter Nathalie, my youngest. She is ill with scarlatina. The spots appeared yesterday. It's nothing to worry about, but she needs careful nursing. And Nathalie's very advanced for her age, very intelligent, but her health has always been delicate.'

'I've only one boy,' said Guénot. 'He plays rolling barrel-hoops and makes little montgolfier balloons by blowing into paper bags.'

'Very often,' Beauvisage contributed, 'it's with objects that aren't toys that children enjoy playing with most. My nephew, Émile, who's only seven, but very intelligent, amuses himself all day long with little squares of wood, with which he constructs buildings . . . Do you partake, citizen? . . .'

And Beauvisage held out his open snuff-box to the two delegates.

'Now we really must set about nabbing our rascal,' Delournel said. He had long moustaches and huge eyes which rolled about. 'I feel just the appetite this morning for a nice piece of aristocratic steak, washed down with a glass of white wine.'

Beauvisage suggested to the delegates that they all went to see his colleague Dupont *aîné* in his shop in the Place Dauphine. He would be sure to know this man, des Ilettes.

So they set off in the keen, morning air, followed by four grenadiers of the Section.

'Have you seen the play *The Last Judgement of the Kings*? Delourmel asked his companions. 'It's worth seeing. The author shows you all the kings of Europe taking refuge on a desert island, at the foot of a volcano which engulfs them all. It's a patriotic work.'

181

At the corner of the Rue du Harlay, Delourmel spotted a little cart, painted as brilliantly as a chapel, being pushed along by an old woman wearing over her coif a hat of waxed cloth.

'What's that old woman selling?' he asked.

The old dame replied herself:

'See messieurs, take your choice. I've beads and rosaries, crosses, images of St Anthony, holy cerecloths, St Veronica handkerchiefs, Ecce Homos, Agnus Deis, St Hubert rings and hunting horns, and all kinds of articles of devotion.'

'It's an arsenal of fanaticism!' Delourmel exclaimed.

And he proceeded to a summary interrogation of the poor woman who gave the same answer to every question:

'My son, for forty years I've been selling objects of devotion!'

The other delegate of the Committee of General Safety, noticing a National Guard passing, asked him to conduct the astonished old woman to the Conciergerie.

The Citizen Beauvisage pointed out to Delourmel that it should rather have been the Committee of Surveillance which had arrested the woman who would then have been brought before the Section; that in addition one never knew nowadays what attitude to adopt towards the old religion so as to be in accord with the views of the government, nor whether it was best to allow everything or forbid everything.

As they approached the joiner's shop, the delegates and the commissary heard angry shouts rising above the hissing of the saw and the grinding of the plane. A quarrel had broken out between the joiner, Dupont *aîné*, and his neighbour the porter Remacle, on account of the Citizeness Remacle, who was continually being attracted irresistibly into the joiner's workshop, whence she would return to the porter's lodge covered with shavings and sawdust. The injured porter went over and kicked the joiner's dog, Mouton, which his own little daugher, Joséphine, was sitting nursing lovingly in her arms. Joséphine was furious and poured a torrent of abuse at her father, while the joiner yelled:

'Miserable coward! That's all you can do – kick a dog!'

The porter picked up his broom and advanced threateningly: 'And I tell you, you're not going to . . .'

He did not finish the sentence since the joiner's plane hurtled close past his head.

At that moment he also caught sight of the Citizen Beauvisage and the waiting delegates. He rushed up to them, shouting:

'Citizen Commissary! You are my witness! You saw this villain just try to murder me!'

The Citizen Beauvisage, in his red cap, the badge of his office, extended his long arms in the attitude of a peace-maker, and said to the porter and the joiner:

'If either of you wants one hundred sols, he has only to inform me where to find a suspect wanted by the Committee of General Safety, a *ci-devant* aristocrat named des Ilettes who is at present earning his living by making marionettes.'

The porter and the joiner both immediately pointed up to Brotteaux's lodging, their only quarrel now being the division of the promised one hundred sols.

Delourmel, Guénot, and Beauvisage, followed by the four grenadiers, by Remacle the porter, Dupont the joiner, and a dozen little ragamuffins of the neighbourhood, filed up the stairs which shook beneath their tread, and finally climbed up the ladder to the attic.

Brotteaux was busy in his garret cutting out dancing figures, whilst Father Longuemare sat opposite him, stringing their limbs on threads and smiling to himself to see form and harmony thus growing under his fingers.

At the sound of the muskets thudding to the floor on the landing, the monk began trembling, not that he was at all the less courageous than Brotteaux, who never moved a muscle, but the monk's habitual respect for conventions had never disciplined him to display assumed self-composure. From the questions put to him by the Citizen Delourmel, Brotteaux understood whence the blow had come and realized a little late how unwise it is to confide in women. Invited to follow the citizen Commissary, he gathered together his Lucretius and three shirts.

'This citizen,' he said, pointing to Father Longuemare, 'is an assistant I have taken on to help me make my marionettes. This is his home.'

But the monk, being unable to produce a certificate of citizenship, was put under arrest with Brotteaux.

As the procession passed in front of the porter's door, the Citizeness Remacle leaning on her broom gave her lodger a look of the virtuous who sees the law dealing out his just deserts to a criminal. The little Joséphine, daintily disdainful, held Mouton back by his collar when the dog wanted to welcome the friend who had given him sugar. A crowd of curious onlookers was filling the Place de Thionville.

At the bottom of the staircase, Brotteaux found himself facing a young peasant girl who was about to go up. She carried a basket full of eggs on her arm and in her hand a flat cake wrapped in a napkin. It was Athénaïs, who had come from Palaiseau to give a token of gratitude to her saviour. When she saw the delegates, the four grenadiers and 'Monsieur Maurice' being taken away a prisoner, she stopped, stupefied, asked if it were true, went up to the commissary and said gently to him:

'You're not taking him away? But it's not possible! ... You can't know him! He's a good man, good as the good Lord Himself!'

The Citizen Delourmel pushed her out of the way and motioned to the grenadiers to go ahead. Then Athénaïs vomited forth at the delegates and the grenadiers a torrent of such foul abuse, of such obscene invective that they could have believed all the closet-pans of the Palais-Royal and the Rue Fromenteau were being emptied on top of their heads. After which, in a voice which filled the entire Place de Thionville and sent a shudder through the crowd of curious onlookers, she yelled:

'Vive le Roi! Vive le Roi!'

XVIII

The Citizeness Gamelin liked old Brotteaux, and taking him
all round regarded him as the most charming and finest man
she had ever known. She had not said good-bye to him when
he was taken away because she would have feared it would
offend the authorities and in her humble condition she had
become used to regarding cowardice as a duty. But she had
received a blow which had completely overwhelmed her.

She could not eat and lamented that she should have lost
her appetitie just when she at last had the means to satisfy it.
She still admired her son; but she no longer dared think of the
terrible tasks he was carrying out and was thankful she was
only an ignorant woman not called upon to judge him.

The poor mother had found an old rosary at the bottom of
a trunk; she did not know how to use it properly, but she
kept fumbling it in her trembling fingers. Having lived to
old age without practising her religion, she was coming to
feel the need of it: she was now praying to God all day long,
in her chimney corner, for her child Évariste and for that
kind Monsieur Brotteaux. Élodie often used to come to see
her: they did not dare look at each other and, sitting side by
side, would talk randomly of things of little interest.

One day in Pluviôse when the snow, falling in heavy flakes,
was darkening the sky and deadening the noises of the city,
the Citizeness Gamelin, who was alone in their lodging heard
a knock on the door. She jumped with fright: for several
months the slightest noise had set her trembling. She opened
the door. A young man of about eighteen to twenty years of
age entered, his hat on his head. He was wearing a bottle-
green greatcoat, the three long collars of which covered his
chest and descended to his waist. He wore top-boots in the
English fashion. His chestnut hair fell in ringlets on to his

shoulders. He advanced into the middle of the studio, as if in order that all the light through the snow-covered skylight might fall on him, and then stood for some moments motionless and silent.

At last, as the Citizeness Gamelin continued to look at him speechless:

'You don't recognize your daughter? . . .'

The old woman clasped her hands tightly.

'Julie! . . . It is you . . . Oh, God, is it possible!'

'Yes, it's me! Oh, kiss me, maman.'

The Citizeness Gamelin clasped her daughter in her arms and one tear fell on the collar of the greatcoat. Then she went on anxiously:

'But – you – here in Paris! . . .'

'Oh, mother, if only I had come alone! . . . Nobody would have known *me* dressed like this.'

The greatcoat did indeed disguise her figure and she did not look very different from a great many young men, who, like her, wore their hair long and parted on the forehead. The delicately cut and charming features of her face, though weary, drawn and weather-beaten, had a bold masculine expression. She was slim, with long slender legs, and she carried herself with an easy poise of distinction; only her light clear voice would have betrayed her.

Her mother asked if she was hungry. She replied she would be very glad of something to eat, and when bread, ham and wine had been set before her, she began eating, one elbow on the table, with the glutton-like beauty of Ceres in the hut of the old woman Baubo.

Then, the glass still at her lips:

'Maman, when will my brother be back? I have come to speak to him.'

The good mother gave her daughter an embarrassed look and did not reply.

'I must see him. My husband was arrested this morning and taken to the Luxembourg.'

The 'husband' she referred to was Fortuné de Chassagne, *ci-devant* aristocrat and officer in Bouillé's regiment. He had fallen in love with her when she was a milliner's assistant in the Rue des Lombards, and had carried her off with him to England where he had fled after the 10th August. He was her lover; but she deemed it better to speak of him as her husband before her mother. Indeed she had come to tell herself that their misfortunes had united them in a bond as strong as wedlock and that theirs was a marriage consecrated by suffering.

More than once they had spent the night sitting together on a bench in one of the London parks, and more than once had they gathered scraps of bread from under the tables of the inns in Piccadilly.

Her mother still made no reply but kept looking at her sadly.

'Don't you hear me, maman? There's no time to lose. I must see Évariste quickly: he's the only one who can save Fortuné.'

'Julie,' her mother said at last, 'it is better you do not speak to your brother.'

'What do you mean? Why not?'

'I mean what I say. It is better you do not speak to your brother about Monsieur de Chassagne.'

'But I must, maman!'

'My child, Évariste has never forgiven Monsieur de Chassagne for his treatment of you. You know how violently he used to speak about him, the names he called him.'

'Yes, he called him my seducer,' Julie answered, with a bitter little laugh, shrugging her shoulders.

'It was his pride that was hurt, my dear. Terribly. He has vowed never to mention Monsieur de Chassagne's name again, and for two years now he hasn't spoken of him or of you. But his feelings are still the same; you know him, he will never forgive you . . .'

'But, maman, Fortuné has married me . . . in London . . .'

The poor mother made a despairing movement with her eyes and hands:

'Fortuné is an aristocrat, an émigré, and that is enough to make Évariste think of him as an enemy.'

'Maman, say what you mean. If I ask him to go to the Public

Prosecutor and the Committee of General Safety and arrange for Fortuné to be released, do you mean he will refuse? . . . But, maman, he couldn't be such a monster as to do that!'

'My child, your brother is an honest man and a good son. But do not ask him. Oh, do not ask him to try to help Monsieur de Chassagne . . . Listen to me, Julie. He does not tell me much, and no doubt I wouldn't understand all he has to do . . . but he is a magistrate: he has principles; he does as his conscience tells him. Do not ask him anything, Julie.'

'I see. Yes, I see you have come to know him now. You know what he is, cruel, vicious, you know he is an evil man, that all he lives for is to satisfy his own vanity and ambition. But you always loved him better than me. When the three of us lived together, you set him up as my pattern, my model. His serious voice always impressed you: to you he had all the virtues. But you always used to blame me; to you I had all the vices, just because I spoke my mind, because I was a bit wild, because I used to go out and climb trees. You could never endure me. It was only him you loved. Well, I hate him, your perfect model! Évariste was always a hypocrite!'

'Julie, Julie, hush! I have been a good mother to you as well. I had you taught a trade. It's not my fault you weren't an honest woman and married out of your station in life. I loved you always and I do still. But you must not speak badly of Évariste. He is a good son. He has always taken care of me. When you left me, my child, when you gave up your work at the shop and went to live with Monsieur de Chassagne, what would have become of me without him? I would have died of hunger and misery.'

'Don't talk like that to me, mother. You know quite well Fortuné and I would have taken care of you, with all our affection, if Évariste hadn't turned you against us. Don't try to justify him! He doesn't know the meaning of kindness. It was just to make me seem hateful to you that he pretended to be kind to you. Him! Love you? . . . Could he love anyone? He's neither the heart nor the mind to. And he's got no talent, not one scrap. To be a good artist, a man must know how to feel tenderness. And he's incapable of that.'

She looked round the studio at the canvases and found them to be neither better nor worse than when she had left home.

'There's his soul! You can see it in his paintings, cold and empty. Look at his Orestes there, with those dull eyes and cruel mouth. That's Évariste himself to the life ... Oh, maman, maman! Can't you understand at all? I can't leave Fortuné in prison without trying to help him. You knew these Jacobins, these patriots, all Évariste's friends. They will kill Fortuné. Oh, maman, little maman, darling maman, I cannot let them kill him! I love him! I love him! He has been so good to me and life has not been kind to us. Look, this greatcoat is one of his. I've no longer a thing to wear. A friend of Fortuné's lent me a jacket and I sold lemonade at Dover while Fortuné worked in a barber's shop. We knew quite well we were risking our lives by coming back to France. But somebody asked us if we would come to Paris on an important mission for them ... We agreed; we would have agreed to carry out a mission for the devil himself if we got paid for it. All our travelling expenses were paid and we were given a banker's draft on a Paris banker. We found his offices closed: the banker is in prison and is going to be guillotined. We hadn't a sou. Everybody we had known and whom we could have asked to help us have fled or are in prison. Not a place we could go to. We slept in a stable in the Rue de la Femme-sans-tête. A kindly boot-black, who slept there on the straw with us, lent Fortuné one of his boxes, a brush and a pot of blacking three-quarters empty. For the last fortnight Fortuné has been keeping himself and me by blacking shoes in the Place de Grève. But on Monday a member of the Commune put his foot on the box to have his boots polished. He'd once been a butcher whom Fortuné had given many a kick on the behind for selling meat at short weight. When Fortuné raised his head to ask for his two sous, this rogue recognized him, called him an aristocrat and threatened him with arrest. A crowd gathered, made up of honest folk with a few scoundrels who started to shout "Death to the émigré!' and called for the gendarmes. Just then I came up with Fortuné's bowl of soup. I saw him being taken away to be imprisoned in the old church of Saint-Jean. I tried to kiss him but they pushed me away. I spent the night on the steps of the church, like a dog . . . They took him away this morning . . .'

Julie could not go on; sobs choked her.

She threw her hat on the floor and fell on her knees at her mother's feet.

'They took him away this morning to the Luxembourg prison. Maman, maman, help me to save him! Have pity on your daughter!'

With her tears streaming down her face, she threw open her greatcoat and, the better to prove herself a daughter and a woman in love, she bared her bosom; and, taking her mother's hand, she pressed them on her palpitating breasts.

'Oh, my dearest daughter, my Julie, my little Julie!' sobbed the Widow Gamelin.

And for some moments she held her face, wet with tears, tight against the girl's cheek.

Neither of them then said a word. The poor mother was searching for some way of helping her daugher, and Julie was watching hopefully the look in those eyes now full of tears.

'Perhaps,' Évariste's mother thought to herself, 'perhaps, if I speak to him, he will relent. He is good, he has a kind heart. If all this political work hadn't hardened him, if he hadn't been influenced by these Jacobins, he would never have started having these cruel feelings which frighten me so because I can't understand them.'

She took Julie's head between her hands:

'Listen, my child. I will speak to Évariste. I'll prepare him for you, so you can talk to each other. The sight of you would be enough to anger him and I'm frightened of how to begin with him . . . And, you see, I know him: anything that offends against morals or the conventions makes him hard. Even I was a little taken aback to see my Julie wearing man's clothes.'

'But, maman, these disguises have become quite common through the terrible state of things making people try to get out of the country. They're used just to escape being recognized, or to get a borrowed passport approved. In London, I saw young Girey dressed as a girl and quite a pretty girl he made as well; and you must admit, maman, his disguise is a more scandalous one than mine is.'

'My poor child, you've no need to try to justify yourself to me, whatever you're wearing. I am your mother; for me you will always be my innocent child. I will speak to Évariste, I will say . . .'

She stopped. She knew in her heart of hearts what her son had become; she knew it, but she did not want to believe it, she did not want to admit it to herself.

'He is good. He will do it for me . . . If I ask him, he will do it for you.'

And the two women, weary to the point of death, fell silent. Julie dropped off to sleep, her head pillowed on her mother's knees as when she was a child, whilst the mother, the rosary between her hands, wept, another *mater dolorosa*, over the calamities she felt creeping closer and closer in the silence of this snow-covered day when everything, footsteps, carriage-wheels, life itself, had become noiseless.

Suddenly, with a quickness of hearing sharpened by anxiety, she heard her son coming up the stairs.

'It's Évariste! . . .' she said. 'You must hide!'

And she pushed the girl into the bedroom.

'How are you today, mother dear?'

Évariste hung his hat on the hat-rack, changed his blue coat for a working jacket and seated himself in front of his easel. For some days he had been working at a sketch in charcoal of Victory laying a wreath on the brow of a soldier who had died fighting for the fatherland. Such a subject would once have called forth all his enthusiasm, but the Tribunal now occupied all his days and absorbed his whole being, whilst his hand had lost its knack from lack of practice and had grown heavy and lazy.

He hummed the *Ça ira*.

'You are singing, my son,' said the Citizeness Gamelin. 'You must be happy.'

'We've reason to be, mother: there's been good news. La Vendée has been crushed, the Austrians defeated; the army of the Rhine has broken through at Lautern and Wissembourg. The day is coming when the triumphant Republic will show its mercy. But why is it that, as the Republic grows in strength, the conspirators have to increase their audacity, and traitors plot in the dark to strike blows against our country just as she is overwhelming the enemies that strike at her openly?'

The Citizeness Gamelin, as she knitted a sock, was watching her son's face over her spectacles.

'Your old model, Berzelius, came to ask for the ten livres you owed him, so I paid him. Little Joséphine had had a stomach ache from eating too much of the jam the joiner gave her. I made some herb tea for her . . . Desmahis has been to see you; he was sorry not to find you in. He wanted to make an engraving of one of your sketches. The good fellow had a look round at your work and was admiring it.'

'When peace comes and the conspiracies are all suppressed,' the artist went on, 'I shall start on my Orestes again. I don't usually flatter myself; but that head is worthy of David.'

And with a majestic sweep he outlined the arm of Victory in the sketch he was working on.

'She holds out her palms,' he said. 'But it would be more beautiful if her arms themselves were palms.'

'Évariste!'

'Yes, maman?'

'I've just had some news . . . guess who about . . .'

'I don't know.'

'About Julie . . . your sister . . . She is not happy.'

'It would be scandalous if she were.'

'My son, don't speak like that: she is your sister. Julie is not bad; there is much good in her and misfortune has increased her goodness. She loves you. Believe me, Évariste, she only wants to live a good, hard-working life and her dearest wish is to be reconciled to us. There's nothing now need stop you seeing her. She has married Fortuné Chassagne.'

'She has written to you?'

'No.'

'How have you had news of her, mother?'

'It has not been by letter, my child; it . . .'

192

He rose and interrupted her in a terrible voice:

'No more, mother! Never tell me they have both returned to France . . . Since they must die, let it at least not be at my hands. For them, for you, for me, let me remain ignorant if they are in Paris . . . Do not force me to know it; otherwise . . .'

'What are you saying, my child? You wouldn't, you wouldn't dare . . .?'

'Mother, listen to me: If I knew my sister Julie was there in that room . . .', and he pointed to the closed door, 'I would go immediately and denounce her to the Committee of Vigilance of our Section.'

The poor mother, white as her coif, let her knitting fall from her trembling hands and murmured in a sighing voice, fainter than the faintest whisper:

'I did not want to believe it, but I see it is true: he is a monster . . .'

And as pale as she, with frothy saliva running from his lips, Évariste fled from the room and ran to find with Élodie oblivion, sleep, the delicious foretaste of nothingness.

XIX

WHILE Father Longuemare and the girl Athénaïs were being interrogated at the Section, Brotteaux was taken by two gendarmes to the Luxembourg prison, where the warder at the door refused to admit him, alleging that there was no room for any more. The old aristocrat was then taken to the Conciergerie and brought into the jailer's office, quite a small room, divided in two by a glass partition. While the jailer was entering his name in the prison register, Brotteaux saw through the window two men, each lying on a tattered mattress, both of them as still as death with glazed eyes that seemed to see nothing. Plates, bottles, and pieces of bread and meat lay around them. They were prisoners condemned to death and awaiting the tumbril to take them to the guillotine.

The *ci-devant* Monsieur des Ilettes was thrown into a dungeon, where from the light of a lantern he could just discern two figures lying on the ground, one brutal in appearance and hideously mutilated, the other gracious and gentle-looking. These two prisoners offered him a share of their straw, and rotten and swarming with vermin as it was, this was better than having to lie on the earth, which was befouled with excrement. Brotteaux sank down on to a bench in the evil-smelling darkness and sat there, his head against the wall, silent and motionless. His misery was such that if he had had the strength he could have beaten his head against he wall until he was dead. He could not breathe. His eyes swam. A prolonged sound, soothing as silence, filled his ears, and he felt his whole being bathed in a delicious nothingness. During one ineffable moment, all became for him a harmony, a serene clarity, a fragrant content. Then he lost consciousness.

When he came to himself, his first thought was to regret having come out of his faint, and philosophical even in the depths of despair, he reflected how he had had to plunge to the depths of a stinking dungeon awaiting execution, in order to enjoy the most exquisite of all the voluptuous sensations he had ever experienced. He tried to lose consciousness again, without success; little by little, on the contrary, he felt the poisonous air of the dungeon filling his lungs and restoring gradually the feeling of being alive, the full consciousness of his unbearable wretchedness.

His two companions, however, were taking his silence as a personal insult. So Brotteaux, sociable as ever, attempted to satisfy their curiosity; but when they discovered he was only what they called 'a political', one of those whose crime was only a matter of words and opinions, they lost all respect and sympathy for him. The offences with which these two prisoners were charged had more solid worth: the elder was a murderer, the other a forger of counterfeit assignats. Both were making the best of their situation and were even finding some satisfaction in it. The thought suddenly struck Brotteaux that above his head the world went on, with its movement, noise, light and life, with the pretty shop-assistants smiling behind their counters piled with perfume and other merchandise, with passers-by happy and at liberty, and the thought deepened his despair.

Night fell, unperceived in the darkness and silence of the dungeon, yet somehow increasing the gloom and oppression. With one leg stretched on his bench and his back against the wall, Brotteaux fell into a deep sleep. And in it he saw himself seated at the foot of a beech tree in full leaf and swarming with singing birds; the setting sun was bathing the river with liquid fire and edging the clouds with deep purple. The night passed. He found himself burning with fever and greedily drained his pitcher of fetid water which only made him feel more wretched and ill.

The jailer who brought the food that day promised to give Brotteaux, if he could afford the cost, the privileges of a prisoner who pays for his accommodation, as soon as there was room, which was not likely to be long. Nor was it; two days later he invited the old aristocrat to leave his dungeon.

With every step he took upwards, Brotteaux felt life and vigour coming back to him, and when he saw a room with a red-tiled floor and in it a bed of sacking covered with a dingy counterpane, he wept for joy. The carved bed ornamented with gilt doves billing and cooing, which he had had made once for the prettiest of the dancers at the Opéra, had not seemed so desirable or promised such delights.

This bed of sacking was in a large room, quite clean, where there were seventeen others like it, each separated by a high partition of planks. The men who occupied these quarters were *ci-devant* aristocrats, bankers, tradesmen and working men, and this suited the old Publican's taste well enough, since he could adapt himself to people of all classes. He noticed that men, cut off like himself from all the pleasures of life and doomed to perish at the hand of the executioner, were joking and laughing and frequently revealing a high degree of wit and humour. Since he was always inclined to take a cynical view of mankind, he attributed the high spirits of his companions to their frivolous bent of mind, which prevented them from taking their situation seriously. He was indeed strengthened in this opinion by observing how the more intelligent among them looked profoundly sad. He noticed before long that wine and brandy largely inspired their gaiety: a gaiety whose source was betrayed by its violent and sometimes almost insane nature. Not all of them possessed courage; but all made display of it. Brotteaux found nothing to surprise him in this: he knew that men willingly boast of their cruelty, their anger, their greed even, but never of their cowardice, because to admit such a thing would put them, whether in a primitive or a civilized society, in mortal peril. 'That is why,' he reflected, 'all nations are nations of heroes and all armies consist only of brave men.'

What contributed even more than the wine and brandy to intoxicate the prisoners and drive them to a frenzy of insanity, was the clanging of weapons and keys, the clash of locks and bolts, the stamping of feet through the door of the Tribunal. There were some who cut their throats with razors or threw themselves out of a window.

Brotteaux had been lodged three days in these privileged quarters when he learnt from the turnkey that Father Longuemare was lying in the filth on the verminous putrefying straw with the thieves and murderers. He had him brought up to the privileged quarters in the same room as himself where a bed had become vacant. Having promised to pay for the monk, the old Publican, who had no large sum of money with him, struck on the idea of making portraits at a crown each. With the help of a jailer, he obtained a supply of small, black frames in which to put the fine little designs made out of hair which he executed with considerable ingenuity. These sold well, being much appreciated by people whose main thoughts were centred on leaving some souvenir to their friends.

Father Longuemare kept cheerful and in good spirits. While he awaited his summons to appear before the Revolutionary Tribunal, he prepared his defence. Though drawing no distinction between his own case and that of the Church, he promised himself he would expose to his judges the scandals and oppressions to which the Church of Christ was subjected by the Civil Constitution of the Clergy; he intended to depict the eldest daughter of the Church in France waging sacrilegious war upon the Pope, the French clergy being robbed, outraged and subjected to the hateful domination of the laity; Christ's true army being despoiled and scattered. He cited Saint Gregory the Great and Saint Irenaeus, quoted numerous articles of canon law and entire paragraphs from the Decretals.

All day long he sat at the foot of his bed, scribbling on his knees, covering with illegible writing candle wrappers, packing paper, newspapers, playing cards, even considering using his shirt after starching it, and dipping stumps of pens worn to the feathers in ink, soot or coffee-grindings. He piled leaf upon leaf, sheet on sheet, and, pointing to this mass of indecipherable scribblings, he would say:

'When I appear before my judges, I shall floor them with the light of understanding.'

And, one day, casting a look of satisfaction at his defence which was growing thicker and thicker, and thinking of these magistrates he was burning to confound with his arguments, he exclaimed:

'I wouldn't like to be in their place!'

The prisoners whom fate had brought together in this jail were either Royalists or Federalists; there was even one Jacobin there; they all held widely differing views as to the right way of government, but not a single one of them possessed the slightest belief in Christianity. Feuillants, Constitutionals, Girondists, all of them, like Brotteaux, considered the Christian God to be a bad thing for themselves but a very good thing for the ordinary people; as for the Jacobins, they were for installing a Jacobin god so that they might justify the rule of Jacobinism on earth by reference to a higher source. But since none of them could believe anybody but a fool could take the conventional revealed religion seriously, and perceiving that Father Longuemare was no fool, they took him for a knave. In order, no doubt, to prepare himself for his martyrdom, he made confession whenever he could, and the more sincerely he did this, the more they judged him an impostor.

It was in vain that Brotteaux assured them of the monk's good faith; Brotteaux himself was judged by them as only believing part of all he said. His ideas were too unusual and so appeared to be an affectation and satisfied nobody. He spoke of Rousseau as a boring rogue. Voltaire, on the other hand, he held to be a man of genius equal to rank with Helvétius, Diderot, or the Baron d'Holbach. In his opinion, the greatest genius of the century was Boulanger. He also thought highly of the astronomer Lalande, and of Dupuis, author of *A Memoir on the Origin of Constellations*.

The wits of the company made a thousand jokes at the expense of the poor Barnabite, the point of which he never saw; his simplicity saved him from every snare. To dispel the suspense which tortured them and to escape the torment of idleness, the prisoners played at draughts, cards and backgammon. No musical instrument was allowed. After supper they would sing or recite verses. Voltaire's *La Pucelle* brought some cheerfulness to their aching hearts and they never tired of hearing their favourite passage repeated. But, unable totally to keep their thought from the appalling vision of what lay before them, they sometimes tried to turn it into an amusement, and in that room of eighteen beds, before they turned in for the night, they would play a game called Revolutionary Tribunal. The parts were allocated according to tastes and aptitudes. While some represented the judges and prosecutors, others were the accused or the witnesses, and others again the executioner and his assistants. The trials invariably ended with the execution of the condemned person, who was laid full length on a bed with his neck under a plank. The scene then moved to hell itself. The most agile of the prisoners, wrapped in white sheets, played the parts of spectral devils. There was a young lawyer from Bordeaux, named Dubosc, short, dark, hunchbacked, bandy-legged, a very devil in appearance himself, who used to come, horned and hoofed, to drag Father Longuemare feet first from his bed, announcing to the culprit that he was condemned to the everlasting flames of hell and doomed past redemption for having set up as the Creator of the universe a Being who was a jealous, vindictive fool and the enemy of human happiness.

'Ha, Ha! Ha, ha!' the devil would shriek horribly. 'So, you old dodderer, you taught that it pleases God to see His creatures wallow in penitence and deny themselves His most beautiful gifts. Imposter, hypocrite, canting humbug, for all eternity you will sit on nails and eat egg-shell crockery.'

Father Longuemare would content himself with replying that such a statement revealed the philosopher's cloven hoof beneath the devil's and that the least imp in hell would know better than talk such foolishness, having at least a passing knowledge of theology and being certainly less ignorant than an encyclopaedist.

But when the ugly Girondist lawyer called him a Capuchin, he turned red with anger and said that a man incapable of distinguishing between a Barnabite and a Franciscan would not know how to see a fly in milk.

The Revolutionary Tribunal was emptying the prisons as quickly as the Committees were filling them; in three months the room containing the eighteen was half-full of new faces. Father Longuemare lost his tormentor. The lawyer Dubosc was hauled before the Revolutionary Tribunal and condemned to death as a Federalist and for having conspired against the unity of the Republic. On leaving the Tribunal, he returned, as prisoners always did, along a corridor that ran through the prison and opened on the room which for three months he had enlivened with his gaiety. As he made his farewells to his companions, he maintained the same air of light persiflage habitual to him.

'Forgive me, monsieur,' he said to Father Longuemare, 'for having hauled you out of bed by your feet. I will never do it again.'

And turning to old Brotteaux, he said:

'Good-bye, monsieur. I go before you into nothingness. I gladly return to Nature the atoms with which she composed me, hoping she will make better use of them in the future, for it must be admitted she didn't make much of a job of me.'

And he went on down to the jailer's room, leaving Brotteaux grieving and Father Longuemare trembling and green as a leaf, more dead than alive to see the ungodly laughing on the edge of the abyss.

When Germinal brought back brighter days, Brotteaux, sensual as ever, tramped down several times each day to the courtyard next to the women's quarters, as near as he could get to the fountain where the female prisoners used to come every morning to wash their linen. An iron railing separated the two quarters; but the bars were not so close together as to prevent hands joining or lips meeting. Beneath the kindly shades of night, loving couples would press against the obstacles between them. At such times, Brotteaux would retire discreetly to the staircase and, seated on a step, he would take his little Lucretius from the pocket of his puce-coloured coat and read, by the light of a lantern, some of that author's stoically consolatory maxims: '*Sic ubi non erimus* . . . When we shall have ceased to be, nothing will be able to move our emotions not even the broken mingled fragments of sky and earth and sea . . .' But, even as he savoured the joy of this deep wisdom, Brotteaux was envying the Barnabite the foolish belief which hid reality from him.

Month by month, the Terror increased. Every night the tipsy jailers with their watchdogs at their heels, would march from cell to cell, howling out names they deliberately mutilated, waking the prisoners and for every twenty victims marked on their list terrifying two hundred. Along these corridors, crammed with blood-stained ghosts, there passed each day without a murmur, twenty, thirty, fifty condemned prisoners, old men, women, young people almost still children, and all of them so widely different in rank and character and opinion that it was impossible not to wonder whether they had not been chosen by a toss of the dice.

And so they went on playing cards, drinking Burgundy, making plans, arranging assignations for after dark at the iron railings. The company, new almost to a man, was now made up largely of 'extremists' and 'irreconcilables'. But still the room of the eighteen beds remained the home of elegance and good breeding: except for two prisoners, named Navette and Bellier, recently transferred from the Luxembourg to the Conciergerie and suspected by the other sixteen of being spies, all were honest men who trusted one another. Glass in hand, they would celebrate the victories of the Republic. Amongst them were several poets, as there always are in any group of people who have nothing to do. The most accomplished of these composed odes on the triumphs of the army of the Rhine, which they recited with great gusto. They were loudly applauded. Only Brotteaux gave feeble acclamation to the victories and to the poets who celebrated them in verse.

'Ever since Homer,' he said one day, 'it's been a strange obsession with poets to celebrate men who fight each other. War is not an art. It's only luck that decides battles. When two generals, both of them imbeciles, face each other, one of them must inevitably be the victor. Just wait! Some day one of these warriors you make a god of, may swallow you all up, like the stork in the fable who gobbles up the frogs.* Ah, then he would be truly a god! For you can always tell the gods by their appetite.'

Brotteaux had never felt himself moved by the glamour of war. He felt no triumph at the victories of the Republic, which he had foreseen. He liked nothing about the new régime, which had been strengthened by military successes. He was a malcontent. Others would have been so with less reason.

One morning it was announced that the Commissaries of the Committee of General Safety were going to make a search of the prisoners' quarters, that they would seize assignats, articles of gold and silver, knives, scissors, that similar proceedings had been taken at the Luxembourg, where letters, papers and books had been appropriated.

Everyone therefore tried to think of somewhere to hide securely whatever he held most precious. Father Longuemare carried off his defence in armfuls and hid it in a rain-gutter, while Brotteaux slipped his Lucretius under the dead ashes in the hearth.

When the Commissaries, wearing tricolour ribands around their necks, arrived they found hardly anything except such trifles which it had been considered judicious to let them discover. On their departure, Father Longuemare ran to his rain-gutter and rescued as much of his defence as wind and water had left. Brotteaux pulled out his Lucretius from the fireplace all black with soot.

'Let us make the best of the present,' he said to himself, 'for the auguries indicate that our time here is now to be short.'

One warm night in Prairial, while above the prison yard the moon floating high in a softly lit sky showed her two silver horns, the *ci-devant* aristocrat was sitting, as was his custom, reading his Lucretius on a step of the stone stairs, when he heard a voice calling to him, a woman's voice, a beautiful voice, and one which he did not recognize. He went down into the courtyard and saw, behind the iron railing, a figure he recognized as little as he had the voice, but which reminded him, in its dim fascinating curves, of all the women he had loved. A flood of silver-blue moonlight fell on the figure and at that moment Brotteaux saw it was Rose Thévenin, the pretty actress from the Rue Feydeau.

'You here, my dear! What a joy for me to see you, but what a misfortune for you. How long have you been here? And why?'

'Since yesterday.'

And she continued very softly:

'I have been denounced as a Royalist. They're accusing me of having conspired to help the Queen escape. As I knew you were here, I've tried to see you at once. Listen, my dear friend . . . for that is what you would so much like me to call you, isn't it? . . . I have powerful friends; I have sympathizers on the Committee of Public Safety itself, I know I have. I will get my friends to help us; they will free me, and then I will get them to set you free.'

But Brotteaux replied urgently:

'By everything you hold dear, my child, do not do anything! Do not write, do not petition; ask nothing of anybody, I beg it of you, let yourself be forgotten.'

As she did not seem to understand what he was saying, he went on more beseechingly still:

'Keep silent, Rose, let yourself be forgotten: in that only lies safety. All that your friends could do would only make things worse for you. Let time work for you. You'll only need to wait a little, a very little I hope, in order to be saved . . . Above all, do not appeal to the magistrates, to a Gamelin. They are not men, they are things: you cannot explain yourself to things. Let yourself be forgotten. If you follow my advice, my dearest friend, I shall die happy knowing I have saved your life.'

She answered:

'I will obey you . . . Do not speak of dying.'

He shrugged his shoulders:

'My life is finished, my child. You must live and be happy.'

She took hold of his hands and laid them on her breasts:

'Listen to me carefully, my friend . . . I only met you once just for a day, and yet I know you are not indifferent to me. And if what I am going to say to you can make you want to live, believe that I say it with all my heart! I will do for you . . . I will be for you . . . whatever you would like me to do or to be.'

And their mouths met in a kiss between the iron railings.

XX

ONE day, as he was sitting on the magistrates' bench in the stiflingly hot courtroom, when there was a particularly long and tedious case before the Tribunal, Évariste Gamelin shut his eyes and allowed his thoughts to wander:

'Evil men, by forcing Marat to hide in holes and corners, turned him into a bird of night, the bird of Minerva, whose dark penetrating eye pierced the recesses where conspirators lurked. Today it is a blue eye, cold and calm, that pierces the dark recesses to discover the enemies of State and denounce them with a cunning unknown even to Marat, the Friend of the People, who now sleeps for ever in the garden of the Cordeliers. The new saviour of our country, as zealous and yet more keen-sighted than the first, sees what no other man can see and when he lifts his finger he spreads terror all around him. He distinguishes the fine shades that almost imperceptibly divide evil from good, vice from virtue, and which but for him would have been confused, to the ruin of liberty and our country; he sees before him always that thin inflexible line he must follow, knowing that on either side of it lie error, evil and crime. The Incorruptible Robespierre shows us how we can help the enemy both by excess of zeal and by lack of it, by persecuting the religious in the name of reason just as much as by using religion to fight the laws of the Republic. Just as much as the villains who murdered Le Peltier and Marat, do those of us harm to the Republic who decree Le Peltier and Marat divide honours, because by doing so we compromise their memory. Our enemy is whoever repudiates the idea of order, wisdom, opportunity; our enemy is whoever outrages public morals, scandalizes virtue, and in the foolishness of his heart, denies God. Yes, fanatic priests deserve to die, but there is also an anti-revolutionary way of fighting fanaticism: adjurers too may be guilty of crime. By moderation, men can destroy the Republic; by violence, they can also destroy it.

'Oh, how terrible are the duties of a judge, dictated by the wisest of men! It is not only open enemies, aristocrats, Federalists, the Orléans scoundrels, we must strike down. There is also the conspirator: the agent of the foreigner is a Proteus, he assumes all shapes and disguises; sometimes he pretends to be a patriot, a revolutionary, an enemy of kings; he pretends to a boldness of heart that beats only for freedom; his voice roars and the foes of the Republic mistakenly tremble. His name was Danton:* his violence was a poor disguise for his hateful moderation and in his base corruption he was revealed at last as our enemy. And that conspirator with the fluent stammer, that man who put into his hat the first cockade of the revolution, that pamphleteer who in his patriotic sarcastic irony nicknamed himself 'The Procureur of the Guillotine'. And his name was Camille Desmoulins.* He revealed himself as a traitor by defending the generals, traitors themselves to their country, and asking clemency for them. And there was Père Duchesne. That vile demagogue who degraded liberty and whose filthy lies raised sympathy for Marie Antoinette herself, he too was a traitor and an agent of the foreigner. There was Chaumette, that mild little man, so popular, so moderate, so well-intentioned and efficient in the administration of the Commune. And he was an atheist! Conspirators and foreign agents, all of them, all those patriotic sans-culottes in red caps and carmagnoles who tried to outdo even the Jacobins in their patriotism.

'And now all these traitors, violent or moderate, all these evil men, Danton, Desmoulins, Hébert, Chaumette, have perished under the axe of the guillotine. The Republic is saved; choruses of praise rise from all the Committees and all the Assemblies for Maximilien Robespierre and the Mountain. All good citizens are raising their voices in homage: "Worthy representative of a free people, blessed Mountain, Sinai, in vain have the children of Baal raised their presumptuous heads: thou hast struck them down with thy thunderbolt of tumultuous wrath . . ."

'And the Tribunal has its share in this chorus of praise. How sweet it is to be virtuous and how dear to the heart of the upright is the knowledge of public gratitude!

'Yet what food for thought, what grounds for anxiety, all these things give! Think! It was not enough thát a Mirabeau, a La Fayette, a Bailly, a Pétion should betray the people! There must needs be also the men who denounce these traitors. Think! All these men who made the Revolution did so only to betray her! These heroes of the first great days of the Revolution were planning with Pitt and Coberg to restore the monarchy in alliance with the Orléans faction and to set up a Regency under Louis XVII. Think! Danton, he was another Monk! Think! Chaumette and the Hébertists, more perfidious than the Federalists who sent them to the guillotine, had conspired the ruin of our country! But what if Robespierre's cold blue eyes discover more traitors, even among those very patriots who sent the traitor Danton and the traitor Chaumette to the guillotine? Where will it stop, this hideous procession of betrayed traitors and this piercing, all-revealing insight of Robespierre the Incorruptible? . . .'

XXI

MEANWHILE Julie Gamelin, still wearing the bottle-green greatcoat, was going every day to the Luxembourg Gardens, where she used to sit on a bench at the end of one of the avenues, waiting for the moment when her lover would appear at one of the windows of the palace. They would make signs to each other and talk together in the silent language they had invented. In this way she learnt that the prisoner had quite a good room and pleasant companions, that he could do with a blanket for his bed, and a kettle, and that he loved his mistress with all his heart.

She was not alone in watching for a beloved face to appear at one of the windows of the palace now turned prison. Not far from her a young mother kept her eyes fixed on a closed window; then immediately she saw it open, she would lift the little child in her arms above her head. An old lady in a lace veil sat for long hours on a folding chair, vainly hoping to catch a glimpse of her son, who, in order not to be overcome at the sight of her, would never stop playing quoits in the prison courtyard until the Gardens were closed and she had to leave.

During these long hours when people took up their position and waited, whatever the weather was like, a middle-aged man, rather stout and very neatly dressed, was always to be seen on a neighbouring bench, playing with his snuff-box or the charms hanging from his watch-guard or unfolding a newspaper which he never read. He was dressed like a bourgeois of the old school in a gold-laced cocked hat, a plum-coloured coat and a blue waistcoat embroidered with silver. He had a respectable air about him, and was musically inclined, to judge from a flute which stuck out of his pocket. Not for one moment did he take his eyes off this apparently good-looking young lad on the nearby bench, smiling at him continually, and when he saw him leave his bench, he would rise himself and follow at a distance. Julie, in her loneliness and misery, was touched by the discreet sympathy shown her by this good man.

One day, as she was leaving the Gardens, it began to rain. The good man came up to her and, opening his huge red umbrella, asked permission to shelter her under it. She answered sweetly, in her clear voice, that she would be very glad to. But at the sound of this voice, and warned perhaps by the subtle smell of a woman, he took himself off quickly, leaving the young woman exposed to the heavy downpour of rain. She suddenly understood, and despite her worries could not prevent herself from smiling.

Julie was living in an attic in the Rue du Cherche-Midi and passing herself off as a draper's shop-boy in search of employment. The Widow Gamelin had been persuaded at last that the girl would be running less risk anywhere else than at her home, had got her away from the Place de Thionville and the Section du Pont-Neuf, and was giving her all the help she could in the way of food and linen. Julie looked after herself, went to the Luxembourg to see her beloved prisoner, and returned to her garret; the monotony of this daily round became a balm to her grief, and, being young and strong, each night she slept soundly and well. She was courageous by nature and accustomed to living adventurously; the dress she wore added perhaps a further spice of excitement, and sometimes she would venture out at night to visit a restaurant in the Rue du Four, at the sign of the Red Cross, frequented by both men and women of all types. There she used to read the newspaper or play backgammon with some tradesman's clerk or citizen-soldier, who would puff the smoke of his pipe in her face. Drinking, gambling, love-making, flourished and fights were frequent. One evening a customer, hearing the sound of hoofs on the pavingstones outside, lifted the curtain, and, seeing the Commander-in-Chief of the National Guard, a certain Citizen Hanriot,* riding past with his adjutant, muttered savagely:

'There goes Robespierre's spying jackass!'

Hearing this, Julie laughed loudly.

But a moustached patriot took offence:

'Anyone who says that is a flaming aristocrat, and I'd like to see him sneeze into Samson's basket!* General Hanriot is a good patriot and if Paris and the Convention ever need defending, he's the one who'll do it. That's what the Royalists can't forgive him.'

He glared at Julie who was still laughing:

'You, you young puppy, take care I don't kick your backside to teach you respect for good patriots!'

But others began to join it:

'Hanriot's a fool and a drunkard!'

'Hanriot's a good Jacobin! Vive Hanriot!'

Sides were taken. Fists began flying. Hats were battered, tables overturned, glasses shattered, the lights went out, the women began to scream. Attacked by several of the patriots, Julie armed herself with a bench, but was knocked to the ground biting and scratching her assailants. From her open greatcoat and her torn shirt her panting breasts appeared. A patrol came running up at the noise, and the young girl aristocrat escaped between the legs of the gendarmes.

Each day tumbrils passed full of victims for the guillotine.

'But I cannot let him die! I love him!' Julie used to say to her mother.

She determined to beg for his life, to go to the Committees and the Section Headquarters, to deputies, to magistrates, to everyone if necessary. She had no woman's clothes to wear. Her mother borrowed a striped gown, a kerchief, a lace coif from the Citizeness Blaise, and Julie, attired as a woman and a patriot, set out to visit one of the judges, Renaudin, in the damp, dismal house in the Rue Mazarine, where he lived.

With trembling steps she climbed the wooden, tiled stairs and was received by the judge in a squalid office, furnished with a deal table and two straw-bottomed chairs. On the walls, the paper was hanging loose. Renaudin, whose black hair was plastered across his forehead, gazed at her with dark eyes, his lips tight above his protruding chin and, signing to her to speak, listened in silence.

She told him she was the sister of the Citizen Chassagne, a prisoner in the Luxembourg, explained as plausibly as she could the circumstances under which he had been arrested, represented him as an innocent man who had been the victim of misfortune, and pleaded for the judge's intervention as urgently as she could.

He remained silent and immovable.

In desperate supplication, she fell weeping at his feet.

The moment he saw her in tears, his face changed: the black pupils of his blood-shot eyes distended and his enormous blue jaws began moving as if drawing saliva into his dry throat.

'Citizeness, what is necessary will be done. Do not upset yourself.'

And, opening a door, he pushed his petitioner into a little sitting-room, decorated in rose-pink colours, with painted panels, porcelain figures, a hanging wall-clock, gilt candelabra, easy chairs, and a sofa covered in tapestry showing a Boucher pastoral. Julie was prepared to do anything to save her lover.

Renaudin was brutal and rapid. When she got up and was readjusting the beautiful dress of Citizeness Élodie, she saw the man's cruel, mocking look, and knew immediately her sacrifice had been useless.

'You promised me my brother's freedom,' she said.

He laughed derisively.

'I said to you, citizeness, that what was necessary would be done, which meant that the law, neither more nor less, would have its way. I said not to upset yourself, and why should you? The Revolutionary Tribunal is always just.'

She thought of throwing herself on the man, biting him, scratching his eyes out. But, realizing this would only result in Fortuné Chassagne's ruin, she rushed from the house and ran to her garret to take off Élodie's besmirched dress. And, there alone, all the night long, she wept and howled with rage and sorrow.

The following day, when she went to the Luxembourg, she found the Gardens occupied by gendarmes, who were turning out the women and children. Sentinels were being posted in the avenues to prevent anyone from communicating with the prisoners. The young woman, who came every day carrying her child, told Julie there was talk of plots in the prison and that the women were being blamed for by meeting in the Gardens they roused people's pity for aristocrats and traitors.

XXII

SUDDENLY a mountain has been piled up in the Tuileries
Gardens. Under a cloudless sky, Maximilien Robespierre
marches, at the head of his colleagues, wearing a blue coat and
yellow breeches, and bearing in his hand a bouquet of wheat-
ears, cornflowers and poppies. He clambers up the mountain
and proclaims the God of Jean-Jacques Rousseau to the vast,
emotionally-roused crowds of Republicans. All is now purity!
Sweetness! Truth! Antique simplicity! Piteous tears!
Bounteous mercy! Human brotherhood!

In vain does atheism still raise its hideous face: Maximilien
seizes a torch; flames devour the monster of atheism and in its
place appears Reason, with one hand pointing to the sky and
the other holding a crown of stars.

On the platform built outside the Palace of the Tuileries,
Évariste weeps silently and gives thanks to God. He sees
opening before him a future of universal joy.

He sighs:

'At last we shall be happy, pure and innocent, if the traitorous scoundrels permit it.'

Alas! The traitorous scoundrels have not permitted it.
There must be still more executions; still more torrents of
tainted blood must flow. Three days after the celebration of
the new alliance and reconciliation between heaven and earth,
the Convention passes the Law of Prairial which suppresses,
with a kind of ferocious brotherliness, all the traditional
forms of law, all that had been devised since the times of
Roman jurists to protect the innocent until proved guilty.
No more sifting of evidence, no more questioning of the
accused, no more witnesses, no more counsel for the defence:
all disappear in the name of love of the fatherland. The
accused, who bears locked up in himself his guilt or his

innocence, is not allowed to say a word before the patriot magistrates, and yet it is in this brief moment that they must decide his case, often complicated and obscure. How can judgment be made now? How recognize in one brief moment the honest man and the scoundrel, the patriot and the enemy of the fatherland? . . .

Gamelin was troubled only for a moment. Quickly he understood his new duties and accommodated himself to them. He saw that these cuts in procedure were indeed inherent in this new and terrible, yet salutary, form of justice, which would no longer be administered by gowned pedants weighing pros and cons at their leisure in their gothic balances, but by sans-culottes judging by patriotic inspiration and seeing the truth in a flash of illumination. Where deliberations and precautions would have lost everything, the impulses of an upright soul would save all. The promptings of Nature, the good mother who never deceives, had to be followed; the heart alone was the true judge, and Gamelin invoked the shade of Rousseau:

'Man of virtue, inspire me with the love of mankind, with the ardour to regenerate all men everywhere!'

His colleagues, mostly, felt the same as he did. They were, for the most part, simple people; and when the law was simplified, they felt more at their ease. Justice, thus curtailed, satisfied them; the pace was quickened and no obstacles were left to confuse them. They confined themselves to inquiring into the opinions of the accused, not conceiving it possible that anyone, except from pure perversity, could think differently from themselves. Believing themselves to possess a monopoly of truth, wisdom and goodness, they attributed to their opponents all error, stupidity and evil. They felt themselves omnipotent: their eyes had seen God.

Their eyes had seen God, these magistrates of the Revolutionary Tribunal. The Supreme Being, acknowledged by Robespierre, flooded them with His pure light. They worshipped, they had faith.

The chair of the accused had now been replaced by a vast

platform able to accommodate fifty prisoners: batches only were dealt with now. The Public Prosecutor would often confuse under the same accusation, or implicate as accomplices, individuals who had never met each other before. The Tribunal, taking advantage of the terrible powers given it by the Law of Prairial, sat in judgment on the supposed prison plots which, coming so soon after the proscription of Danton and the Commune, were made by cunning adversaries to appear to be its result. In fact, to make apparent to the world the two primary characteristics of a conspiracy fomented by foreign gold against the Republic: excessive moderation on the one hand and excessive zeal on the other, both self-interested, they had brought together under the same accusation two very different women, the widow of Camille Desmoulins, the lovable and charming Lucille, and the widow of the Hébertist Momoro, the complaisant friend of all. Both of them, to further the analogy, had been placed in the same prison, where they had wept together on the same stone bench; both of them, to complete the analogy, had climbed the scaffold together. The symbol was too ingenious, a masterpiece of equilibrium doubtless conceived by some lay brain, but credited to Robespierre. This representative of the people was honoured with being the author of every incident, happy or unhappy, that happened in the Republic, with every eventuality connected with laws, morals, manners, weather, harvests or epidemics. Unjust of course, but an injustice not unmerited, for this man, this little, spruce, cat-faced dandy was all-powerful in the eyes of the people . . .

One particular day the Tribunal was despatching a batch of prisoners involved in the great plot, thirty or more from the Luxembourg, all of whom had been submissive victims but were not pronounced Royalists or Federalists of the most heinous type. The prosecution relied almost entirely upon the evidence of a single informer. Gamelin, glancing along the prisoner's benches, recognized Fortuné Chassagne among the accused. Julie's lover, pale and thin through long confinement and his face appearing less handsome in the glare of light that filled the hall, still maintained something of his former presence and proud bearing. His eyes met Gamelin's and they filled with a look of contempt.

Overcome by a cold fury, Gamelin rose, asked in a calm voice permission to speak, and, fixing his eyes on the bust of the Roman Brutus, which gazed down on the Tribunal, he said:

'Citizen President, although there may exist between one of the accused and myself ties which, if they were acknowledged, would be ties of relationship by marriage, I hereby declare that I shall not refuse to act in this case. The two great Romans did not decline to do their duty when for the salvation of their country and the cause of freedom, one of them had to condemn his son, and the other to strike down his adopted father.'

He sat down again.

'There's a scoundrel if there ever was one,' Chassagne muttered, bitterly.

The public remained unmoved, either because it was tired of high-flown rhetoric, or because it thought that Gamelin had triumphed too easily over feelings of natural human affection.

'Citizen Gamelin,' said the President, 'by law, a refusal by a magistrate to act in any case should be handed in writing twenty-four hours before the opening of the case. Anyway, you have no reason to withdraw: a patriotic magistrate is above human passions.'

Each prisoner was questioned for three or four minutes, and in every instance the verdict of death resulted. The magistrates gave their decision without speaking, simply by a nod of the head. When Gamelin's turn came, however, he rose to pronounce his opinion.

'All the accused,' he declared, 'are guilty, and the law must take its course.'

As Gamelin was descending the staircase of the Palais de Justice, a young man wearing a bottle-green greatcoat and who looked about seventeen or eighteen years of age, stopped him abruptly. The lad wore a round hat, tilted on the back of his head and framing his fine pale face in a dark aureole.

Facing the magistrate, in a terrible voice filled with passion and despair, he shrieked:

'Monster! Murderer! I am a woman, so strike me, you coward! Have me arrested! Have me guillotined! Your name is Cain! I am your sister!'

And Julie spat in his face.

The crowd of tricoteuses and sans-culottes was relaxing its revolutionary viligance by this time; its civic ardour was becoming much cooler: with the result that Gamelin and his aggressor found themselves surrounded only by a confused uncertainty. Julie fought her way through the crowd and escaped into the dusk.

XXIII

ÉVARISTE GAMELIN was tired but could not relax; twenty
times a night he would awake with a jump from sleep full of
nightmares. It was only in the blue bedroom, in Élodie's
arms, he was able to find a few hours' sleep. He talked and
cried out in his sleep and often awoke her; but she could make
nothing of what he said.

One morning, after a night when he had seen the Eumeni-
des, he woke terror-stricken and weak as a child. The dawn
was piercing the bedroom's windows with its pale arrows.
Évariste's hair, tangled across his forehead, covered his eyes
with a black veil: Élodie, beside his pillow, was gently smooth-
ing it straight. She was looking at him, this time with a
sister's tenderness, as she wiped with her handkerchief the
sweat from the unhappy man's ice-cold brow. At that moment
he recalled the beautiful scene in the *Orestes* of Euripides,
which he had tried to portray and which, if he could have
finished it, would have been his masterpiece: the scene where
the unhappy Electra wipes away the saliva that froths on her
brother's lips. And it seemed to him that he was hearing
Élodie also saying in a gentle voice: 'Listen to me, my dear
brother, whilst the Furies still leave you master of your
reason...'

And he kept thinking:

'All the same, I am certainly no parricide. On the contrary,
I have acted like a pious son in shedding the impure blood of
the enemies of my fatherland.'

XXIV

THE trials of those accused of plotting whilst in prison seemed endless. Forty-nine more of the accused filled the benches. Maurice Brotteaux occupied the right-hand corner of the top row, the place of honour. He was dressed in his puce-coloured coat, which he had brushed carefully the day before and mended the pocket which his Lucretius had frayed a little. Next to him sat the woman Rochemaure, painted, and powdered, brilliant yet horrible. Father Longuemare had been placed between her and the girl Athénaïs, who had regained, at the Madelonettes prison, the freshness of youth.

On the benches other prisoners, unknown to these four, had been packed by the gendarmes: lawyers, journalists, *ci-devant* aristocrats, and others of the former bourgeois class. The Citizeness Rochemaure caught sight of Gamelin on the magistrate's bench. Although he had not replied to her urgent letters and repeated messages, she had not given up hope and threw him a look of supplication, attempting to appear fascinating and pathetic at the same time. But the cold look he gave her dispelled any illusion she might still have.

The clerk of the court read out the writ of accusation, which, brief in its reference to each individual, was still a lengthy document owing to the large number of the accused. It began by giving a general outline of the plot concocted in the prisons to drown the Republic in a blood-bath by the slaughter of the Representatives and of the people of Paris, and then, taking each in turn, it went on:

'One of the most pernicious authors of this abominable conspiracy is the man named Brotteaux, *ci-devant* des Ilettes, collector of taxes under the tyrant. This individual, who was remarkable even in the days of the tyranny for his dissolute conduct, is a living proof that immorality and bad living are the greatest enemies of Liberty, and of the happiness of the people: in brief, after misappropriating the public revenue and wasting in debauchery a large part of the people's money, this individual connived with his former concubine, the woman Rochemaure, to enter into correspondence with émigrés and with traitorous intent to inform agents of foreign countries of the state of our finances, the movements of our troops, and the fluctuations of public opinion.

'Brotteaux, at this period of his despicable existence, was living in concubinage with a prostitute he had picked out of the mud in the Rue Fromenteau, the girl Athénaïs. He had easily won her to his purposes and employed her to foment the counter-revolution by insolent shouts and indecent speeches.

'Several remarks made by this nefarious man will clearly indicate to you his pitiful opinions and his pernicious aims. Speaking of this patriotic Tribunal, today called upon to punish him, he declared insultingly:

The judges of the Revolutionary Tribunal, with their black hats and plumes, are modelling themselves on that William Shakespeare, so admired by Englishmen, who introduces crude buffoonery in the midst of his most tragic scenes.

'He was also forever preaching atheism, as the best means to degrade the people and drive them into immorality. In the Conciergerie prison, where he was confined, he used to deplore the victories of our valiant armies as being the worst of calamities, and he used to try to throw suspicion on the most patriotic generals, crediting them with tyrannous ambitions.

'The woman Rochemaure, a *ci-devant* aristocrat and concubine of Brotteaux, is no less culpable than he. Not only was she in correspondence with foreign agents and in the pay of Pitt himself, but in complicity with swindlers, such as Jullien (of Toulouse) and Chabot, both associates of the *ci-devant* Baron de Batz. She also helped that reprobate Brotteaux in all sorts of cunning ways to depreciate the shares of the Company of the Indies, by buying them at cheap prices, and then by equally cunning ways raising the market price to the ruin of private and public funds. Confined at La Bourbe and at the Madelonettes, she continued in prison to conspire, to play the market in stocks and shares, and to do all she could by corrupt means to suborn judges and magistrates.

'Louis Longuemare, *ci-devant* aristocrat, *ci-devant* Capuchin, had had a long career of crime before committing the acts of treason for which he has to answer here. He lived in shameful promiscuity with the girl Gorcut, known as Athénaïs, under the same roof as Brotteaux, and he is the accomplice of the said girl and the said *ci-devant* aristocrat. During his imprisonment at the Conciergerie, he continued every day to write pamphlets aimed at subversion of public liberty and order.

'It can be stated with regard to Marthe Gorcut, known as Athénaïs, without fear of contradiction, that prostitutes such as she are the greatest cause of public immorality and that they are a disgrace and insult to society, abhorred by all right-thinking people. But what purpose is served by speaking at length of these revolting crimes which all the accused confess to so shamelessly? . . .'

The prosecution then proceeded to pass under review the forty-five other prisoners, none of whom were known by Brotteaux, Father Longuemare, or the Citizeness Rochemaure, except for their having seen several of them in the prisons, yet who were all included with the four first-named in 'this odious plot, unequalled in the history of our country'.

The writ of accusation concluded by demanding the death-penalty for all involved.

Brotteaux was the first to be questioned.

'You confess to conspiracy?'

'No, I have never conspired in any plots. Every word in that writ of accusation I have just heard is false.'

'You see: you are conspiring still, at this very moment, against the Tribunal.'

And the President passed on to the woman Rochemaure, who answered with quibbling, tearful and despairing protestations.

Father Longuemare said he stood entirely in the hands of God. He had not even brought his written defence.

To all the questions put to him he replied with an air of resignation. Only when the President referred to him as a Capuchin did his old spirit flash out:

'I am not a Capuchin,' he said. 'I am a priest and a monk of the Order of Barnabites.'

'That's the same thing,' the President replied, jovially.

Father Longuemare looked at him indignantly:

'One cannot conceive a more extraordinary error,' he exclaimed, 'than to confuse a Capuchin with a monk of the Order of Barnabites, which derives its constitution from the Apostle Paul himself.'

This was greeted with bursts of laughter and hooting from the public.

Father Longuemare, taking this derision to mean a denial of his assertion, announced that he would die a member of the Order of St Barnabas, whose habit he wore in his heart.

'Do you admit,' the President demanded, 'having conspired with the girl Gorcut, known as Athénaïs, who accorded you her miserable favours?'

At this question, Father Longuemare raised his eyes sorrowfully heavenwards and replied with a silence which conveyed the astonishment of a naïve heart and the gravity of a man of religion who fears to utter empty words.

'You, the girl Gorcut,' demanded the President of the young Athénaïs, 'do you admit having conspired with Brotteaux?'

She replied gently:

'Monsieur Brotteaux, as far as I know, has never done anything but what is good. There should be more, many more, men like him, because there cannot be any better. Those who say the opposite are mistaken. That is all I have to say.'

The President asked her if she admitted having lived in concubinage with Brotteaux. The expression had to be explained to her since she did not understand it. But, when she did gather its implication, she replied that that had rested only with him, but that he had never asked it of her.

The public galleries roared with laughter and the President threatened the girl Gorcut that he would refuse to hear her if she answered again in such a cynical way.

So she called him a lying, sour-faced, old cuckold and spewed out such a torrent of abuse at him, the judges and the magistrates, that the gendarmes had to drag her from the bench and push her out of the hall.

The President then proceeded to question briefly the rest of the accused, taking them in the order in which they were seated on the benches. One, named Navette, pleaded that he could not possibly have plotted in prison since he had only been there four days. The President observed that the point deserved consideration, and begged the citizen magistrates to make a note of it. A certain Bellier said the same, and again the President commented in his favour to the magistrates. His mildness was interpreted by some as a praiseworthy scrupulousness, by others as payment in recognition of these men's talents as informers.

The Deputy Public Prosecutor spoke next. All he did was to amplify the details of the writ of accusation and then to put to the magistrates the question:

'Has it been proved that Maurice Brotteaux, Louis Rochemaure, Louis Longuemare, Marthe Gorcut, known as Athénaïs, Eusèbe Rocher, Pierre Guyton-Fabulet, Marceline Descourtis, etc., etc., are guilty of a conspiracy whose aims were assassination, starvation, the forging of assignats and counterfeit coin, in order to bring about civil war, the abolition of representative government and the restoration of the monarchy?'

The magistrates withdrew into the chamber of deliberation. Their vote was unanimous: guilty; except in the cases of Navette and Bellier, whom the President, and following his lead, the Public Prosecutor, had separated from the rest. Gamelin explained his decision thus:

'The guilt of the accused is self-evident: their punishment is necessary for the safety of the nation and they themselves ought to desire to be punished as the only means of expiating their crimes.'

The President pronounced sentence in the absence of those it concerned. In these great days, contrary to what the law prescribed, the condemned were not recalled to hear the verdict read, no doubt for fear of the effects which their despair might have on such a large number of people. A needless fear, so wide and general had become the submissiveness of the victims! The clerk of the court went down to the cells to read the verdict, which was listened to with such silent impassivity that it had become common to compare those condemned during Prairial to trees marked down for felling.

The Citizeness Rochemaure declared herself to be pregnant. A surgeon, who was also one of the magistrates, was ordered to examine her. She was carried out fainting.

'Ah!' sighed Father Longuemare. 'These judges and magistrates deserve all our pity: the condition of their souls is truly deplorable. Their confusion is such that they even mistake a Barnabite for a Franciscan.'

The executions were to take place the same day at the Barrière de Trône Renversé.* The condemned, their toilet completed, their hair cropped and their shirts cut away at the neck, were packed like cattle in the small room separated from the jailer's office by a glass partition, to await the executioner.

When presently he and his assistants arrived, Brotteaux, who was quietly reading his Lucretius, placed the marker at the page he had reached, shut the book, put it in the pocket of his coat, and said to the Barnabite:

'Reverend Father, what enrages me is that I shall never now convince you. We are both of us going to sleep our last sleep, and I shall not be able to pull you by the sleeve and wake you and say to you: "You see: you no longer can know or feel; you are inanimate. That which follows life is like that which precedes it."'

He wanted to smile; but a terrible despair gripped his heart, filled his whole body with pain, and he came near to fainting.

He went on, all the same:

'Father, I have let you witness my weakness. I love life and I cannot leave it without regret.'

'Monsieur,' replied the monk very gently, 'be mindful, then, of the fact that you, who are a braver man than I, are troubled more by death than I. What does that mean, if not that I see the light which you do not yet see?'

'It could also mean,' said Brotteaux 'that I regret leaving life because I have enjoyed it more than you, who have made it resemble death.'

'Monsieur,' said Father Longuemare, his face going even paler, 'this is a solemn moment. May God help me! It is certain we shall die without spiritual comfort. It must be that in time past I have received the Sacraments with a lukewarm and thankless heart, that heaven should deny me them today, when I have so great a need of them.'

The tumbrils were waiting. The condemned were piled into them, with their hands tied. The woman Rochemaure, whose pregnancy had not been confirmed by the surgeon, was hoisted into one of the tumbrils. She recovered sufficiently to watch the crowd of onlookers, hoping against hope to find someone to save her. The crowd was less dense than formerly, and the excitement less extreme. Only a few women screamed: 'Death! Death!' or mocked those about to die. The men mostly shrugged their shoulders, looked away and kept silent, either out of prudence or respect for the law.

A shudder passed through the crowd as Athénaïs appeared. She looked like a child.

She bowed her head in front of the monk:

'Monsieur le Curé,' she said to him, 'give me absolution.'

Father Longuemare gravely murmured the words of the Sacrament, and then said:

'My daughter, you have fallen into grave spiritual peril; but how can I not offer to the Lord a heart as simple as yours!'

She climbed lightly into the cart. And there, with breasts flaunted and childish head held high, she shouted:

'Vive le Roi!'

She made a little sign to Brotteaux to sit beside her. Brotteaux helped the Barnabite climb up and seated himself between the monk and the innocent prostitute.

'Monsieur,' Father Longuemare said to the philosophical epicurean, 'I ask you one favour: this God in whom you do not yet believe, pray to Him for me. It is possible that you may be nearer to Him than I am myself: a moment and we shall know. Only one second, and you may have become one of the Lord's most dearly beloved children. Monsieur, pray for me.'

While the wheels of the tumbrils rolled on, making a grinding noise on the pavingstones of the long Faubourg-Antoine, the monk was reciting in his heart and with his lips the prayers for those dying in agony.

Brotteaux was recalling the lines of the poet of nature: *Sic ubi non erimus* . . . Tied up as he was and shaken by the jolting of the infamous cart, he maintained his tranquil air and even succeeded in appearing so much at his ease as to be without a care. Beside him, Athénaïs, proud to die thus like the Queen of France, gazed haughtily at the crowd, and the old aristocrat, contemplating with a connoisseur's eyes the young woman's white breasts, was filled with regret for the light of day.

XXV

WHILE the tumbrils, surrounded by gendarmes, were rumbling along on their way to the Place du Trône Renversé, taking Brotteaux and his accomplices to their death, Évariste sat, deep in thought, on a bench in the Garden of the Tuileries. He was waiting for Élodie. The sun, low on the horizon, was piercing the thickly leafed chestnut trees with its golden arrows. At the gate of the Gardens, seated on its winged horse, the statue of Fame blew its everlasting trumpet. The newspaper boys were shouting the news of the great victory at Fleurus.

'Yes,' Gamelin was thinking, 'victory is ours. And we have paid a heavy price for it.'

In his mind he could see those defeated generals wandering about over there, like lost ghosts, in the blood-stained dust of the Place de la Révolution where they had perished. And he smiled, reflecting proudly that, but for the severities in which he had taken his share, the Austrian horses would today be eating the bark of the very trees beside him.

He exclaimed to himself:

'Beneficent Terror! Oh, blessed Terror! At this very moment last year, our heroic armies were defeated, the soil of the fatherland invaded, two-thirds of the country in revolt. Today, our armies, well-equipped, well-trained, commanded by able generals, are on the offensive, ready to spread Liberty throughout the whole world. Peace reigns over all the Republic ... Oh, beneficent Terror! Saintly Terror! Holy Guillotine! At this very moment last year, the Republic was torn by opposing factions, the hydra of Federalism threatened to devour her. Today, a united Jacobinism spreads its might and wisdom throughout the Republic...'

He was, nevertheless, filled with gloom. His forehead had become deeply lined; his mouth bitter. He thought to himself: 'Once we used to say: *To conquer or to die*. We were mistaken, it was *To conquer and to die*, we should have said.'

He looked around him. The children were building sandcastles. The citizenesses, on their wooden chairs under the trees, were sewing or embroidering. The passers-by, in coats and breeches of strange elegance, busy thinking of their business or pleasures, were making for home. And Gamelin felt himself alone among them: he was neither their compatriot not their contemporary. What had happened to them? How was it that indifference, weariness, disgust even, had replaced the enthusiasm of those first beautiful years? It was obvious that all these people around him never wanted to hear the Revolutionary Tribunal mentioned again and turned their eyes away at the sight of the guillotine. Having become too provocative in the Place de la Révolution, it had been banished to the far end of the Faubourg Antoine. Even there the passage of the tumbrils was greeted with murmurings. It was even said that voices had shouted: 'Enough!'

'Enough, when there were still traitors and conspirators! Enough, when the Committees had to be reformed and the Convention purged! Enough, when scoundrels were disgracing the name of National Representative! Enough, when they were even plotting in the Revolutionary Tribunal itself to bring about the downfall of Robespierre! For, though to even think of it was horror, it was yet only too true! Fouquier himself was weaving the plots, and it was simply to ruin Robespierre that he had sacrificed fifty-seven victims with solemn ceremony, having them led to their death each wearing the red shirt of a parricide. To what sort of criminal pity was France yielding? It would be necessary to save her from it in spite of herself, and when she cried: 'Have mercy!' to stop our ears and to strike. Alas! Fate had decided that the fatherland should curse its saviours. Well, let it curse us, so long as we save it!

'It is not enough to sacrifice aristocrats, financiers, poets, a Lavoisier, a Roucher, or an André Chénier. It is not enough to sacrifice other more obscure victims. We must strike at these all-powerful criminals who with their hands full of gold and dripping with blood are plotting the downfall of Robespierre, those are the men we must remove: the Fouchers, the Talliens, the Roveres, the Carriers, the Bourdons. We must deliver the fatherland from all its enemies. If Hébert had triumphed, the Convention would have been overthrown and the Republic hastened to the abyss; if Desmoulins and Danton had triumphed, the Convention would have been ready to surrender the Republic to the aristocrats, the financiers and the generals. If the Fouchés and the Talliens, and such monsters gorged with blood, should triumph, France will be overwhelmed in a flood of infamy and crime ... You are sleeping, Robespierre, while criminals drunk with fury and fear plan your death and the death of Liberty. Couthon, Saint-Just, what delays you from denouncing these plots?

'In the old days the Royal monster kept his power by imprisoning four hundred thousand people, by hanging fifteen thousand, by breaking three thousand on the wheel every year and yet the Republic hesitates to sacrifice a few hundred heads to secure its domination. Let us shed rivers of blood and save the fatherland ...'

While he was thinking such thoughts, Élodie came running up to him, pale and agitated:

'Évariste, what is it you have to tell me? Why couldn't you have come to the *Amour Peintre*? Why have you made me come here?'

'In order to say good-bye to you forever.'

She said she didn't understand, he must be out of his mind ...

He stopped her with a very slight gesture of his hand:

'Élodie, I am no longer able to accept your love.'

'Stop it, Évariste! Don't say such things!'

She begged him to walk with her: people could see them, overhear them, where they were.

He walked beside her for about twenty paces and then went on, very calmly:

'I have dedicated my life and my honour to my country. I shall die hated by many, and I shall leave you nothing except the memory of a man despised and execrated . . . How can we love each other? Is it possible that I am able to love anyone?'

She said he was mad; that she loved him, would always love him. She was ardently sincere; yet she also knew as well as he, better than he, that he was right. But she refused to recognize it.

He continued:

'I have nothing to reproach myself with. What I've done, I'd do again. For the sake of my country, I've put myself beyond the pale of humanity: I can never belong again. No. I cannot! Because my great task is not yet finished. If you say I can still forgive, still show mercy – I say, do conspirators show mercy, do traitors forgive? Scoundrels who betray their fatherland are multiplying unceasingly; they come out from below ground, from across our frontiers: young men, who would have done better to perish with our armies, old men, children, women, all appearing on the surface so innocent and so pure. And when we have sacrificed them on the altar of the fatherland, more of them appear, and more, and more . . . So you must see there is no other course for me but to renounce love, joy, all the sweetness of life, even life itself.'*

He fell silent. Made for the joys of peaceful pleasures, Élodie had for many a day now found herself horrified to discover, under the kisses of her tragic lover, that she was obtaining a voluptuous delight out of the thought of the blood he shed: she made no reply. Évariste drank as from a bitter chalice the silence of the young woman.

'You see it yourself, Élodie: we are on the edge of a precipice. Our deeds devour us. Each hour, each day, stretches out as if it were a year. I shall soon have lived a hundred years. Look at my face! Is it the face of a lover? A face to be loved? . . .'

'Évariste, you are mine, I am going to keep you; I will not let you go.'

The very tone of her voice expressed self-sacrifice. He felt it. She herself felt it.

'Élodie, will you be able to bear witness, one day, that I lived faithful to my duty, that I was upright of heart and pure of soul, that I desired only the public good; that I was by nature kind and tender? Will you be able to say: "He did his duty?" No! No, you will not say that! And I do not ask that you will say it. Let the memory of me perish! Sufficient to me is the glory that in my own heart I know I did my duty; to others there is only the shame that surrounds me. If you love me, bury my name in eternal silence.'

At that moment, a child of eight or nine, playing with its hoop, bumped against Gamelin's legs.

He lifted the boy roughly in his arms:

'Child! You will grow up to be free and happy, and you will owe it to the infamous Gamelin. I am steeped in blood so that you may be happy. I am cruel, that you may be kind. I am pitiless so that tomorrow all Frenchmen will embrace one another with tears of joy.'

He pressed the child to his chest.

'Little one, when you are a man, you will owe to me your happiness and your innocence; and, if ever you hear my name mentioned, you will curse it.'

And he put the child down, who ran off in terror to cling to the skirts of his mother, who was hurrying up to rescue him.

The young mother, in a gown of white lace and possessing a graceful and aristocratic charm, led her son away with a haughty air.

Gamelin turned towards Élodie with a wild look in his eyes:

'I held that child in my arms; perhaps I shall have his mother sent to the guillotine.'

And he strode away quickly under the symmetrically lined trees.

Élodie remained a moment motionless, staring at the ground. Then, suddenly, she raced after her lover, and in a frenzied fury, her hair coming dishevelled like a Maenad, she seized hold of him as if to tear him in pieces and shouted at him in a voice strangled with blood and tears:

'All right, then! Oh, my beloved, send me too, send me to the guillotine! Have my head also put beneath its knife!'

And, at the thought of the knife cutting through her neck, her very flesh melted in an ecstasy of sexual horror.

XXVI

As the sun of Thermidor was setting in a purplish, blood-red sky, Évariste was wandering, deep in gloomy thought, in the Marbeuf Gardens, now a national park and frequented by the Parisian idlers. There were stalls for the sale of lemonade and ice-cream, wooden horses and shooting galleries were provided for the younger patriots. Beneath a tree, a little boy, obviously a Savoyard, in rags and wearing a black cap, was making a marmot dance to the shrill notes of his hurdy-gurdy. A man still young, slight of figure, in a blue coat, his hair powdered, and with a large dog at his heels, stopped to listen to this rural music. Évariste recognized Robespierre. He recognized at once that pale, thin face, hardened and wrinkled with lines of suffering. And he thought:

'What a weight of weariness and grief has left its imprint on that forehead! How painful a thing it is to work for the happiness of mankind! What is he thinking about at this moment? Does the sound of that mountain music bring relief from the cares of State? Is he thinking he has made a pact with death and the hour of reckoning is approaching? Is he meditating a triumphant return to the Committee of Public Safety, from which he withdrew with Couthon and Saint-Just, weary of being held in check by a seditious majority? What hopes, what fears, are turbulent behind that impenetrable face?'

But Robespierre smiled at the boy and in a quiet, gentle voice asked him several questions about his native valley and the humble home and parents which the poor child had left behind him.* Then he threw him a small piece of money and strolled on. After a few steps, he turned round to call his dog, who was sniffing at the marmot and baring his teeth at the bristling little creature.

'Brount! Brount!' he called.

Then he plunged down one of the gloomy paths.

Gamelin, out of respect, had not approached the lonely walker; but as he gazed after the thin figure disappearing into the night, he sent this mental prayer after him:

'I have seen your sadness, Maxmilien; I have understood your thoughts. Your melancholy, your weariness, and even that look of fear engraved on your face, everything about you says: "Let the Reign of Terror end and that of Fraternity begin! Frenchmen, be united, be kind, be good. Love you one another . . . ." So be it, then! I shall support your plans, in order that you, in your wisdom and goodness, may be able to end our civil discord, our fratricidal hate, and turn the executioner into a gardener who will, for all time to come, cut off only the heads of cabbages and lettuces. With my colleagues of the Tribunal, by exterminating all conspirators and traitors, I will pave the way to clemency. We will redouble our vigilance and severity. No culprit will escape us. And when the head of the last enemy of the Republic has fallen under the knife, then it will be possible for you to be merciful without committing a crime, then you will be able to inaugurate the reign of Virtue and Innocence throughout the land, oh, father of your country!'

The Incorruptible was already far away. As he turned the far end of the tree-lined alley, two men untidily attired in round hats and nankeen breeches, one a tall, lean man with a blur in one eye and resembling Tallien, looked at him from the corners of their eyes, and passed on, pretending not to have recognized him. When they had proceeded far enough to be out of hearing, they muttered to each other:

'There he goes – King, Pope, God! Yes, that's what he is – God; and Catherine Théot is his prophetess.'

'Dictator, traitor, tyrant, you mean! But there is still more than one Brutus left!'

'Let the scoundrel tremble! The Tarpeian Rock is near the Capital!'

The dog Brount ran towards them. They said no more and hastened their steps.

XXVII

You sleep, Robespierre! The hour to strike is passing, precious time is running out . . .

At last, on the 8 Thermidor, in the Convention, the Incorruptible rises and speaks. Sunshine of the 31st May, are you going to shine a second time? Gamelin waits and hopes. Is Robespierre going to drag from the benches which they dishonour these law-makers more guilty than the Federalists, more dangerous than Danton? . . . No! Not yet! 'I cannot' he says, 'bring myself to clear away completely the veil which hides this profound mystery of iniquity'. But this distant flash of lightning, though striking none of the conspirators, frightens all of them. Sixty of them, at least, will not now dare sleep in their beds. Marat would denounce traitors by name, point his accusing finger at them. The Incorruptible hesitates, and, from that moment, it is he who is the accused . . .

That evening, at the Jacobins, the hall is filled to suffocation, the corridors, the courtyard, are crowded.

They are all there, the loud-voiced friends and the silent enemies. Robespierre reads them the speech the Convention has heard in fearful silence and the Jacobins greet it with excited applause.

'It is my dying testament,' Robespierre declares. 'You will see me drink the hemlock with fortitude.'

'I shall drink it with you,' answers David.

'All of us will!' shout the Jacobins, and they separate without deciding anything.

Évariste, whilst the death of Robespierre was being prepared, slept the sleep of the disciples in the Garden of Gethsemane. Next day, he attended the Tribunal where two sections were sitting. That on which he served was trying twenty-one accused of being implicated in the plot at the

Lazare prison. The case was still proceeding when the news arrived: 'The Convention, after sitting for six hours, has accused Maximilien Robespierre, Couthon, Saint-Just, together with Augustin Robespierre and Lebas who have demanded to share the fate of the first three accused. The trial of the five accused is now proceeding before the bar of the Convention.'

News is also brought, the news that the President of the Section sitting in the next court, the Citizen Dumas, has been arrested on his bench, but that the case goes on. Drums can be heard beating the alarm, and the tocsin peals from the churches.

Évariste is still on his bench when he is handed an order from the Commune to present himself at the Hôtel de Ville to sit on the General Council. To the sound of the bells and the drums, he and his colleagues record their verdict and he runs home to embrace his mother and get his scarf of office. The Place de Thionville is deserted. The Commune of the the Section is afraid to vote either for or against the Convention. People keep close to walls, slip down side streets, sneak indoors. The call of the tocsin and the general alarm is answered by the noise of shutters being barred and doors bolted. The Citizen Dupont *aîné* has hidden himself in his shop; Remacle the porter has barricaded himself in his lodge. Little Joséphine holds Mouton in her trembling arms. The widowed Citizeness Gamelin bewails the cost of food, which has caused all this trouble. At the foot of the stairs, Évariste meets Élodie out of breath, the locks of her black hair clinging to her moist neck.

'I've been looking for you at the Tribunal, but you had left. Where are you going?'

'To the Hôtel de Ville.'

'You mustn't! It will ruin you. Hanriot has been arrested ... the Sections won't do a thing to help. Even the *Section des Piques,* Robespierre's own Section, will do nothing. I know it for certain: my father belongs to it. If you go to the Hôtel de Ville, you will be throwing your life away for nothing'.

'You want me to be a coward?'

'Bravery is to be faithful to the Convention and to obey the law.'

'The law is dead when scoundrels triumph.'

'Évariste, listen to your Élodie; listen to your sister; come, sit beside her so that she can soothe your troubled heart.'

He looked at her: never had she seemed to him so desirable; never had her voice sounded so seductively, so persuasively in his ears.

'Come, two steps, only two steps, my dear.'

And she pulled him towards the raised platform on which stood the pedestal of the overturned statue. Benches surrounded it, occupied by strollers of both sexes. A dealer in fancy goods was offering his laces, a seller of cooling drinks, carrying his cistern on his back, was ringing his bell; little girls were playing. The parapet was lined with anglers, motionless, rod in hand. The weather was stormy, the sky overcast. Gamelin leant on the low wall and looked down at the little island below, pointed like the prow of a ship; he listened to the wind whistling in the tree tops, and felt his soul filled with an infinite longing for solitude and peace.

And, like a delicious echo of his thought, he heard the sigh of Élodie's voice:

'Oh, my dear, do you remember those fields and how you wanted to be a justice of the peace in some little village? Yes, that would be happiness.'

But above the roar of the wind in the trees and the voice of the girl beside him, he heard the tocsin and the beating of the drums, the distant tramp of horses and the rumbling noise of cannons being drawn along the pavingstones.

Two paces from them, a young man, chatting with an elegantly dressed citizeness, said:

'Have you heard the latest? . . . The Opéra has opened in the Rue de la Roi.'

Meanwhile the news was spreading: Robespierre's name was being whispered with a shudder, for men feared him still. And the women, on hearing the muttered news of his fall, quickly concealed their joy.

Évariste Gamelin seized Élodie's hand and then quickly dropped it again brusquely.

'Adieu! I have involved you in my terrible affairs, I have ruined your life forever. Adieu! May you be able to forget me!'

'Make sure,' she said to him, 'you don't go home tonight: come to the *Amour Peintre*. Don't ring the bell; throw a stone at my shutters. I'll come and open the door myself; I'll hide you in the attic.'

'You will see me return in triumph, or you will never see me again. Adieu!'

As he approached the Hôtel de Ville, Évariste heard the well remembered roar of the great days rising to the grey sky. In the Place de Grève the clash of arms, the glitter of uniforms, Hanriot's cannon lined up. He climbs the grand staircase, and, entering the Council Hall, he signs the attendance register. The General Council of the Commune, by the unanimous vote of the four hundred and ninety-one members present, declares itself for the five accused.

The Mayor has the Table of the Rights of Man brought in, reads the article in which it is written: 'When the Government violates the Rights of the People, revolution is for the people their most sacred duty.' And the Mayor of the Commune, the first Magistrate of Paris, announces that the Commune's answer to the Convention's act of violence is to raise the people of Paris against the Convention.

The members of the General Council take oath to die at their posts. Two of the Commune's officers are directed to go out into the Place de Grève and summon the people to join their magistrates in saving the fatherland and Liberty.

Members search for one another, exchange news, give advice. Among these councillors, few are artisans. The Commune assembled here is what the Jacobin purge made it: judges and magistrates of the Revolutionary Tribunal, artists such as Beauvallet and Gamelin, well-to-do householders and college professors, citizens and tradesmen of means, powdered heads, fat stomachs, gold watch-chains, but very few sabots, striped trousers, carmagnoles and red caps.

These bourgeois councillors are numerous and determined. But, when one comes to think of it, they are about all that Paris possesses of true Republicans. They are making their stand in the city's Town Hall, as on a rock of liberty, but an ocean of indifference surrounds them.

Good news arrives, however. All the prisons, where the five accused have been taken, have opened their doors and let out their victims. Augustin Robespierre, released from La Force, is the first to enter the Hôtel de Ville and is welcomed with cheers. It is learnt at eight o'clock that Maximilien Robespierre, after much persuasion, is coming also to the Hôtel de Ville. Everybody awaits him, he is going to come, he is coming; an overwhelming roar of acclamation shakes the vaulting of the old municipal palace.

He enters, followed by twenty armed men. This little man, thin, spruce, in blue coat and yellow breeches: it is he. He takes his seat. He speaks.

On his arrival the Council immediately orders the façade of the Hôtel de Ville to be illuminated. Where he is, the Republic is. He speaks in a thin voice, choosing his phrases with elegance. He speaks lucidly, at length. Those listening to him, who have staked their lives on his head, realize, to their horror and dismay, that this is a man of words, a man of committees and tribunals, incapable of resolute decision and of revolutionary action.

They lead him into the Hall of Deliberations. Now they are all there, these illustrious accused: Lebas, Saint-Just, Couthon. Robespierre speaks. It is half past midnight: he goes on speaking. Meanwhile, Gamelin, in the Council chamber, his forehead pressed against a window, looks out with anxious eyes: he sees the smoke rising from the flaming torches into the gloomy night. The cannons of Hanriot are lined up in front of the Hôtel de Ville. In the almost completely black Place de Grève an anxious crowd surges, in uncertainty and suspense. At half past twelve torches are seen coming round the corner of the Rue de la Vannerie, escorting a delegate from the Convention wearing the insignia of office. He unfolds a paper and reads, by the light of the torches, the decree of the Convention outlawing all members of the rebellious Commune, all members of the General Council who have abetted it, and all citizens who respond to its appeal.

Outlawed! Death without trial! The mere thought turns the most determined pale. Gamelin feels an icy sweat on his forehead. He watches the crowd hastening with all speed from the Place de Grève.

And turning his head he finds the Council chamber, but a moment ago packed with members, now almost empty.

But they have fled in vain: their signatures witness to their presence.

It is two o'clock in the morning. The Incorruptible is in the adjoining hall deliberating with the Commune and the accused representatives.

Gamelin looks out in despair on the dark Place de Grève. By the light of the lanterns he can see the wooden candles above the grocer's shop knocking together like nine-pins; the street lamps sway and swing: a strong wind has sprung up. A moment later, it begins to pour with rain: the square below is now entirely empty; those whom the dreadful decree of the Convention did not scatter, have now fled from the rain. Hanriot's cannons are abandoned. And when flashes of lightning reveal the troops of the Convention debouching simultaneously from the Rue Antoine and from the Quai, the approaches to the Hôtel de Ville are deserted.

At last Robespierre has decided to appeal from the decree of the Convention to his own Section, the Section des Piques.

The General Council sends for swords, pistols, guns. But the clash of arms and breaking glass fills the building. The troops of the Convention sweep like an avalanche through the Hall of Deliberations and into the Council Chamber. A shot rings out: Gamelin sees Robespierre fall, his jaw shattered. He himself seizes his knife, the cheap knife which one day during the famine, had cut a loaf of bread in half for a starving mother and her child, and which one beautiful summer's evening on a farm at Orangis had lain in Élodie's lap as they played forfeits; he opens it and tries to plunge it into his heart, but the blade strikes a rib and closes on the handle. The catch gives way and two of his fingers are cut. Gamelin falls, the blood pouring from his wounds. He lies motionless, but feels himself becoming colder and colder. Feet trample on him and over the tumult of the terrible fighting above him, he hears distinctly the voice of the young dragoon, Henry, shouting:

'The tyrant is no more! His slaves are broken! The Revolution can continue in majesty and terror!'

Gamelin fainted.

At seven in the morning, a surgeon sent by the Convention dressed his wounds. The Convention was full of solicitude for Robespierre's accomplices: it did not want any of them to escape the guillotine. Gamelin, artist, ex-magistrate, ex-member of the General Council of the Commune, was carried on a stretcher to the Conciergerie prison.

XXVIII

On the 10 Thermidor, while Évariste, after a feverish sleep on a palliasse in a dungeon, was awakening to a sudden realization of indescribable horror, Paris in all her spacious beauty lay smiling in the sunshine; hope was surging once more in prisoners' hearts; tradesmen were light-heartedly opening their shops, the bourgeois were feeling themselves wealthier, young men happier, women more beautiful, all as a result of the fall of Robespierre. Only a handful of Jacobins, a few constitutional priests and some old women were trembling to see the Government taken over by the wicked and the corrupt. A delegation from the Revolutionary Tribunal, composed of the Public Prosecutor and two judges, was on its way to the Convention to congratulate it on having put an end to the plots. The Assembly had decided that the guillotine was to be set up again in the Place de la Révolution. It did not want the wealthy, the fashionable, the pretty women to have to go out of their way to witness the execution of Robespierre, which was to take place that day. The dictator and his accomplices had been outlawed: it sufficed therefore that their identity should be verified by two officers of the Commune and they could then be handed over immediately by the Tribunal to the executioner. But a difficulty arose: the verifications could not be put into legal form, since the whole Commune itself had been outlawed. The Assembly therefore authorized identification by ordinary witnesses.

The accused were dragged to their death, accompanied by their chief accomplices, amid shouts of joy and of fury, amid curses, laughter and dancing.

The next day, Évariste, who had regained some of his strength and could almost stand, was taken from his cell, brought before the Tribunal and put on the platform where so many victims, illustrious or obscure, had previously sat.

Now it groaned under the weight of seventy persons, most of them members of the Commune, and some of them magistrates, like Gamelin, who had also been outlawed. Again he saw the magistrates' bench, where he had been accustomed to lean at ease, the place where he had terrorized unhappy prisoners, the place where he had had to endure the look in the eyes of Jacques Maubel, of Fortuné Chassagne, of Maurice Brotteaux, and the pleading eyes of the Citizeness Rochemaure who had secured for him the position of magistrate and whom he had rewarded with a sentence of death. Again he saw, dominating the daïs where the judges sat, the busts of Chalier and Marat and that same bust of Brutus which he had once invoked. Nothing was altered, neither the axes, the fasces, the red caps of Liberty on the wallpaper, nor the insults shouted by the tricoteuses in the galleries to those about to die, nor the soul of Fouquier-Tinville, implacable, laboriously leafing through his deadly papers, the perfect Public Prosecutor, sending his friends of the day before to the scaffold.

The Citizen Remacle, porter and tailor, and the Citizen Dupont *aîné*, joiner, of the Place de Thionville, member of the Committee of Surveillance of the Section du Pont-Neuf, identified Gamelin (Évariste), artist, ex-magistrate of the Revolutionary Tribunal, ex-member of the General Council of the Commune. For so witnessing, they received an assignat of a hundred sols from the funds of the section; but since they had had ties of neighbourliness and friendliness with the accused, they found it embarrassing to meet his eyes. Anyway, it was a hot day: they were thirsty and in a hurry to get away to drink a glass of wine.

Gamelin found it an effort to climb into the tumbril: he had lost a lot of blood and his wound was giving him great pain. The driver whipped up his old horse and the procession began amidst a storm of booing.

Some women recognized Gamelin and shouted at him:

'Now it's your turn to have a drink of blood! Massmurderer for eighteen francs a day! ... He's not laughing now: just look how pale he is, the coward!'

They were the same women who had used to mock at the

conspirators and the aristocrats, the extremists and the moderates whom Gamelin and his colleagues had sent daily to the guillotine.

The tumbril turned into the Quai des Morfondus, and proceeded slowly towards the Pont-Neuf and the Rue de la Monnaie: they were being taken to the Place de la Révolution, to the scaffold where Robespierre had died. The horse was lame; every minute the driver had to flick him about the ears with his whip. The crowd of spectators, happy and excited, kept delaying the progress of the escort. Everybody wanted to congratulate the gendarmes, who had to keep reining back their horses. At the corner of the Rue Honoré, the insults increased two-fold. Young people, seated at tables in the fashionable restaurants, ran to the windows, their napkins in their hands, and shouted:

'Cannibals! Man-eaters! Vampires!'

The tumbril having plunged into a pile of garbage which had not been removed during the two days of disorder, the *jeunesse dorée* exploded with delight.

'The waggon's bogged down! ... That's where they belong, stinking Jacobins!'

Gamelin was thinking, and it seemed to him that he understood.

'I die a just death,' he thought. 'It is just that we should receive these insults hurled at the Republic, for we should have safeguarded her against them. We have been weak; we have allowed ourselves to be too indulgent. We have betrayed the Republic. We have deserved our fate. Even Robespierre, pure and saintly as he was, sinned by being too mild, too merciful; his faults are wiped out by his martyrdom. By following his example, I have betrayed the Republic; she perishes: it is just that I die with her. I did not shed enough blood: let my own blood flow! Let me perish! I have deserved it ...'

As he was thinking thus, he caught sight of the sign of the *Amour Peintre,* and a flood of bitter-sweet memories overwhelmed him.

The shop was shut, the venetian blinds of the three windows

242

on the first floor were drawn tight. As the tumbril passed in front of the window of the blue bedroom, a woman's hand, wearing a silver ring, pushed aside the edge of the blind and threw towards Gamelin a red carnation. His bound hands prevented him from catching it but all his heart went out to it as the symbol and likeness of those sweet red lips whose fragrance had used to refresh his mouth. His eyes filled with tears and his whole being was still suffused with the charm of this farewell when he saw rising into sight in the Place de la Révolution the knife of the guillotine dripping with blood.

XXIX

It was Nivôse.* Five months had passed and summer had turned to winter. Masses of floating ice blocked the Seine, the basins of the fountains in the Tuileries Gardens were frozen. The north wind swept waves of hoarfrost along the streets. White steam breathed from the horses' nostrils, and people would glance as they passed at the thermometers at the doors of the opticians. A shop-boy was wiping the condensation from inside the windows of the *Amour Peintre* and the curious glanced in at the prints on show: the vogue was for Robespierre squeezing a heart, shaped like a lemon, into a cup to drink the blood, and for huge allegorical designs with such titles as the *Tigrocratie de Robespierre*: representing hydras, serpents and other horrible monsters let loose on France by the tyrant. Other were entitled the *Horrible Conspiration de Robespierre,* the *Arrestation de Robespierre,* the *Mort de Robespierre.*

One day, after the midday dinner, Philippe Desmahis entered the *Amour Peintre,* his portfolio beneath his arm, and handed to the Citizen Jean Blaise a stippled engraving, the *Suicide de Robespierre,* which he had just finished. The engraver had sardonically etched Robespierre as hideously as he could. The French people were still not satiated with memorials enshrining the hate and horror felt for the man who had been made the scapegoat for all the crimes of the Revolution. However, the print-seller, who knew his customers, informed Desmahis that in future he was going to give him military subjects to engrave.

'We shall be all demanding conquests and victories, swords, generals, waving plumes. We are out for glory. I feel it; my heart beats wildly when I hear of the exploits of our brave armies. And when I feel something, everybody else usually feels the same. What we need now is warriors and women, Mars and Venus.'

'Citizen Blaise, I've still two or three of Gamelin's drawings at my lodging, the ones you gave me to engrave. Are they urgent?'

'No, no, not at all.'

'Talking about Gamelin, I saw all the poor devil's canvases yesterday on a second-hand dealer's stall in the Boulevard du Temple. There was even his *Orestes* and his *Electra*. The head of Orestes is very like Gamelin's and it's really very fine. The arm as well is superb. The dealer told me he had no difficulty in getting rid of such canvases to artists to paint over them ... Poor Gamelin! He could have been an outstanding genius, perhaps, if he hadn't taken to politics.'

'He'd the soul of a criminal!' replied the Citizen Blaise. 'I proved that, on the very spot where you're standing, when his craving for bloodshed was still held in check. He never forgave me for it ... Oh, he was a real scoundrel!'

'Poor fellow! He was certainly sincere. It was those fanatics who ruined him.'

'You are not defending him, I hope, Desmahis! ... A man like that!'

'No, Citizen Blaise, I'm not defending him.'

The Citizen Blaise tapped the handsome Desmahis on the shoulder:

'Times have changed. We can call you "Barbaroux", now the Convention is pardoning those still standing accused ... I've been thinking, Desmahis. You'd better do me an engraving of Charlotte Corday.'

A tall, beautiful, brown-haired woman wrapped in furs, entered the shop and gave the Citizen Blaise a little intimate and discreet nod. It was Julie Gamelin; but she no longer used that dishonoured name: she now called herself the 'Citizeness Widow Chassagne' and wore, under her cloak of fur, a red tunic in honour of the red shirts of the Terror.

Julie had at first felt a certain distaste for Évariste's mistress; anything to do with her brother was hateful to her. But the Citizeness Blaise, after Évariste's death, had given refuge to his unfortunate mother in the attics of the *Amour Peintre*. Julie had also found safety there; then she had obtained employment again at the fashionable milliner's shop in the Rue des Lombards. Her short hair, *à la victime*, her aristocratic air, her mourning attire, had gained her the sympathies of the *jeunesse dorée*. Jean Blaise, whom Rose Thévenin had now almost finished with, offered her his affections, which she accepted. Julie, however, still had a liking for wearing men's clothes, as she had done during the tragic days only a few months past. She had had a fine *muscadin* outfit made for her and often went, with an enormous baton in her hand, to have supper at some tavern at Sèvres or Meudon with one of the girl assistants from the milliner's shop. Inconsolable after the death of the young aristocrat whose name she had taken, this masculine Julie found the only solace for her sadness in outbursts of savage fury, and whenever she met any Jacobins, she would set the passers-by on to them with threatening shouts of death. She found little time left to give to her mother, who told her beads all day alone in her room, too overcome by the tragic end of her son even to feel sorrow. Rose Thévenin had now become the constant companion of Élodie, who got on very well indeed with both her two stepmothers.

'Where is Élodie?' asked the Citizeness Chassagne.

Jean Blaise indicated that he did not know. He never did: he made it a point of honour not to.

Julie had come to take Élodie to visit Rose Thévenin at Monceaux, where the actress now lived in a little house with an English garden.

At the Conciergerie prison, Rose Thévenin had made the acquaintance of a big army contractor, the Citizen Montfort. After being released by the intervention of Jean Blaise, she had obtained a pardon for the Citizen Montfort who, no sooner free, began provisioning the troops again and speculating in land in the Pépinière district. The architects Ledour, Olivier and Wailly were building good houses there, and the land tripled in value in three months. Since the time of their imprisonment together in the Luxembourg prison, Montfort had been Rose Thévenin's lover: he had now given her a little house near the Tivoli and the Rue du Rocher, which was extremely expensive but cost him nothing, the sale of the neighbouring properties having already reimbursed him several times over. Jean Blaise was a man of the world; he thought it best to put up with what he could not prevent: he abandoned Rose Thévenin to Montfort without quarrelling with her.

Soon after Julie had arrived at the *Amour Peintre*, Élodie came down into the shop dressed in her best clothes, but under her cloak, despite the coldness of the weather, she was naked except for her white dress; her face had become paler than it used to be, her figure thinner, her eyes had a languidly inviting look and her whole body spoke of sensual pleasure.

The two women set off to visit Rose Thévenin, who was expecting them. Desmahis accompanied them: the actress was consulting him about the decoration of her new townhouse and he was in love with Élodie who had by this time more than half decided to put an end to his suffering. When the two women passed near Monceaux, where the victims from the Place de la Révolution were buried under a layer of lime, Julie said:

'It's all right during this cold weather, but in the spring the smell from this ground will poison half the city.'

Rose Thévenin received her two friends in a drawing-room decorated *à l'antique,* the couches and chairs being designed by David. Roman bas-reliefs copied in monochrome adorned the walls, above statues, busts and candelabra of imitation bronze. Rose was wearing a straw-coloured, curled wig. At that time wigs were all the fashion: six, twelve or eighteen being included in a bride's trousseau. A dress *à la Cyprienne* clung to her body like a sheath.

Throwing a cloak over her shoulders, she led her friends and the engraver into the garden, which Ledoux was designing for her, but which as yet was only a chaos of bare trees and plaster. She showed them, all the same, Fingal's grotto, a Gothic chapel, with a bed, a temple, and a waterfall.

'Over there,' she said, pointing to a clump of fir trees, 'I would like to raise a memorial to that unfortunate Brotteaux

247

des Ilettes. I was not indifferent to him. He was a lovable man. The monsters slaughtered him: I wept for him. Desmahis, you will design me an urn on a column for him.'

And she continued, almost without a pause:

'It is really too bad . . . I wanted to give a ball this week; but all the violins are booked up three weeks in advance. They have dancing every evening at the Citizeness Tallien's.'

After dinner, Rose Thevénin's carriage took the three friends and Desmahis to the Théâtre Feydeau. All the most elegant in Paris were there. The women, hair *à l'antique* or *à la victime*, in very open dresses, purple or white and spangled with gold; the men in very tall, black collars, their chins disappearing into enormous white cravats.

The bill announced *Phèdre* and the *Chien du Jardinier*. The entire audience demanded the hymn dear to the *muscadins** and the *jeunesse dorée*, the *Réveil du Peuple*.

The curtain rose and a little man, short and fat, appeared on the stage: it was the celebrated Lays. He sang in a fine, tenor voice:

'*Peuple français, peuple de frères!* . . .'

The wild storm of applause that broke out set the crystals on the chandeliers tinkling. Then murmurs were heard and the voice of a citizen in a round hat in the pit replied with the *Hymne des Marseillais:*

'*Allons, enfants de la patrie!* . . .'

His voice was drowned with howls; voices shouted:

'Down with the Terrorists! Death to the Jacobins!'

And Lays was recalled to sing for a second time the hymn of the Thermidorians, who had brought Robespierre to the scaffold:

'*Peuple français, peuple de frères!* . . .'

In every theatre the bust of Marat was to be seen, on a column or a pedestal. At the Théâtre Feydeau his bust stood on a small pillar, on the 'prompt' side, against the masonry which formed the stage.

While the orchestra was playing the overture to Phèdre, a young *muscadin* pointed his cane at the bust and shouted:

'Down with Marat!'

The whole audience took up the cry:

'Down with Marat! Down with Marat!'

Some with louder voices dominated the tumult:

'It's a disgrace to have that bust still standing there!'

'Shame on us that we allow that infamous Marat to reign everywhere! His busts are as numerous as the heads he wanted to cut off!'

'Venomous toad!'

'Blood-thirsty tiger!'

'Vile serpent!'

Suddenly an elegantly dressed member of the audience climbs on to the edge of his box, gives the bust a push, and knocks it to the ground. The plaster head shatters into pieces amongst the musicians in the orchestra, amid the cheers of the audience, who jump to their feet and burst forth singing the *Réveil du Peuple*:

'*Peuple français, peuple de frères! . . .*'

Among the most enthusiastic singers, Élodie recognized the pretty dragoon, the little lawyer's clerk, Henry, her first love.

After the performance, the handsome Desmahis summoned a cabriolet and escorted the Citizeness Blaise back to the *Amour Peintre*.

In the carriage, the artist took Élodie's hand between his and said:

'You know very well, Élodie, I love you.'

'I know, because you love all women.'

'I love them in you.'

She smiled:

'I should be taking on a huge task, despite all the black, blond and red wigs that are the fashion, if I tried to be all sorts of woman for you.'

'Élodie, I swear to you . . .'

'What! Are you going to take an oath on it, Citizen Desmahis? You must be either very naïve, or else suppose I am.'

Desmahis found himself without a ready reply, and she congratulated herself on defeating him at his own game of witty repartee.

At the corner of the Rue de la Loi, they heard singing and shouting and saw shadows dancing wildly round a brazier. It was a gang of elegant young hooligans, who, on coming out of the Théâtre-Français, had set light to a guy representing Marat.

In the Rue Honoré, the driver of their cabriolet knocked his cocked hat against a burlesque effigy of Marat, hanging from a street lamp.

The driver took it as a great joke, and turning to his passengers told them how, only the night before, the tripe-seller in the Rue Montorgueil had smeared blood over a bust of Marat saying: 'That's the stuff he liked,' and how some little boys, about ten years old, had thrown the bust into a sewer, and how wittily the citizens had then shouted: 'That's the right Panthéon for him!'

Meanwhile, from all the eating houses and lemonade-stalls people could be heard singing:

'*Peuple français, peuple de frères! . . .*'

They arrived at the *Amour Peintre*.

'Good-night,' Élodie said, as she jumped from the cabriolet.

But Desmahis pleaded so tenderly and with such persuasive urgency, that she had not the heart to leave him at the door.

'It's late,' she said. 'You can only stay a moment.'

In the blue bedroom, she threw off her cloak and stood in her white dress *à l'antique*, which revealed all the warm shapeliness of her body.

'Perhaps you need warming,' she said. 'I'll light the fire. It's all ready.'

She struck the flint and put a lighted match to the fire.

Philippe took her in his arms with that gentle finesse which reveals great strength, and she felt in it a sweetness she had never known before. Then, as she was yielding beneath his kisses, she pulled herself away, saying:

'Wait.'

Slowly she unwound her hair before the mirror on the mantelpiece; then she looked with great sadness, at her left hand, at the little silver ring bearing the face of Marat, now so battered and worn it could hardly be seen. She looked at it until she could no longer see it through the tears in her eyes. Then she took it off gently and threw it into the flames.

Tears and smiles, tenderness and love, gave brilliance to her beauty as she turned and threw herself into Philippe's arms.

Night had long fallen when the Citizeness Blaise opened the door of her apartment for her lover and said to him softly in the darkness:

'Good-bye, my love! This is the time my father usually returns. If you hear any noise on the staircase, run up quickly to the top floor and don't come down until you're quite sure there's no danger of being seen. To get the door on to the street opened, knock three times on the concierge's window. Good-bye, dear heart! Good-bye, my soul!'

The last burnt-out logs were glowing in the fireplace. Élodie let her happy, tired head fall back again upon her pillow.

NOTES

Page 27. Jacques Louis David, the most famous artist of the period, was a supporter of Robespierre and a member of the Convention.

Page 27. *Section* Revolutionary Paris had been divided into 48 Sections each with considerable autonomy.

Page 27. *Palais de Justice* The Revolutionary Tribunal met in the Palais de Justice on the Ile de la Cité. Close to it was the prison, the Conciergerie.

Page 27. The *carmagnole*, a short jacket, together with red, blue and white striped trousers, was the uniform of the *sansculottes*. (See note following.)

Page 28. *Federalist* The Girondins became known as the Federalists since they were suspected of wanting to destroy central government in Paris and establish a Federal system.

Page 28. *Culottes* (breeches) had been the respectable pre-revolutionary form of apparel. When the Revolutionaries adopted trousers they were contemptuously referred to as *sansculottes*, a name which they became proud to be known by.

Page 30. *Ça ira!* The repetitive refrain to one of the Revolutionary songs went 'Ah ça ira ça ira ça ira ça ira.' Its nearest equivalent would be: 'Ah, things will start to hum, to hum, to hum.'

Page 34. *collector of revenue and taxes* The collection of taxes under the old régime had not been undertaken directly by the Government. It had been delegated to aristocrats, many of whom amassed vast fortunes.

Page 41. *that Austrian woman* The Austrian Archduchess Marie Antoinette, daughter of the Empress Maria Theresa, had married Louis XVI of France. As Queen of France she had, largely undeservedly, become an object of popular hatred long before the Revolution.

Page 43. *Assignats* were originally interest-bearing bonds. They gradually became a form of paper money and greatly depreciated in value owing to a flood of forged *assignats*, many from England. In this case, an *assignat* for five livres would be worthless.

Page 63. *Place de la Révolution* Now the Place de la Concorde.

Page '92. *magistrate* In the original, the word is 'juryman'. 'Magistrate' has been substituted throughout this translation since Gamelin's powers in this position went far beyond those of a member of a jury in this country. He and his colleagues were allowed, by decree of the Convention, to refuse to permit the defence to complete its case if they considered they had heard enough evidence to decide on their verdict. They were, in effect, both judge and jury.

Page 99. *plot of the Capet* Refers to the youngest son of Louis XVI. Though there were attempts to rescue him he had not escaped from the Temple prison. He probably died there.

Page 118. *God-eaters* This expression was contemptuously applied to Christians, and was in common usage, at the time.

Page 129. *Madame Royale* 'Madame Royale' was the title of Louis XVI's eldest daughter. This rumour was rife at the time.

Page 137. Élodie uses the same words at the end of the book. (See Introduction.)

Page 148. *Vendémiaire* The new revolutionary calendar came into effect in 1790 on the first anniversary of the Republic. The 11 Vendémiaire was the 2 October.

Page 169. *The Twenty-one* The leaders of the Girondins.

Page 179. *the 24 Frimaire* the 14 December 1793.

Page 201. France ironically makes Brotteaux prophesy what would in fact be done by Napoleon.

Page 205. *Danton* had been the ally of Robespierre but when he began to advocate a more moderate policy and to oppose further shedding of blood Robespierre had him arrested and guillotined.

Page 205. *Camille Desmoulins* Another friend of Robespierre, Desmoulins was guillotined with Danton, for the same reason.

Page 208. The National Guard commanded by General Hanriot was Robespierre's chief source of military power.

Page 209. *Samson's basket* Samson and his son were the chief executioners.

Page 223. *Barrière de Trône-Reversée* The guillotine had been moved to the outskirts of Paris because the people were turning against public executions. It was taken back to the Place de la Révolution for the execution of Robespierre.

Page 229. *So you must see . . . even life itself* There is a striking

parallel between these words of Gamelin's and those uttered by
by Macbeth (Act V, iii):

> ... honour, love, obedience, troops of friends,
> I must not look to have; but, in their stead,
> Curses, ...

This is emphasized shortly after when Gamelin tells the child in
the park that one day he will curse his, Gamelin's, name.

Page 231. This meeting of Robespierre with the little Savoyard
boy is based on fact: and Brount was, in fact, the name of Robespierre's dog.

Page 244. *Nivôse* January 1795.

Page 248. *muscadins* The young men of the *jeunesse dorée* who ran
riot in the streets of Paris after the death of Robespierre.

READ MORE IN PENGUIN

In every corner of the world, on every subject under the sun, Penguin represents quality and variety – the very best in publishing today.

For complete information about books available from Penguin – including Puffins, Penguin Classics and Arkana – and how to order them, write to us at the appropriate address below. Please note that for copyright reasons the selection of books varies from country to country.

In the United Kingdom: Please write to *Dept. EP, Penguin Books Ltd, Bath Road, Harmondsworth, West Drayton, Middlesex UB7 0DA*

In the United States: Please write to *Consumer Sales, Penguin Putnam Inc., P.O. Box 12289 Dept. B, Newark, New Jersey 07101-5289.* VISA and MasterCard holders call 1-800-788-6262 to order Penguin titles

In Canada: Please write to *Penguin Books Canada Ltd, 10 Alcorn Avenue, Suite 300, Toronto, Ontario M4V 3B2*

In Australia: Please write to *Penguin Books Australia Ltd, P.O. Box 257, Ringwood, Victoria 3134*

In New Zealand: Please write to *Penguin Books (NZ) Ltd, Private Bag 102902, North Shore Mail Centre, Auckland 10*

In India: Please write to *Penguin Books India Pvt Ltd, 11 Community Centre, Panchsheel Park, New Delhi 110017*

In the Netherlands: Please write to *Penguin Books Netherlands bv, Postbus 3507, NL-1001 AH Amsterdam*

In Germany: Please write to *Penguin Books Deutschland GmbH, Metzlerstrasse 26, 60594 Frankfurt am Main*

In Spain: Please write to *Penguin Books S. A., Bravo Murillo 19, 1° B, 28015 Madrid*

In Italy: Please write to *Penguin Italia s.r.l., Via Benedetto Croce 2, 20094 Corsico, Milano*

In France: Please write to *Penguin France, Le Carré Wilson, 62 rue Benjamin Baillaud, 31500 Toulouse*

In Japan: Please write to *Penguin Books Japan Ltd, Kaneko Building, 2-3-25 Koraku, Bunkyo-Ku, Tokyo 112*

In South Africa: Please write to *Penguin Books South Africa (Pty) Ltd, Private Bag X14, Parkview, 2122 Johannesburg*

READ MORE IN PENGUIN

Penguin Twentieth-Century Classics offer a selection of the finest works of literature published this century. Spanning the globe from Argentina to America, from France to India, the masters of prose and poetry are represented by Penguin.

If you would like a catalogue of the Twentieth-Century Classics library, please write to:

Penguin Press Marketing, 27 Wrights Lane, London W8 5TZ

(Available while stocks last)